Stay low. Keep your head down. One false move and it's curtains.

I fell out of the lounge chair onto the ground. And then I was crawling. No, dragging myself along the grass like a soldier under fire. The landscape around me blurred as I moved closer to the edge of the bluff. I dragged myself on, closer, closer to the edge. As if I was being lured by a siren.

No, not lured, I thought, my head clearing for an instant. I wasn't dragging myself. I was being dragged. Someone was tugging at me. Pushing me. And the cliff was coming up on me.

Terror gripped me. I tried with all my might to pull myself away, but a wave of cold black washed over me, paralyzing my limbs. Then I heard the echo of a scream.

It was me. Hands were grabbing at me. I opened my eyes and stared straight down the jagged mountain cliff. I felt doomed. Lost.

Dear Reader,

This month we welcome you to a new venture from Silhouette Books—Shadows, a line designed to send shivers up your spine and chill you even while it thrills you. These are romances, but romances with a difference. That difference is in the fear you'll feel as you journey with the heroine to the dark side of love . . . then emerge triumphantly into the light. Who *is* the Shadows hero? Is he on the side of the angels? Sometimes. But sometimes neither you nor the heroine can be sure and you wonder, *Does he want to kiss me—or kill me?*

And what a lineup of authors we have for you. This month we're bringing you *four* tantalizing, terrifying titles by authors you won't be able to resist. Heather Graham Pozzessere is known to romance readers everywhere, but in *The Last Cavalier* she demonstrates an ability to spook you that will . . . well . . . haunt you long after you've turned the last page. In *Who Is Deborah?*, Elise Title gives her heroine amnesia, leading her to wonder if the man who claims they are married is telling the truth. Because if he's not, what on earth happened to his real wife? Lee Karr's *Stranger in the Mist* mingles past, present and future into a heady brew that will leave you guessing until the very end. And in *Swamp Secrets*, Carla Cassidy creates one of the darkest—and sexiest!— heroes I've seen in a long, long time.

And that's only the beginning! Because from now on we'll be bringing you two Shadows novels every month, novels where fear mingles with passion to create a reading experience you'll find nowhere else. And the authors who will be penning these books are some of the best anywhere. In months to come you'll find books by Jane Toombs, Helen R. Myers, Rachel Lee, Anne Stuart, Patricia Simpson, Regan Forest and Lori Herter, to name only a few. So now, step into the shadows and open yourself up to romance as you've never felt it before—on the dark side of love.

Yours,

Leslie J. Wainger
Senior Editor and Editorial Coordinator

ELISE TITLE

Who is Deborah?

SILHOUETTE® *Shadows*™

Published by Silhouette Books New York
America's Publisher of Contemporary Romance

SILHOUETTE BOOKS
300 East 42nd St., New York, N.Y. 10017

WHO IS DEBORAH?
Silhouette Shadows #2

Copyright © 1993 by Elise Title

ISBN: 0-373-27002-X

First Silhouette Books printing March 1993

All the characters in this book have no existence outside the imagination of the author and have no relation whatsoever to anyone bearing the same name or names. They are not even distantly inspired by any individual known or unknown to the author, and all incidents are pure invention.

® and ™: Trademarks used with authorization. Trademarks indicated with ® are registered in the United States Patent and Trademark Office, the Canada Trade Mark Office and in other countries.

Printed in the U.S.A.

ELISE TITLE

lives in Hanover, New Hampshire, with her husband Jeff, son David, daughter Rebecca and miniature poodle Jazzy. Writing is her full-time career, with over forty romances published in the past eight years. This last year has been particularly exciting as her novel, *Too Many Husbands,* is being made into a feature film starring Geena Davis. This year, she is contributing to the launch of Silhouette Shadows. Elise says, "When I'm not at my computer, I love taking long walks, reading, going to the movies and spending time with my terrific family."

To Sherie, for being more than a great editor

CHAPTER ONE

It all began the day I discovered I was Deborah Steele. I awoke early that morning, just after dawn—a sharp break in my routine of sleeping till noon. Usual, at least, for the past two months. Before then... Well, that was something else.

I remember waking anxious and disoriented, crying out in a low, broken voice as I heard a clap of thunder. I hated thunderstorms.

Lightning flashed across my drawn window shade and I was overwhelmed by feelings of panic and helplessness. I pulled my pillow over my head, blocking out sight and sound, curling up my whole body as if once again I was fending off...

Fending off what? That was the problem. As Dr. Royce had told me time and again, over the past two months, I wouldn't allow myself to remember. I suppose he was correct. I was afraid. Everyone is afraid at times; but this fear lived inside me like a malignant virus for which there was no cure.

Tears spiked my eyes, dread mingling with frustration and desperation. I squeezed my eyes shut, praying for the awful feelings to pass, for the storm not to come, and most of all, for someone to find me—to find me in the truest sense. Because I felt lost. Completely and utterly lost.

By midmorning, I had managed to pull myself together. The sky was gray and overcast but it wasn't raining yet. Maybe the storm wouldn't materialize, after all. Maybe I'd make it through the day without unraveling. Not a lot to ask for. I could have asked for more. Much more. But I was working hard on not asking for things I wasn't likely to get or setting myself up for disappointment. Which is why what happened later that day threw me for such a loop...

I was in my usual corner of the occupational-therapy room, my easel set up by a large window that let in the northern light. I stood there painting, as I did every afternoon between the end of my group-therapy meeting and dinner. There were other patients scattered about the large space, busy at projects, some of them chatting as they pounded clay or wove baskets. But I kept to myself. Not that I mingled much at any time of the day, but this was my special time, a time just for me. Two precious hours when I could lose myself in other worlds. Two hours when I could forget the hospital, the tedium, the persistent prodding, the endless frustration, the awful loneliness and the ineffable sense of loss.

Painting was my joy and my salvation. I loved the smell of the oil paints and even the turpentine. When I painted— only when I painted—did I somehow feel connected to myself. While all the other hours of my day dragged by, these two golden hours seemed to pass in the blink of an eye. I knew they had passed when I heard a familiar voice behind me.

"It's very good."

The pleasant, approving voice belonged to John Harris, my art therapist. The tall, gangly young man with a shock of red hair stood just off to my right, observing my painting with one of his thoughtful looks.

It was a look I had come to know well over the past two months. I returned his look with one he'd seen often enough before—a look at once guarded and sardonic. "Yes, but that isn't the point, is it?"

He smiled good-humoredly. "Not the whole point."

I didn't respond. I set my brush down and joined him in his study of my canvas—a landscape with a still, blue sky dotted with clouds suspended over a mountain scene. And, as in each of my paintings, there was a single human figure—a young woman with flowing blond hair. This one standing on the top of the mountain, with the wind blowing at her back and looking out to the west. No, not merely looking; searching. I knew this as did John, even though—as in all my paintings—the woman was faceless.

"Tell me about her," John said gently. I was in 'real time' again, hospital time, prodding time.

"You always ask me that. Why?"

He reacted to the added edge in my voice. "It's the weather, isn't it?"

"I suppose," I replied noncommittally.

He gestured to the woman on the canvas. "Does she like the mountains?"

"I'm really not sure. Or maybe she's the one who isn't sure."

He smiled and I offered up a quick, wry smile in return.

"What do you think would happen," he asked in that measured voice that always made me uneasy, "if you painted her to look like you? Your face, I mean?"

Instinctively, my hands flew to my face. I could feel the tremor radiating from my fingers against my warm cheeks. "But this isn't really... *my* face."

A ribbon of color—ruby red—squeezed from a tube of paint flashed before my eyes. Only it wasn't paint. It was... blood. Ruby-red blood. My blood. Hot and moist and fetid, blurring my vision. And with the image came a violent spasm of shock. That first glimpse of myself in the hospital before the plastic surgeon had put me together again—in a fashion.

John gave me a sympathetic look. "It's very possible that you don't look all that different than you did before."

My temples began to beat like a drum. "But I don't know that, do I?" I snapped at him. "Because I haven't the foggiest notion what I looked like before." A dam seemed to burst in me. "Why have any face at all when I'm faceless inside? Anyway, if this is my face, why hasn't anyone come forward to identify me? I ran a photo of myself for over a week in the newspaper with the biggest circulation in New York. No one recognized me, did they?" I finished bleakly.

"Katherine..."

My defenses collapsed, despair washing over me. "Even the name isn't mine. Made up out of thin air like everything else about me."

He looked distraught at my outburst and I felt a stab of guilt. My predicament wasn't John's fault.

"I'm sorry. It is the weather. I woke up early. I've been wound up all day. Sometimes I wish..."

"What do you wish?"

"That the police had just left my bruised and battered body on the sidewalk that rainy night."

I could hear the rain again, pounding in my head. That was all I could remember of that night. That, and then waking up a few hours later in the emergency room of the New York General, with a sweet-faced, young policeman gazing anxiously down at me. I could picture him perfectly.

"You must have fought back hard," the policeman had said, a touch of awe in his voice.

My own voice seemed to have dried up. When I'd finally managed to speak, I discovered it wasn't easy to move my lips. My face was swathed in bandages. Later I was informed that I'd suffered a concussion and that both my nose and jaw had been broken. But at that moment I wasn't concerned about my mutilated face. Terror had gripped me. "Was I...?"

Before I'd had to say the word *raped,* he'd hurriedly shaken his head. I'd felt a rush of relief. It hadn't lasted long—just until he'd started to question me and to my horror, I hadn't been able to give him any answers. Not only had I been unable to tell him anything about the assault, I'd even forgotten my name. I couldn't remember anything. My mind was a complete blank. And the police had little to go on, since I'd been found without any identification on me, in a dark alley in a commercial district of the city.

The doctors tried to assure me that once the trauma wore off, my memory would gradually return. But it hadn't. I'd undergone plastic surgery to have my nose and jaw restructured, and then I'd been moved to the psychiatric ward of the hospital.

"Katherine."

John Harris's voice drew me from my reverie. I saw that Dr. Royce was standing beside John. I'd been so wrapped up in my thoughts I hadn't even seen my psychiatrist come in. He was staring at my painting and then he turned to me.

"Mountains," he murmured. "Interesting."

I sensed some hidden import in the tone of his voice that made the muscles between my shoulder blades tighten. This was odd, because the distinguished-looking psychiatrist generally had the opposite effect on me. I'd developed something of a crush on the soft-spoken, good-looking, kindly doctor. Sometimes, when I was particularly depressed, I would fantasize that he had a special fondness for me, as well. Sometimes I even wondered if it was all a fantasy. To my surprise, I found myself wondering it at that moment. I wasn't sure why. I thought it might be the heightened tenderness and concern I detected in his warm brown eyes. Ironically, instead of being pleased, I felt a flash of alarm. Something was troubling him. Something was wrong.

"What is it?" My voice was a bare whisper.

"Let's talk in my office," he said, in a soothing tone. Only it didn't soothe me at all.

I was glad his office was just a few doors down from the O.T. room.

I didn't realize I was holding my breath until he shut his office door, and I finally exhaled. I spun around to face him. "Please. Tell me."

He nodded, gesturing to a big, comfortable gray-tweed armchair. For the past two months, I'd spent an hour every other day in that chair, in therapy.

I managed a lopsided smile as I moved to the chair. "All of a sudden, my legs feel like jelly."

Dr. Royce took the matching armchair that was a few feet from mine, forgoing his usual seat behind his desk. I was completely convinced that something big was brewing. I felt both nervous and excited.

"Someone's come to see you."

No sooner had he said those words than tears instantly flooded my eyes. I thought I must be hearing things. But I could see from the doctor's sober expression I'd heard correctly. "Who?" I managed to eke out.

He put off answering for a moment—his way of giving me a chance to gather myself. There was an electric coffeepot on a table near him. He poured a cup and handed it to me. My hands were trembling badly as I took it from him, but I sipped the hot, strong brew gratefully. Then I plucked out some tissues conveniently placed by my chair and wiped my eyes and blew my nose.

"His name is Greg Eastman."

Dr. Royce fixed his gaze on me as he said the name. If he expected some reaction, a ray of light to dawn, I disappointed him. Not to mention my own sorry disappointment. The name meant absolutely nothing to me.

"Who is he? How... How does he know me?"

"He's a private investigator." A faint smile curved the psychiatrist's lips. "He recognized you from the photo you ran in the paper."

I started to smile, too. "He *recognized* me? Then . . . then my face isn't . . . I haven't . . . changed. . . ."

"Not enough for him not to recognize you."

There was something I didn't understand. "Are you saying he wasn't sure, at first? Is that why he's waited . . . ?"

"No. He told me he was out of town when your photo ran in the paper, but his secretary had, as a matter of practice, clipped it out and filed it in his Missing Persons folder. The minute he saw it . . ." Dr. Royce paused for a moment. "He knew it was you."

I waited, as if suspended, for him to tell me who I was. I will never forget that wait. A part of me felt it was interminable; another part of me was afraid for it to conclude. Discovering my identity could be as frightening as not knowing it at all.

When Dr. Royce finally spoke, there was such solemnity in his voice that the hairs on my forearms literally stood on end. "He says your name is Deborah Steele."

I stared at him blankly, not knowing what to say to this announcement, how to react. It was the strangest sensation. I suddenly went numb all over.

"Deborah." I tried the name out for the first time. It sounded as foreign and removed from me as the name Katherine—as any name I might have pulled out of a hat.

My hand was shaking so, I only barely managed to set my coffee cup down on the table. "Is he sure?"

"Naturally, he wants to see you in person, but . . . I think he's pretty certain. He knew you. Quite well, he says. He knew . . . that you painted."

My eyes widened.

"And he brought along a photograph."

"Of . . . her?" I couldn't think of *her* as *me*.

Not yet. It was all too unreal. I wasn't even sure I wouldn't wake up any moment and find out this was all some wild, impossible dream.

"The similarities are striking."

I sensed he was holding something back. "And the differences? Are they striking, too?"

It was the only time I ever saw Dr. Royce blush. "Naturally... there are some differences. The nose and jawline..." His voice trailed off.

I had a feeling there were more profound differences, but I wasn't sure I was ready to hear what they were. "This private detective—Greg Eastman—you say he knew me."

Dr. Royce leaned forward a little. I braced myself. As it turned out I needed bracing.

"He's not merely a private investigator. He's a close friend of... your husband." He exhaled a breath. "Nicholas Steele."

Husband? My heart began to pound and a line of perspiration broke out across my brow. I could feel the color drain from my face. I must have looked ghastly, because Dr. Royce's expression became etched with concern.

"It's a lot to take in. Don't expect to do it all at once," he cautioned in that comforting voice he used whenever I became overly agitated.

"Husband?" This time I said the word aloud, but it still didn't sound real. Or possible. I looked at my bare ring finger. Had I worn a wedding band before the attack? Had it been stolen, along with everything else I had on me? But, I didn't feel... married. I felt so... detached. I stared incredulously at Dr. Royce. "You say his name is... Nicholas Steele?"

He was watching me closely. "Does it sound familiar to you?"

I started to shake my head, but then I stopped abruptly, my heartbeat accelerating. "I... don't know. It does... ring a bell. I... I think I've heard the name... before."

Could this be that first chink in the armor? If it was, I would have expected to see some sign of pleasure in the doctor's face. I didn't. If anything, his expression took on a more somber cast. I was crestfallen.

"Nicholas Steele is a writer," he said gently. "His novels are bestsellers. You might have seen some of his books here at the hospital or seen an ad for one of them in a newspaper." He paused. "On the other hand, it is possible you may—"

I shook my head then. "No," I said, cutting him off. "I must have seen his name on a book or in the newspaper. It certainly doesn't conjure up any images."

"Maybe that's just as well."

As soon as the words had slipped out of his mouth, I could see that he regretted them.

He smiled awkwardly. "I only meant ... He writes horror novels."

By this point my head was swimming. How could I, the victim of a horror so traumatic I'd erased it and everything that came before it from my mind, be the wife of a famous—for all I knew, infamous—writer of ghoulish deeds? It was utterly perverse and incredible. I had to be dreaming—an insane nightmare.

"You don't believe this, do you? You don't think I'm the wife of a man ... like that?"

Dr. Royce donned a fatherly expression. "Like what? Just because he writes horror stories doesn't mean—"

"I can't even imagine reading a horror novel. I can't believe I ... I ever did."

"Wives aren't required to be fans of their husbands' work."

"You think I'm Deborah?"

"I talked with Mr. Eastman for close to two hours. He was very candid, and he gave me a great number of details that I must say sounded credible." He hesitated, and my body tensed. "He also told me that Nicholas Steele lives in a small town about three hours north of here. Sinclair. It's in the Catskill Mountains.''

I finally understood his remark back in the O.T. room when he was looking at my landscape. ''I wasn't painting any particular mountain. I... I couldn't have been.''

''Not on a conscious level,'' he went on, in an almost-chatty tone. I knew he was trying to calm me down, but even he had to know that wasn't a likely prospect. Still, though my head was spinning with it all, I tried to concentrate on his words.

''Mr. Eastman has a getaway cottage up in Sinclair,'' Dr. Royce was saying. But I wanted to hear about Nicholas Steele, this writer of horror stories, this man who was supposedly my husband. Or did I?

''Eastman spends most weekends and summers there. He's known Steele for more than five years. They're tennis partners and Eastman says he's even been acknowledged in a couple of Steele's books for giving him technical advice. From what he said, I gather he and Steele are very good friends.''

''And what about me?'' There. I'd said it. *Me.* Not her. *Me.* It was the strangest feeling, yet not altogether unpleasant.

I saw that Dr. Royce didn't miss the shift in pronouns. ''Nicholas Steele was, according to Eastman, a dyed-in-the-wool bachelor until he was off in St. Martin doing some research on a book and met 'the girl of his dreams.' That's a direct quote from Mr. Eastman.''

I found myself smiling, but then the incredulity of it all made me stop abruptly.

Dr. Royce continued. ''When he returned to Sinclair three weeks later, he had a bride with him.''

''A whirlwind courtship, marriage on a tropical island... It sounds like something out of a romance novel.'' But, better a romance than a horror novel.

"That was just over two years ago," he told me quietly. "And then, two and a half months ago, Deborah Steele disappeared."

"Disappeared?" I echoed, and shivered.

Dr. Royce's gaze fixed on me. "She left the house to catch the train down to Manhattan for a shopping trip and…and that was the last that was heard of her. Eastman says he spent a month working both with the police and on his own, trying to trace her. Finally he returned to Sinclair, since he thought it was possible she could have met with some kind of accident or foul play before ever getting on the train. After getting nowhere in Sinclair, either, he came back to Manhattan and—"

"Saw the picture of me in his file."

Dr. Royce nodded. I found myself nodding back inanely, the whole time feeling completely adrift. Eventually I asked, "Now what?"

"Mr. Eastman wants to see you, talk to you. I told him I would talk with you first and that I'd suggest you let all this…news…sink in for a day or two, or however long you need. There's no rush. I know all this is an enormous shock to your system—"

"Is he still here?"

Dr. Royce hesitated. "Yes, but—"

"I want to see him."

"Katherine—"

"But it isn't Katherine, is it?"

He scowled. "For you, it still is. You can't take on a new name and a whole new identity in a matter of minutes. It will take time. And there's still the possibility that he's wrong."

"All the more reason for us to meet right away," I insisted.

I could see that Dr. Royce wasn't particularly pleased with my refusal to take his advice. Now it was I who leaned closer. "I must know. You do understand that."

He nodded. "My only concern is for your welfare. Too much, too soon—"

"I'm stronger than I appear." I laughed softly, experiencing a ripple of surprise. "I didn't know that myself until just now."

"I did," he said, a smile curving his lips. And in that smile I saw genuine caring. I think that's where much of my strength came from. Little did I know that very soon, I'd have to call on that strength in spades.

CHAPTER TWO

I tried to compose myself as I waited in Dr. Royce's office for Greg Eastman to come in. Dr. Royce had wanted to wait with me, to stand by me during the meeting and give me moral support. Or maybe artificial respiration if I passed out! But I'd been adamant about wanting my very protective doctor to leave me on my own. I think my assertiveness surprised him. It surprised me even more. I didn't really understand my sudden spurt of boldness, writing it off as partly desperation, partly the need to begin to stand on my own two feet.

My two feet, however, weren't holding me up all that well. They felt like a cross between rubber and marshmallows. I sat down in the armchair. I folded one hand over the other. I crossed my bare legs at the ankles. I took deep breaths. Nothing helped. My heart was racing. My palms were sweaty. I was a nervous wreck.

I kept thinking, you should be happy. This is what I'd dreamed about for months. Finally, someone's come for me—someone who knows me, someone who's bringing me the greatest gift possible: myself. Not that it couldn't be some terrible mistake. This private investigator might come in, see me, and realize I wasn't Deborah Steele, after all. Suddenly I was fervently praying that wouldn't happen. In those last waiting moments, I found myself longing to be Deborah Steele. For if I wasn't Deborah, I was once again...nobody. I didn't truly exist. Even the idea of being married to a man whose mind must be steeped in hor-

ror fiction didn't prevent me from my longing to be
Deborah. I focused on what Dr. Royce had told me—the
whirlwind courtship and marriage on a tropical island, the
romance of it all. Oh, if I could be Deborah, the girl of this
man's dreams . . .

I couldn't keep my anxiety or my anticipation at bay for
more than a few moments. This meeting with Greg Eastman could hold the key to unlocking my past. And my future. Whatever had gone on before, whatever lay ahead, had
to be better than the awful blankness, the loneliness that
consumed me almost every waking moment here in the
hospital. At least, that's what I told myself at the time.

When he stepped into the office after what felt like an
eternity but was probably no more than ten minutes, I
popped up like a puppet whose strings had been abruptly
tugged hard.

Greg Eastman smiled. "Please. Sit down."

Self-consciously, I followed his request. My boldness
having deserted me altogether, I could manage little more
than a quick glance at the private investigator. It was long
enough, though, to know that he looked utterly unfamiliar
to me. I felt incredibly disappointed as I stared down at my
hands.

When I think back on that first meeting with Greg, it was
his smile that I remember most. Sympathetic, charming,
coaxing at turns. His grab bag of smiles didn't quite put me
at ease—that would have been impossible—but they did give
me some comfort. I think I must have been expecting some
hard-boiled shamus right out of a detective novel. Greg was
nothing like that. He was clean-cut and attractive, with
close-cropped sandy blond hair, regular features, and that
engaging smile.

His next words broke the awkward and extended silence.
"This must be quite a shock for you, Deborah."

The name rolled so easily and naturally off his lips that my head jerked up.

"Am I...her?" My mouth was dry. The words came out like a harsh croak.

"After they made you, they threw away the mold." Immediately after uttering the glib remark, he looked contrite. "Sorry. It's just that I'm so incredibly relieved to see you. Dr. Royce has explained everything to me, Deborah. The assault, the injuries you suffered, the memory loss that resulted. But it's going to be all right. Now, you can begin to really heal. I've come to take you home, Deborah."

Home. I had promised myself I wouldn't break down, but it was all too much. *Home.*

My sudden burst of tears filled Greg with alarm. He didn't seem to know what to do, what to say. After a few attempts to calm me with words and pats on my shoulder, he finally just kept handing me tissues until I got my bearings again.

"I'm sorry," I mumbled, horribly embarrassed.

"Don't be. It's probably the best thing for you."

The best thing for me. No. The best thing for me would be to remember being Deborah.

"Did the headshrinker fill you in?" Greg asked. He gave me a quirky smile in response to my blank look. "Sorry. The psychiatrist."

I repeated by rote what Dr. Royce had told me. "He said that you knew me from Sinclair. In the Catskill Mountains three hours north of here. You have a getaway cottage there. You're a friend of Nicholas Steele's. You've known him for five years. You're tennis partners."

I continued in a monotone. "Nicholas was married for two years and then two and a half months ago his wife, Deborah, disappeared. You saw my photo in the newspaper clipping and recognized me as Deborah Steele." I might have been giving a canned speech at a conference. Nothing that I said had any foundation in reality for me. I felt like I was talking about someone else altogether. Deborah and Nicholas. They were both no more than phantom beings. I felt no connection to either of them.

Greg leaned forward, his elbows resting on his knees, palms capturing his square chin. He seemed unfazed by my mechanical presentation.

"You must have been mugged the first day you got to the city," he said. "I checked out the area where they found you. At night, it's a pretty desolate spot, but there are a few designers who have lofts in that neighborhood. You always had a thing for searching out new fashion designers. The best-dressed woman with the most original wardrobe in Sinclair. Not that Sinclair's exactly a fashion mecca, but we do have our country-club set." He winked, clearly expecting to garner a little laugh or a smile from me at the very least.

But my mouth was stuck in a tight line. To make matters worse, I became horribly self-conscious about the drab cotton print sundress that hung loosely on my narrow frame. My meager wardrobe, culled from the hospital's thrift shop with a few hand-me-downs from a couple of nurses tossed in, was about as far from designer wear as one could get. I was certainly not the fashion plate of the New York General.

Greg leaned a little closer. I squirmed under his scrutiny, thinking he, too, was none too impressed with my attire, nor with my whole appearance. But how I looked and what I was wearing turned out not to be what was on his mind. "I know all this must be hard for you, but it's hard for me, too, Deborah. You really don't remember anything? Anything at all?"

Slowly, I shook my head. "This feels very unreal. I don't even know whether to believe any of it. I keep thinking...you must have made a mistake."

"No mistake," he said confidently. And then he added, "Maybe this will help." He withdrew a photo from a manila envelope and extended it toward me. As much as I wanted to look, I felt frozen to the spot. I couldn't even reach out my hand to take the photo from him.

Eventually he laid it in my lap, facing me.

Still, it took several long moments for me to manage to lower my eyes to it.

It was an eight-by-ten glossy of a blond-haired woman in a bikini, smiling provocatively into the camera as she posed on the bow of a sailing sloop. What emerged most from the shot was the vibrancy of her coloring—the healthy, glowing golden sweep of hair, the tanned skin, the glamorous red lipstick, the vibrant blue eyes that sparkled with such youth and vitality.

Was this me? A me in happier times? Had my blue eyes ever shone like that? Had my blond hair ever looked so lustrous? Had I ever been so carefree? So curvy?

Incredible as it was, the similarities were undeniable. Not just that our eye color and hair shade matched, but it was there in the shape of the eyes. And in the mouth. Even our noses weren't all that different. The jawlines... Well, they weren't the same. Hers seemed to jut out more, giving her an air of defiance. It went with the seductive glint in her eyes. She seemed so sure of herself. And maybe a little full of herself, as well. That was the heart of the difference between us. I was certain that was what Dr. Royce saw, too, when he examined the photograph.

"You just need to put on a bit of weight, get out in the sun again, and—"

"Tell me about her," I said, cutting him off.

He looked slightly startled. Then he smiled. "Well, she's beautiful, vivacious, fun loving..."

But those were all qualities I could see myself in the photo. I wanted to know about the parts of her—of me?—that I couldn't see.

My disappointment must have shown on my face, because he gave me a tender smile. "You always looked very sure of yourself, but you didn't always feel that way. Not by half. We were good friends, Deborah. You...confided in me. You told me how important painting was for you. You talked about how lonely you were as a child."

"My family...?"

A flicker in his hazel eyes told me it was a sad story. "Your father walked out on you when you were a small child. You always wished you could at least picture him in your mind, but you couldn't. Your only memory of him was of a red plaid shirt he'd worn. You used to...tear up a little and say, 'Can you imagine remembering nothing at all about your father but a dumb old shirt?'"

I hung on every word Greg spoke, struggling to make them mean something to me. I could feel for this sad child, but I couldn't identify with her as being a part of myself.

"And my mother?"

He sighed. "She died when you were nine. You went to live with a maiden aunt in Omaha. I always used to tease you that no one really lived in Omaha."

"And...and what would I say?"

"You'd say, 'I didn't live there, Greg. I existed there. Just barely, at that.'"

I sat very still, tears slipping down my cheeks. It sounded so much like the feeling I had here in the hospital. This was the first real connection I felt to Deborah.

"I honestly think that once you're with Nick at Raven's Cove, it will all come back to you," he said in a soft murmur.

"Raven's Cove?"

Greg grinned. "From Edgar Allen Poe's 'The Raven.' An appropriate name for the abode of a renowned spook writer. Not that Nick takes any of that nonsense seriously. I think it was his cousin who named the place."

"His cousin?"

"Second cousin once removed, or something like that. Lillian. She sort of looks after things. Very quietly and unobtrusively. You needn't worry about old Lill."

"I'm worried about everything," I confessed readily. "I don't think I'm really able to take it all in."

He went to reach for my hand, but instinctively I jerked it away. Even though I remembered nothing about the assault, it had left me with an uneasiness about being touched. I started to apologize, knowing Greg meant only to comfort me, but he waved off my apology.

"Deborah, listen to me. You don't belong here. You won't get well here. And that's what you want, isn't it?"

Of course, he had to know I wanted that more than anything.

I asked shakily, "Have you... spoken with him already?" I couldn't say his name yet. *Nicholas? Nick? Darling?* I felt my cheeks redden.

"Yes."

"He's... expecting me?"

"Yes."

"Were you so certain I'd come?"

"As certain as I was that you were Deborah. And now I'm more certain than ever. I'll say it again. Deborah Steele is one of a kind. Since you can't know that, take it from someone who does." It was a warm compliment and I sensed no seductiveness in it. Here, I started to think, was someone whom I might be able to trust. Trust wasn't something that had been coming easily to me. I got the feeling from the little Greg had told me, it never had. But I must have trusted him in the past. He'd said I'd confided in him.

"It's going to be all right, Deborah. I promise."

I managed a small smile. "I have to confess, Mr. Eastman—"

"Greg. I've been Greg ever since we first met, two years ago. What do you confess, Deborah?"

Her smile deepened a little. "I confess, Greg, that your confidence is a bit contagious."

He smiled back—a smile at once charming and ingenuous. "Progress already. Won't Dr. Royce be pleased." He rubbed his hands together. "I'll phone up to Nick and let him know we'll be on our way." Then, realizing I might feel he was moving too fast, he hastened to add, "As soon as you're ready."

Having all but sealed my fate, I felt a flurry of nervous anticipation. No amount of sitting around the hospital would make me any more ready than I was. Not that I was the least bit ready psychologically, mind you.

"I just need to pack and tell Dr. Royce—"

"Good," Greg said cheerily. "Then we'll make it up to Raven's Cove in time for dinner."

The rain started as Greg guided his sunny yellow Miata sports car onto the New York State Thruway. Flicking on his windshield wipers, he asked, "Are you okay?"

"It's just...the rain," I replied, not knowing whether Dr. Royce had told him anything about that.

"It should clear up," he said with an overabundance of confidence that the cloud-laden skies didn't support.

But it wasn't only the rain. It was my growing sense of unease. All I could think, now that I was actually on my way, was that I shouldn't have jumped into this so impulsively. Dr. Royce had tried to talk some sense into me. He'd even suggested phoning Nicholas and having him come down to the hospital to meet with me a few times . . .

"Why didn't he come?"

Greg gave me a blank look.

"Nick." I felt somehow foolish speaking his name.

"I only just told him about finding you a few hours ago. And his editor was up there. He would have come... Would you rather he'd have...?"

"No. I don't know," I answered shakily. Saying that, I was struck by how little I knew about Nicholas Steele. It was beyond me at that point to think of that stranger, a writer of macabre stories, as my husband. In my rush to begin my real life again, I'd pushed this rather crucial but certainly troubling part of it aside.

Greg must have picked up on my distress, because he started to tell me about him. "I should have brought along a picture of Nick. I could have pulled off a jacket cover from one of his books lying around my office." He winked at me. "I'm not only a close friend, but an avid fan. Well, let me ease your worries. He's real easy on the eyes. Tall, dark and Hollywood handsome. Although I'm always teasing him about getting a haircut. He keeps it long and pulled back in a ponytail. A real rogue pirate. Women find him witty, charming and incredibly sexy, and most men are envious as hell of him."

"Are you?" I turned scarlet. "I'm sorry. That was a stupid, inappropriate question. Please forgive me."

Greg merely laughed. "It wasn't stupid or inappropriate. You always did have a habit of speaking your mind, Deb. Loss of memory notwithstanding, there's no reason that should have changed about you. And the answer is yes. As envious as the next guy." There was a slight pause, a quick glance in my direction, as he added, "Maybe more so."

My face remained flushed, but Greg seemed amused, letting the innuendo slide by.

"Not that Nick's perfect, mind you. He can be a bit intimidating until you get to know him. He's very self-contained, exceptionally disciplined, an impossible perfectionist.''

I gave him a nervous look.

Greg quickly attempted to alleviate my anxiety. "A perfectionist when it comes to his work, that is. He sets incredibly high standards for himself, but he's not one of those people who expects those around him to necessarily follow suit," he assured me, following the remark with a dry laugh. "Otherwise we'd never have become friends."

I gave the private investigator a curious look. He laughed again. "Compared to the illustrious Nicholas Steele, I'm just an ordinary slob, Deb."

I didn't think he was ordinary, but I didn't say that. I didn't say anything. "We should be there in another hour or so," Greg said a few minutes later.

Another hour? So soon? As if to amplify the mounting tension I was feeling, the rain began falling harder and the car was buffeted by the accompanying winds. The quick, steady rhythm of the windshield wipers seemed to mirror my rapid heartbeat. What had I gotten myself into?

My silence, and no doubt my rigid posture, clued Greg in to my anxious mood. Without thinking, he reached out and patted my knee in what I knew was meant to be a calming gesture. Still, I couldn't suppress my automatic response.

My sharp cry of alarm at his touch nearly cost Greg control of the car. He managed, after a few panicky moments, to pull over. There was a truck stop up ahead on the highway. He drove into the parking lot. Both of us were shaken up at this point.

"I'm sorry." We both said the same words at the same time. Greg laughed. I managed a weak smile.

"We can go inside, get a cup of coffee and wait the storm out," he offered.

I shook my head, chiding myself for overreacting. I had to somehow get it into my head that every touch wasn't a threat. Even though all memory of the assault was absent from my mind, I was paranoid. The storm and this trip only heightened it.

I took in a deep breath, exhaling slowly as Dr. Royce had taught me. I could feel some of the color return to my face. "I'm all right now. Please, let's go." I felt foolish and self-conscious and was greatly relieved when Greg started for the exit ramp without a word.

To my amazement and I'm sure Greg's relief, by the time we neared Sinclair a little over an hour later, the skies had cleared. When we approached the small main drag of the quaint mountain town, the streets were actually dry, the descending sun casting a warm golden hue over the picture-postcard landscape.

The setting, far from stirring any memories, was completely unfamiliar to me, but my spirits perked up nonetheless. There was something warm and friendly and easygoing about the village. Good vibes, I thought, smiling.

Greg was delighted with the change in me. "You're already looking more like your old self," he commented, his eyes sparkling.

The remark gave me a surprising little thrill.

We were approaching a quaint, barnboard red-shingled convenience store. "Could we stop for a minute?" I asked. "I'd like to pick up a few things. I made do with very little at the hospital." I was thinking some cosmetics were in order, and some perfume would be nice. What scent, though? What did "Deborah" wear? Did "my husband" have a preference?

Greg drove into the small parking area in front of the convenience store. "I'll fill up across the street and be back here in a few minutes."

As I opened the car door to step out, I was tempted to ask him about the perfume, but then felt foolish and embarrassed.

"Do you need some money?" he asked.

"Oh ... No. I have ... enough," I said, hurriedly stepping out and waving as Greg pulled out.

Actually, I'd been penniless at the hospital, a ward of the state. The only reason I had money on me now was that I'd accepted a small loan from Dr. Royce. Despite the fact that he was against my leaving the hospital so precipitously, he'd insisted that I not go off empty-handed. I felt funny about accepting the money, but I was touched, too. For a moment, I wished I'd discovered I was Dr. Royce's wife, not Nicholas Steele's. I suppose most patients have special feelings for their therapists. And I suppose the converse is true of some therapists, as well. It certainly was true of Dr. Royce—even though the money he loaned me wasn't actually his, but came out of an emergency hospital kitty. I promised to pay it back as soon as possible, not thinking at the time that it meant having to ask Nicholas Steele for the money. Or did I have some money of my own?

A little bell jingled over the glass-and-wooden door as I stepped into the shop that on the inside gave the appearance of an old-fashioned general store. There was even a bulletin board near the cash register where locals tacked up folksy announcements, photos, and notices of items for sale.

I was relieved to see that other than the young girl at the register, there were only a couple of customers in the shop—a pair of middle-aged women chatting and browsing over at the book-and-magazine rack. The prospect of being around a crowd of people made me feel skittish. I had voiced that concern to Greg at one point while we were driving up. I worried that such a rich and celebrated author as Nicholas Steele would surround himself with some sort of literary "in" crowd. Greg, however, had assured me that Nick led what most people would call a very reclusive life. He valued his solitude, had few close friends, dispatched sycophants with practiced ease, never gave big parties. Greg also insisted that, sought-after though Nicholas was, he, too, felt uneasy and out of place in large groups. Of course, a certain amount of that was required to promote sales of his books. But, fortunately, Greg had added, Nicholas Steele's horror novels were so popular at this point that they basically sold themselves, allowing him to be very selective about the guest appearances and such that he now rarely made.

The cosmetics rack turned out to be in the aisle that was directly on the other side of the book-and-magazine rack. Feeling overwhelmed by the wide assortment of choices for lipstick, blush, eye shadows, eyeliners and face powders, I could do little more than stare at it all.

I was only vaguely conscious of the conversation between the two women at the book rack until I heard one of them say, "Nicholas Steele."

"*Night Cries* is his latest," the other was saying in a raspy voice. "Of course, that won't come out in paperback for months. I put my name on the waiting list for it at the library the day it came out in hard cover. It was weeks before my turn came up. And then, I foolishly went and made the mistake of starting the darn thing right before bed. I was so terrified I couldn't sleep a wink that night. And I still can't go up into my attic without Tom."

"I don't care what any of those celebrity magazines say about the man, I think Nicholas Steele must be a little mad himself, don't you think?" her friend replied. "I mean, what person in his right mind could even come up with such gruesome plots?"

My whole body was trembling as I heard a soft chuckle. "Well, we devour every one of them, Joan," the raspy-voiced woman countered. "So what does that say about us and all of Nicholas Steele's other fans? We may gasp in horror, lose sleep, but we keep turning the pages as fast as we can."

"It's not the same thing, Alice," Joan argued. "Besides, he looks...weird. That dark hair pulled back severely from his face in a ponytail. Those eyes. I've never seen anyone with truly black eyes before. Why, you can't even see where the irises leave off and the pupils begin. He gives me the willies."

"I don't know," Alice mused. "I think he's rather medieval looking. His features are so arresting and unusual. He looks like he stepped out of a history book. Or some swashbuckling movie. On the few occasions I've spotted him in town, I found myself thinking he ought to be wearing a dark cloak, rapier sword in hand, riding a white charger down Main Street."

"Hiding in the shadow of doorways seems more appropriate," Joan said dryly. "Or lurking in a rat infested dungeon like that madman, Olafson, in his book, *Only the Dead.*"

"Oh, please, I get goose bumps just thinking about that book."

"I tell you, Alice, Nicholas Steele has a warped mind. It's no wonder that wife of his ran away like she did. Can you imagine living with that man?"

There was another soft chuckle from Joan. "I don't know. It could be rather exciting. Even . . . dangerous."

I couldn't believe what I was hearing. Surely this couldn't be the same man Greg had told me about? He'd made Nick sound so appealing and glamorous. He'd said women adored him. Not if they perceived him as weird and frightening, surely. But hadn't I conjured up a frightful image of Nicholas Steele myself when Dr. Royce first told me he was a horror novelist?

I was so caught up in the conversation and my response that I was completely unaware of having been approached by the cashier.

"Is there something I can help you with?" the young woman inquired politely.

I swayed at the sound of her voice, having to grip one of the cosmetic racks to keep my balance. Several of the items toppled to the floor.

"Say, are you okay?" the cashier asked anxiously, looking as if she expected me to collapse and have some sort of a fit.

With every ounce of strength I could muster, I pulled myself together and nodded. Then, without a word, I hurried to the exit. Just as I made it to the door, I heard one of the women saying to her friend, "Why, I don't believe my eyes."

"What? What?"

"Isn't that Deborah Steele?"

The bell that had seemed to make a friendly jingle when I'd entered the store, sounded more like it was tolling ominously as I made my retreat.

CHAPTER THREE

I must have looked a sight as I fled the general store, so in embarrassment, I turned my face away from Greg as I got into his sports car. Meanwhile, snippets of those two women's conversation kept echoing in my mind. *He must be a little weird himself... Those eyes... It's no wonder that wife of his ran away....*

Ran away? But I didn't run away. Greg had told me I'd gone on a shopping trip. He'd made it sound so...mundane. Why would he lie to me? Why?

I couldn't still my trembling. Had he lied? And if he'd lied about that, why not about other things?

No, no, I told myself, refusing to give in to my paranoia. What did those two silly gossips know? Greg was Nick's friend. My friend. Why would he lie to me?

"Don't tell me you couldn't find what you needed in Gus's," Greg said, his attention on the traffic as he pulled out of the parking area and turned left on Main Street.

"What?" I dabbed at the perspiration on my brow. "Gus's?"

"Gus used to own the convenience store. Sold it about fifteen years ago, but all the locals still call it Gus's."

"Does...Nick?"

"Nick's probably the only one in Sinclair who doesn't know what they call the store. He's oblivious to such mundane tidbits."

"Is he?"

"When you're the local celebrity, as Nick is, you can't help but cause a bit of a stir every time you come into town. Nick's not the type who likes a fuss being made over him. And he hates all the gossip—"

"Gossip?" I jumped on the word.

Greg grinned. "Sure, there's always gossip. It goes with the territory. Nick understands that. He tries to act like he's impervious to it, but I know him well enough to know it bugs him."

"What...kind of gossip?" I could hear the tremor in my voice, but I hoped Greg wouldn't pick it up.

"Oh, everything from Nick being a sorcerer to a vampire. For a while there was a rumor floating around town that he was a direct descendant of Dr. Frankenstein."

He chuckled. "And then there was the one that he kept a wild tiger as a pet and fed it live rats. I guess when you're gossiping about a horror writer, it's easy to imagine all sorts of ghoulish nonsense. And I suppose Nick's appearance and demeanor only encourage it. All of which delights his publishers because it translates into more book sales. They love the mystique that swirls around Nick. I mean, just think if the famous horror novelist, Nicholas Steele, looked like a dreary accountant."

"What about...me? Was there...gossip about me, as well?"

I'm not sure if it was the question itself or something in my voice that made him slow the car to a stop and look over at me with concern. "Deborah, what is it? You're white as a ghost. Are you having second thoughts?"

A hoarse laugh escaped my lips. "Second, third and fourth."

He gave me a broad, easy smile. "It's only natural. I suppose it must feel to you something like one of those arranged marriages with a total stranger."

"Something very much like that."

"Does it help any to tell you that there must be thousands of women out there who'd give anything to be in your shoes?"

My glance skipped down to my shoes—a pair of worn, scuffed, white pumps. "I can't imagine anyone wanting to be in these shoes."

Greg laughed. "They aren't your usual style, I'll admit that. If we'd thought about it earlier, we could have stopped along the way. There are a couple of dress shops in Sinclair, but the whole street closes down by five."

"That's all right." I was feeling uncomfortable enough in "my" outfit—well, as much mine as anything I possessed.

"What do you think of that place across the street? It's pure Greek Revival. On a small scale, of course." He pointed to an attractive whitewashed cottage. My mind wasn't on town architecture and I gave it the barest of nods, muttering a brief pleasantry about its cheerful appearance.

"It's my home away from home. I'm settling in for the whole summer, so if you get lonely or just want to drop by when you're in town..." As he spoke, he pulled out onto the road again and headed north of the town.

"Was I often lonely in . . . the past?"

"When Nick's working on a book, he pretty much withdraws from humanity for whole spurts of time. If Lillian didn't bring him in his meals, he'd probably waste away to nothing and never even notice."

"Why Lillian?"

"What do you mean?"

"Why didn't . . . I bring him in his meals?"

Greg shrugged. "You probably did sometimes. It's just that Lillian does all the cooking and she has a tendency to be a bit of a mother hen around Nick."

"Is she much older than him?" And then I realized I didn't even know how old this husband of mine was. I wasn't even sure how old I was, for that matter. I asked Greg.

"Nick's thirty-seven and I recall him once mentioning that Lillian was a couple of years younger than him. You'd never know it to look at her. When I first met her I thought she was his spinster aunt. Maybe forty-five, even fifty."

"And me?"

"Poor Deb. It just hit me how totally devastating it must be for you to have no memory whatsoever. Not even to know how old you are. It's really tragic."

I was feeling pretty tragic by then, and must have looked it because he quickly donned an upbeat tone. "You turned twenty-six on April seventeenth. But you don't look a day over twenty-five."

"If you want to win my trust, Greg, you mustn't tell such bald-faced lies."

I was surprised to see hurt cross his features. "I thought I had won your trust, Deborah. A long time ago. But, of course, I see that I have to begin all over again. Rest assured, I will."

There was no smile on his face now, and a deep crease stretched across his brow.

I felt guilty for doubting him and for making that snippy remark. He didn't deserve it. I might not remember anything of our past relationship, but I could sense his genuine caring.

With a cloudless blue sky overhead, the Miata began climbing a narrow winding mountain road about a mile past Greg's cottage. This was the way to Raven's Cove. To Nicholas Steele. I was feeling better about Greg by then, but I was a complete nervous wreck about my imminent arrival "home."

Greg made small talk about the surrounding landscape as we ascended the mountain. I knew it was an effort on his part to get my mind off what lay ahead, but that was all I could think about. In the middle of his waxing poetic about the beauty and the joys of country life, I abruptly cut him off.

"Has he always written horror stories?"

Greg had to smile. "You weren't listening to a word I said, were you?"

"Not a word," I admitted sheepishly.

"Okay, you want more dope on Nick. Sure, I can understand that. Let's see. Did he always write horror stories? I'm not sure. The horror genre is certainly where Nicholas made his name. He did confess to me on a couple of occasions that he'd like to try his hand at something else, something altogether different, but... it's difficult. His fans would be terribly disappointed if they didn't get their Nicholas Steele 'horror' fix each year."

The voices of the two women in Gus's came to mind.

"Was I a fan?"

"Sure, you were. Oh, I don't know that you read all his books, but what I'm saying is... you supported him."

"And he, in turn, supported me?"

Greg gave me a teasing, lopsided smile. "In the style to which any woman would love to be accustomed."

I flushed. "I didn't mean that. I meant... my work. My painting."

To avoid answering my question, Greg turned all of his attention to driving carefully on the narrow, curving road. I realized then that he'd done that once before, when he'd failed to answer my question about whether there had been any gossip about me. *It's no wonder she ran off like she did.* Had that been pure rumor? Had an innocent shopping jaunt and my disappearance gotten distorted into something hinting of menace and treachery?

"You're going to be blown away when you see Raven's Cove. It's really something." He gave me a warm smile. "I suppose it will be like seeing it for the first time all over again.''

''Was I…'blown away'…when I saw it before for the first time?''

Greg laughed. ''I'm the wrong one to ask about your first impressions of the place. You'll have to ask Nick that question. When the infatuated groom brought you home, he didn't want anyone else around.''

Infatuated. I experienced a fluttery sensation. ''Even his cousin?'' I asked innocently.

''Lillian? Oh, she doesn't count. She's part of the woodwork up in Raven's Cove.''

I doubted Lillian, or anyone for that matter, would appreciate such an unflattering, even callous description. I was a little disappointed in Greg for saying it, but then I told myself no one was perfect and I was probably being hypersensitive. Was it any wonder? We were nearing the top of the mountain, nearing the awesome Raven's Cove. Despite Greg's enthusiasm about the place, I couldn't help imagining a dark, foreboding mansion that would come looming out of the clouds like a portentous apparition, like something from one of Nick's own horror novels.

I looked out at the lush, wild terrain, suddenly aware that in the whole drive up the mountain I hadn't spotted a single other home or building of any sort.

''Doesn't anyone else live on the mountain?'' I asked Greg.

''Not very likely. Nick owns the whole kit and caboodle. Bought it so he could protect his privacy.''

He gave me a reassuring look. ''Don't worry. You won't be completely alone. I drop in at Raven's Cove a lot.'' He smiled at me. ''You'll probably get to thinking I'm a pest.''

''No I won't,'' I assured him so quickly that I flushed. ''I mean—I think you're…very nice.'' My amendment, I was sure, only served to deepen the pinkness in my cheeks, but then I spotted something reflected in Greg's features that made me wonder if I'd always thought Greg nice. Had there been times when I had considered him a pest? Or, were there times when I'd felt he was *too* nice? Those disturbing thoughts led me back again to the nature of my relationship with my husband.

"Greg, were we—Nick and I—happily married?"

When he didn't reply right away, my heart started to race. "Tell me. You . . . you must," I said in a shaky voice.

"Deborah, listen to me."

Listen? I was hanging on his every word.

"I pride myself on being an expert observer of people," he went on. "That goes with being a private investigator. And I'm very successful at my work."

I didn't question that. He'd found me, hadn't he?

He pulled the car to a stop and turned to face me. "There isn't a doubt in my mind that you have always been in love with Nick. From the first moment I saw you two together to that last day when you took off, you loved him. Trust me on that."

I stared at him. "It wasn't just a shopping trip, was it?"

Greg closed his eyes and then opened them again slowly. "You got a little miffed at him. Even the happiest of married couples have their spats. You and Nick were no exception."

"What did we fight about?"

"I thought if I told you that you'd left in a huff that day, you wouldn't . . . come back. And I felt I owed it to Nick and to you to bring the two of you back together. When . . . When your memory comes back, Deborah, I know the two of you will smooth things out."

"What things?" I asked stiffly.

He rubbed his eyes. "You sometimes got on Nick's case about not . . . paying you enough attention. I told you when he's working on a book, he pretty much closes himself off from the outside world. You resented it at times. It was only natural. And you were young, wanted to have fun, go places. Sometime you got lonely, bored, and craved a little more attention from Nick. Anyway, you'd planned this sailing trip. Just you and Nick. A kind of second honeymoon, I guess. And then Nick told you at the last minute that he had to cancel because of some revisions he felt he needed to do on his book. You got pissed—''

"You were there?"

He looked away. "For part of the row. I left before you did." When he turned back to me, there was a pained expression on his face. "Maybe if I'd stuck around I could have...calmed you down. Knowing Nick, the angrier you got, the more...restrained he got. You probably ended up good and frustrated—''

"You're telling me I walked out on Nick?"

"It wasn't like that, really. We both knew you'd be back, probably with a pile of new clothes and a new hairstyle. If nothing had...happened to you."

"And how did Nick feel about all this?"

Greg's lips compressed. "Nick isn't one for sharing his feelings. Or showing them, for that matter. If you ask me, I think he's actually very vulnerable and kind of puts up a wall to protect himself. Not that I claim to be Freud or anything."

"What did he say when you told him you'd found me? That you were bringing me...home?" The word *home* nearly stuck in my throat.

Greg sighed. "He said he'd wait supper for you."

We stared at each other in silence. It was Greg who broke it. "Give him a chance, Deborah. Give yourself a chance. And know one thing for certain. I'll always be there for you. You knew that in the past. And I want you to know it again now."

But I didn't know what I knew in the past—about Greg, about Nick, about anything. And I was equally, if not more so, in the dark about the present. As for the future—it was impossible to even consider.

The house was nothing like I'd conjured up in my mind. It wasn't the dark, ominous, Victorian-style mansion I'd fantasized. Raven's Cove, nestled into the crest of the mountain like it had been carved into the granite, was a wonder of modern architectural design. All glass and cedar, the house was built on several levels jutting down the cliffside, each level having access through sliding-glass doors to its own landscaped terrace. While it inspired no memories for me, I couldn't help but be captured by the visual if stark beauty of the place. My spirits managed to lift a bit. Maybe Nick would even greet me with open arms—the prodigal wife returned; the girl of his dreams. Maybe his love would be the key to unlocking my memory. Now I was the one sounding like I'd stepped out of a romance novel. How naive and innocent I was, then. Or, maybe it was just desperation. Desperation to belong, to feel wanted, to have a real home, to be loved and cherished.

A gravel path swung around to the main entrance of the house with its oversize double front doors fitted with smoky etched glass around cedar frames. The right door opened just as Greg pulled the car to a stop.

"Ah, the welcome committee," Greg muttered dryly.

My gaze fell on a tall, somber, middle-aged woman who stepped over the threshold, her face expressionless—except for her eyes. Even from this distance, I could recognize a look of undisguised reproach and wariness evident in her dark, lackluster eyes.

Greg appeared at my side of the car, opening the door and temporarily obscuring my view of the woman I presumed to be Nick's cousin, Lillian. Greg reached out for my hand to assist me in getting out, then, probably remembering my previous distressing reaction to physical contact, thought better of it, and let his hand drop. He couldn't know this, but for once, I'd have welcomed his touch. I felt in great need of someone to hold on to just then; someone who was no longer a complete stranger to me at least, someone who didn't regard me with such overt displeasure as the woman at the door.

After a moment's hesitation, I alighted from the car without assistance, while Greg stepped around to the trunk to retrieve my small case—the sum total of my possessions. I felt very much like a sorry waif as I nervously ascended the fan-shaped slate steps to the front door under the watchful eye of the solemn, spare-figured, tight-lipped Lillian. Not even a grudging smile of greeting. A welcoming committee, indeed! Why, the woman went so far as to step back inside the house before I even reached the door! And without saying so much as a word.

As we followed Lillian inside, I glanced anxiously over at Greg, but he merely presented me with another of his lop-sided smiles and an encouraging wink that did little to buoy my plummeting spirits.

"Well, here we are, home at last," Greg said cheerily to Lillian, ignoring the woman's dour expression.

"He's in the den. Working," Lillian responded stiffly, her voice cold and dismissive.

"Then I'll just go and rouse him from his 'work,'" Greg replied, undaunted.

Panicked to see my one ally take off, I nearly ran after him. But that would have meant running right into Nick—looking like a scared rabbit, no doubt. Better to calm down a bit and wait for him to come to me.

Not that it was easy to calm down, left alone with the austere and silent Lillian. I considered easing the tension by saying something, but was at a complete loss. Nor was

Nick's cousin any help. Lillian merely stood there in the vast marble-floored hallway giving me a cold, piercing look, not uttering a word, her proprietary manner making itself markedly clear. It was as though the woman was going out of her way to intimidate me—at which she was succeeding nicely.

The question was, why? Did I look so different that she was suspicious of whether I truly was Deborah? Did she think Greg had made a mistake? Or was Lillian giving me this cold reception because she resented my return? Had the two of us not gotten along in the past? If so, my bet was it was a case of mutual dislike. And then the thought struck me: Had Lillian been jealous of me? Was Nick more than just a cousin to her? Had she liked having him all to herself again these past two months? Pampering him? Bringing him his meals? Never making demands on his time, I surmised. Not the way I had.

I felt a flash of irritation. At least the woman could have the decency to speak her mind. I was even building up the courage to confront her. Anything seemed better than this tense, silent face-off. But, as if Lillian suspected I was about to say something, her lips curved slightly in what could hardly be called a smile, and, still without a word, she abruptly turned and took off down the hall, disappearing through a door at the far right.

Left alone, I fought to regain my composure before my next and very likely even more traumatic encounter ensued. While I waited for the arrival of "my husband," I regarded the large, sparsely decorated sunken living room to my right. The far wall was all window and sliding-glass doors, affording a spectacular view of the surrounding mountains and the sky, now streaked with brilliant slashes of red, purple and orange as the sun sank lower toward the horizon.

Pulling my gaze from the breathtaking vista beyond the windows, I focused my attention on the room itself. While there were few furnishings, each item was tastefully placed and reflected an expensive and refined taste. There was nothing large, cumbersome or gloomy here. The eclectic mix of modern pieces and antiques worked beautifully. A few modern paintings hung on the white walls. I recognized the artists, all quite celebrated. There was nothing here painted by an amateur; nothing of Deborah's—mine—in sight.

Despite the attractiveness of the room, it had the same starkness as the exterior of the house. It was all too meticulous. All *too perfect*. And there was an awful heaviness in the air, producing a chill that had nothing to do with temperature, but with something indefinable, something cloying and . . . sinister.

Paranoia rearing its ugly head again, I chided myself. I was getting carried away, letting some silly gossip I'd overheard in town distort my perspective, color my feelings. Color them *ruby red*. The blood-red shade flashed unbidden into my mind.

I was already trembling badly when I heard a door open behind me. Then footsteps on the cold, ungiving marble. Whirling around, I came face-to-face with him at last. The celebrated author of horror novels.

I saw now that the two customers back at the general store had been right about Nicholas Steele. He was everything they had said—and more. The inky blue-black eyes that shone with an inner, mysterious glow, the striking, angular features, the arrogance and pride of his tall, stately carriage, the glistening black hair pulled back from his face, and held by a leather band at his nape. "Medieval," one of the women had described him. Yes, I thought. It was as if this man were somehow from a darker, more dangerous, perhaps more reckless period of history.

With an air of desperation, I looked past him, hoping to see Greg. But the private investigator had remained inside the den. His own decision? Or Nick's? Whichever, it was clear to me that this was to be a private meeting between the two of us. A happy reunion? A callous dismissal? I had no idea. Those dark, mesmerizing eyes of his gave nothing away. He stood now no more than three feet from me. Except for the description of him I'd overheard in the shop, I in no way recognized this man who was supposedly my husband. And there was absolutely nothing in his look that indicated recognition of me as his wife.

He continued his silent survey, much as his cousin Lillian had done a few minutes earlier. But with Lillian, I had felt a mixture of intimidation, discomfort and irritation. My feelings were altogether different now. It was as if I were being tossed pell-mell into white-water rapids, rushing precariously closer to a waterfall. I could even hear the roar of the water in my ears, feel the danger engulfing me. But I felt helpless to stop my course—a course I had so impulsively set in motion the moment I'd agreed to come here to Raven's Cove and Nicholas Steele. Why, oh, why, hadn't I listened to Dr. Royce, followed his advice? If I'd seen Nicholas Steele at the hospital, looking at me the way he was looking at me now—silent, appraising, utterly unsettling—would I ever have come here? I really don't know. Even today, it's a question I can't answer for certain.

But one thing I knew then: I longed to look away, run away, escape this man, this cloying house, but I was so transfixed by his riveting, mesmerizing scrutiny of me that I could do nothing but remain frozen in place.

Well, not quite frozen. I began to sway. In a daze, I saw him reach out toward me. An instant later, his large hand rested on my shoulder. His touch—it was like fire and ice all at once. I opened my mouth to speak, to cry out, but then his face began to multiply before my eyes; worse still, to spin. Spinning and spinning, faster and faster. And then, mercifully, blackness descended as I fainted dead away.

CHAPTER FOUR

A sound of chirping birds broke through my sleep. I fought waking up, rolling onto my stomach and pulling the covers over my head to block out the light. It was far too bright. How could that be? I always slept with my shades drawn. Always in the hospital, that was. Before that... Well, there was no before that.

Sleep was my refuge, my escape from tension, anxiety, tedium. Early to bed, late to rise. That was my pattern. I knew, just as the doctors did, that it wasn't a real solution to my problem: but then, there didn't seem to be a solution.

Or did there? The question jabbed at me, and, in a minute, I was completely awake. And disoriented. Where was I? Last I remembered, I was standing in the vast white-marble-floored hallway of Raven's Cove, staring into those mesmerizing blue-black eyes of Nicholas Steele. And then I had gotten so dizzy....

My eyes shot open, my head still beneath the cover. I saw that I was now in a big, roomy bed made up with exquisitely soft linens. I also saw that I was no longer in the dress I'd had on. I was wearing a delicate cotton nightgown. Who had carried me to bed? Undressed me?

Slowly, warily, I drew the covers down from my eyes, blinking in the brightness of the room. A spacious, sunny room it was, with floral paper on the walls, a large bay window offering a spectacular vista of sky and mountains, an hand-painted antique armoire, a lovely chintz chaise longue coordinated to match the wallpaper...

My gaze stopped dead at the chaise, and I drew in a gasp. Sitting there, silent, his dark eyes giving me a measured, unflinching look, was none other than Nicholas Steele himself. Shaken though I was to find him there, somehow I wasn't surprised.

"What...happened?" I managed to say after I saw that he was not about to be the one to break the silence.

"You fainted." His voice had a deep resonance about it. A commanding voice. It suited him, I thought. As did its faintly mocking tone.

Bristling, I found myself replying in a tone that matched his. "Yes, I know that. I mean, after I fainted."

Something changed in his features. It was very subtle, but I noticed it. I could not, however, interpret its meaning.

He rose from the chaise. Standing, he seemed even more compelling. It wasn't merely his physique, but rather a presence about him, a strength and sureness of will that that radiated.

I was about to give up on getting an answer, when he replied matter-of-factly, "I carried you upstairs. Then you were tucked into bed where you slept a rather drugged sleep through the night. You missed one of Lillian's excellent roasts."

I was stunned to learn that it was the next day. How long had he been sitting there watching me? I felt a cold chill. "I'm not on any drugs, if you're concerned—"

"I'm not."

There was a prolonged silence. To my surprise, this time he broke it. "I imagine you're hungry."

I shook my head. Food was the furthest thing from my mind. "Did you...?" I glanced down at my nightgown.

"Did I what?"

I silently cursed the warmth I knew was rising in my cheeks. And him, as well, for forcing me to spell it out. Did he deliberately want to embarrass and humiliate me? Because he was still angry about our fight? About my walking out on him? Had he suffered and now wanted to make me suffer in turn? Although, to look at him now, there was no sign of suffering.

I drew in a breath. "I am hungry."

Was that actually a hint of a smile I detected on those otherwise grim lips?

"I'll have Lillian bring you up a tray." He started for the door, not even bothering to ask what I wanted to eat. But, of course, he had to know what his wife ate for breakfast.

My mind, however, wasn't on the menu. I was remembering my previous intimidating encounter with Lillian. I didn't want to begin my first and, for all I knew, last morning in Raven's Cove having to confront dour cousin Lillian if I could avoid it.

"Nick?" I called out to him as he opened the door.

He turned, his expression suddenly dark. I was taken aback.

I saw that he had no intention of volunteering the cause of his glaring disapproval. He simply waited for whatever else I intended to say.

"What's wrong?" I asked finally.

"Is there something wrong?" A sardonic expression replaced the dark look.

I felt a flash of fury. He was deliberately baiting me. "You didn't appear to approve of my calling you by your given name," I said rather stiffly, having no idea if that was the reason for his dark look. As I discovered, it was.

"My given name is Nicholas."

"Greg calls you Nick."

"Only to annoy me."

"I see," I answered quietly.

"You did occasionally call me Nick," he said with a slightly upward curve of the corners of his mouth that wasn't quite a smile. "But only in the throes of passion."

I flushed, looking away.

After a brief silence, he went on. "What was it you wanted to say?"

I was surprised to hear a softer tone in his baritone voice. Nicholas Steele was, I thought, one of those disturbingly mercurial people capable of constantly throwing you off your guard. Just when you thought you knew what to expect of him, he would toss you a curveball.

"I was going to say that I'd prefer to have breakfast downstairs." Hopefully, I prayed, not under the watchful eye of cousin Lillian.

He nodded disinterestedly. Again he started to leave the room. At the door, though, he abruptly turned back to me.

"You've changed a great deal."

There was such portent in his voice that I gasped audibly. "You're not sure, are you? At first I thought your rude behavior had to do with your being angry at me still. Greg told me that we'd argued and that I'd walked out."

"Did he?"

"The moment I first saw you, I sensed that you weren't at all sure whether you wanted me here. But it isn't because you're still angry. You aren't sure I'm ... her. You think I might not be ... Deborah."

"Do you always tell people what they're thinking?"

"Did Deborah?" I shot back, having no idea where my courage was coming from.

He gave me a long, appraising look. "Yes, as a matter of fact."

"You seem to be in almost as much of a predicament as I find myself in," I said.

"It looks that way, doesn't it?" He paused. "While you and Greg were driving up here, I phoned the New York

General and had a chat with your psychiatrist, Dr. Royce.
He's apparently quite solicitous about your welfare. Did you
know he was particularly fond of you?''

I didn't miss the cutting edge in his voice. "He's particularly fond of all his patients," I replied archly, foolish
enough to think I'd have the last word. Needless to say, I
hadn't.

"And are all of his patients particularly fond of him?" he
asked dryly, his dark gaze fixed on me. Oh, how I willed
myself not to flush, but it was beyond my control. He
seemed to get some perverse pleasure out of seeing me embarrassed, and I thought to myself, this certainly wasn't the
captivating man Greg described to me—a man whom
women supposedly found witty and charming. I was decid-
edly not charmed. As for his reported sex appeal, I dis-
missed even the possibility of that entirely. He was rude,
insinuating and cruel. I may have once been the girl of his
dreams, but I couldn't imagine that Nicholas Steele had ever
been the man of my dreams. Of my nightmares, was more
like it.

"It's Dr. Royce's opinion that however you might once
have been, both in terms of your appearance and personal-
ity, he believes it's quite conceivable, even probable, that
you could appear and act quite differently now."

"Am I so different than I—than Deborah—was?" There
was a little catch in my voice. Greg had so convinced me I
was Deborah, I'd begun to fully believe it myself. Nicholas's doubts took me completely unaware.

Since I didn't expect a smile, that was just what he threw
me. It was like a break in dark clouds. "Not completely
different. You share a low tolerance for frustration."

"You mean she found you frustrating?" I tossed back
cheekily.

His smile faded. I saw that I had clearly overstepped my
bounds. As if I had even the vaguest idea what my bounds

were, under such strange, not to mention strained, circumstances.

"You look remarkably like Deborah, though a little paler, a little thinner," he said, his tone formal and analytical now. "Your hair's a bit darker, but then perhaps you haven't spent much time out in the sun during your hospitalization." There was a long pause. "Deborah was a real sunworshiper. She was always taking herself off to sunny shores."

"Alone?"

He gave me a curious look. "Not always."

"You went with her sometimes, then?"

"That isn't what I said." His tone was wry and insinuating.

I flinched visibly. "Maybe if you weren't always so busy writing and revising your horror novels, your relationship with your wife would have been . . . closer."

He laughed harshly. "Deborah never minded my working. It left her free to pursue her own pleasures, unencumbered."

This was certainly not the picture of Deborah that Greg had painted for me. Nicholas was describing a spoiled, willful, and possibly unfaithful vixen. A sharp contrast to the loyal but lonely young wife whose only crime was that she craved a bit of attention from her workaholic husband. So, which picture of "Deborah" was the accurate one? Which of the two men was I to trust?

As I was suffering this torment of doubt, Nicholas was giving me another of his long, assessing looks. "In the end, maybe it's not so important whether *I'm* certain you're Deborah as that *you* are."

"Still, this is your home," I said. "Either way, you can always ask me to leave."

"You never needed my permission in the past."

And, I realized with relief, I didn't need it now. I could leave of my own free will. And very likely not be missed at all. But then I glanced at Nicholas, catching him unaware, for once. There was a hint of sadness there in those dark, uncompromising eyes. It was there for only an instant, but it made me think back to Greg's remark that Nicholas was really quite vulnerable behind that mask of arrogance he wore so well.

He gripped the doorknob. "I think you'll find the atmosphere and amenities of Raven's Cove at least as pleasant as the hospital," he commented offhandedly, the mask again solidly in place. "And I can assure you that as long as you're here, you won't be required to engage in any activities that displease you," he added.

Though his expression was bland, I felt sure I understood the meaning behind this comment. But could I believe him? Right now he had some doubts about my identity. I told myself it was understandable. I was certainly not a carbon copy of the Deborah I'd seen in that photograph. Not by a long shot. But, if he came to be convinced I was Deborah—whether or not my memory ultimately confirmed it for me—wouldn't he expect me, as his wife, to sleep with him? Would it even matter to him that in my eyes he would still be a stranger?

Despite feeling the heat spread again over my cheeks, I eyed him with a touch of defiance. "Who undressed me? And put me in this nightgown?"

He laughed dryly, giving me a rueful, condescending look. "Lillian. Who did you think?"

Without waiting for an answer, he exited the room. Only after he'd gone did I realize that I was shaking. Admittedly short as my memory was, I couldn't recall another instance of a person making me feel the way Nicholas Steele did. I felt that he was the most exceedingly dangerous man I had ever encountered. And the most compelling.

As I showered in the spacious and lavish private bathroom adjoining the bedroom, I considered packing my few belongings and taking the first train back to the hospital. A few minutes later, returning to the bedroom, I was even further convinced that I should leave. There on my bed was a hardcover book. *Night Cries*. Nicholas's latest horror novel. The cover alone—a woman, faceless save for a wide, screaming mouth, her arms outstretched, superimposed on a midnight-black background—terrified me.

I stared at the book with revulsion. Had Nicholas dropped this off for me? A token of his... Of his what? There was a tremor in my hands as I finally lifted the book from the bed. At first I meant only to stick it away in a drawer, unable to bear the hideously pained image on the cover. But as I took hold of the book, I found myself compelled to open it. I selected one page at random—just to see what made this master of the macabre so renowned.

A harsh cawing broke the stillness of the night. Then silence. The silence of death. Creeping behind the trunk of a large elm, he lay in wait for her. He knew he would not have to wait long. A few minutes later, he heard the crunch of leaves underfoot. He smiled. Not a very pleasant smile. He had sometimes wished he had one of those ordinary faces with their ordinary smiles. The kind of face people trusted. A face women trusted...

She let out a sharp cry when he stepped out from his hiding place. But then she laughed softly, wantonly.

"Silly man. You nearly scared the living daylights out of me."

He knew, in the darkness, she could not yet make out who it really was she had come to meet for this little rendezvous. But she would. In time, she would. The anticipation filled him with delight. Oh, how he longed to hear her crooning voice turn into a whimper. What pleasure he would take as the wantonness bled from her face and gave way to terror, her gut tightening like a fist. *Please, please, don't hurt me,* she would cry.

He would hurt her. But he would take his sweet time. He would toy with her. He would show her who was in charge; who had been in charge right from the start.

Forgive me, she would cry. He would laugh at her. Didn't she know, that forgiveness wasn't in his nature...?

I let out an audible gasp, slamming the book shut. And then, as if the closed book were some kind of lethal viper, I flung it across the room. It slammed against the wall, then landed front cover facing up on the royal blue carpet—that horrible faceless woman, her mouth opened in a scream, arms outstretched. Now I understood. The woman was crying out in the agony of mental and physical torment, pleading for forgiveness, begging for her life. I rushed over, grabbed up the book and stuck it in the top drawer of a bureau.

How vile and gruesome! What kind of mind...? I realized I was echoing the sentiment of one of the female customers I'd overheard yesterday at Gus's. And then another of the women's remarks replayed in my head. *He has to be a little mad himself...*

Ignoring the armoire with its large assortment of expensive, fine looking designer clothing, I hurriedly pulled a creased sundress from my suitcase, shaking out the wrinkles as best I could. I closed the case, leaning on it for support. This situation was impossible. The man who might possibly be my husband frightened and mystified me. His cousin, who clearly bore me no good feelings whatsoever, only added to the impossibility of my remaining. To stay, surrounded by suspicion, not even knowing if I belonged, was madness itself. And even if I were to discover that I was

Deborah, maybe I had left Raven's Cove and my husband for good reason. Maybe I'd never meant to return as Greg had implied. However I examined my dilemma, the solution was the same: Get dressed and leave at once.

But I couldn't just leave. Raven's Cove was perched on the top of a mountain. It had to be a good five miles of winding roads to its base, and another five, at least, to town. I couldn't very well hike it, heavy suitcase in hand. Nor did I feel at all comfortable about asking Nicholas to drive me. I wanted no further confrontations with the intolerable Nicholas Steele. And no others with Lillian. I supposed I could telephone to Greg and ask him . . . But he seemed so bent on my giving my new—or to his mind, old—surroundings a fighting chance. He would very likely try to dissuade me from my impulsive decision. And I didn't know if I had the strength to argue. My only other option was to call for a cab. Surely there was a taxi service in Sinclair.

There was a phone by the side of my bed, but no phone book in sight. I dialed Information. To my relief, there was one cab company in town. I received a busy signal on my first three attempts, but finally got through on my fourth try.

"Sinclair Cab," a nasal voice snapped.

"Yes, I'd like a cab to the train station," I replied in a hushed whisper, as if someone might be listening. My gaze strayed involuntarily to the bureau where I'd put Nicholas's frightful book. "Right away."

"Address?"

I hesitated. "Raven's Cove."

There was a drawn-out silence.

"Is... Is there something...wrong?" I asked finally. The response took me aback.

"You must be her."

I rubbed a sweaty palm on my dress. "Excuse . . . me?" I was getting my first taste of what small-town life was about.

It was clear that word had already spread through Sinclair about my arrival at Raven's Cove. Or, as at least a couple of the townsfolk and Greg believed, my *return*. For all I knew, Nicholas shared their belief and was just getting some perverse amusement out of voicing doubts as to my identity. Again, I wondered if it was payback for my having walked out on him. Maybe he held other misdeeds against me, as well. He'd certainly implied some indiscretions on my part.

"You say the railroad station?" the dispatcher asked.

"Yes."

"You planning to catch a train?"

"Yes."

"Where to?"

I thought it was none of the dispatcher's business.

After a pause, he said, "Next train out's at eleven. Goes to New York City. Express."

"Fine."

"Not even nine. You don't need a cab for a while yet."

I was about to tell him I was in a hurry, but stopped myself, realizing how odd that would sound since I'd be stuck waiting at the train for close to two hours. Besides, I didn't want this nosy dispatcher spreading rumors. I could just hear the townsfolk buzzing away. *Wanted to get out of there in a real hurry, she did. Sounded scared out of her wits. Guess it's true about that Steele fellow being mad . . .*

In as level a voice as I could manage, I said, "I do have a few errands to do in town first. Do you think you could get a cab up here by ten?"

"I got one driver out sick and my other guy's got a pickup in town in ten minutes. A gal who's going over to Carlisle. Better make it ten-fifteen. Just to be on the safe side."

The safe side.

There was no safe side about it, I thought as I hung up, frowning.

After I was dressed, I searched in my purse for my hair-brush. It wasn't there. I realized that I must have left it back at the hospital. Crossing to a mirrored dressing table, I searched there for a brush. The surface of the dressing table had a pristine tidiness about it. Save for a small collection of ornate and very beautiful blown-glass perfume bottles that sat on a mirrored silver tray, there were no other personal effects to be seen.

Still shaky and weak, I sat down at the table. I opened the top drawer. Inside was not only the brush that I needed, but a framed eight-by-ten photograph, half hidden by some blank embossed stationery. For all my trepidation, my curiosity got the best of me. Nervously, I removed the photo from the drawer, waiting a moment for my breath to steady before actually looking at it.

There was certainly nothing gruesome about the photo. Far from it. It showed a couple embracing on a white sandy beach under a palm tree. Deborah and Nicholas. The shade fell across Deborah's face, clouding her image. But Nicholas's face was in full sunlight, as was his tanned, athletic body clad only in a pair of black swimming trunks.

I almost didn't recognize him. Could the grim, patronizing, disdainful man who inspired such anxiety and worse in me, and the smiling figure in the photo, truly be one and the same? Oh, I had caught a quick glimpse of Nicholas's smile, and it had most definitely softened his features. But the smile he wore in this photo utterly transformed his face. Up until now, I had thought Nicholas imposing, striking, but not really good-looking. Not in any traditional sense. His features were too strong, too harsh. But in the photo he looked heart-stoppingly handsome. Perhaps because the smile he was bestowing on Deborah was so adoring, so filled with love. No. More than love. *Adulation.*

I wiped tears from my eyes. Instead of placing the photo back in the drawer, I set it on top of the dressing table. It

held such fascination for me. And something else. A sense
of loss. So that was what my tears were about. If I was
Deborah, then I questioned whether I would ever again see
such love in Nicholas's face. And if my memory returned
and I proved not to be Deborah, then I'd never know what
it must have felt like to have been so cherished and adored.
All I would know was envy.

I lifted out the sterling-silver-handled hairbrush from the
drawer. A beautiful object. Why had it been left behind?
Had I been so angry when I walked out, that I took almost
nothing with me? I realized, despite Nicholas's doubts, I was
already incorporating Deborah into my identity. After all,
I had no other. And somehow, for all the discrepancies between Greg's vision of Deborah and Nicholas's, I *felt* like
her. And, much to my consternation, I even felt I could have
fallen wildly, deeply in love with the man in the photograph
on the dressing table.

As I brushed my hair, I noticed the perfume bottles beside the photo. Finishing with my hair, I gingerly lifted one
of the bottles up and carefully removed the sculptured-glass
top. I sniffed it cautiously, as if it might be tainted.

The scent was strongly floral and cloying. My nose crin-
kled as I hurriedly closed the bottle. It wasn't something I
would wear at all. Was that a clue? Did it mean I mustn't be
Deborah? And again the question, did it even matter now?
Now that I was resigned to leaving Raven's Cove?

I put the bottle back on the tray. Of course, I might have
received the perfume as a gift and not cared for it. I tested
the other scents. Unlike the first one, these were more
pleasant. One in particular—a perfume with a slightly pun-
gent fruity aroma—was especially pleasing. I felt tempted to
put a few dabs behind my ears.

"He doesn't care for Intoxication."

The remark was so strange that for a moment I didn't
even connect it to an actual voice. The information had been

supplied by Lillian, who was standing at the open door. She'd had the gall to step in without even bothering to knock. Had it been Lillian, not Nicholas, who'd put his book in my room while I'd been in the shower? In any case, both cousins certainly seemed too comfortable about walking into my room unannounced and uninvited.

Unnerved by Lillian's sudden appearance, I accidentally let the exquisite glass perfume bottle drop from my hand. It hit the corner of the dressing table, shattering on contact. The scent, far stronger now as it spilled out on the table and carpeting, permeated the air, making me feel queasy. I stared down at the shattered glass with dismay, then bent to pick up the shards.

A scornful smile colored Lillian's expression, not improving it, as she crossed the room in long, gliding steps and brushed me aside with a dismissive wave of her hand. Silently and thoroughly, the gaunt woman set to the task I'd begun. If the heavy scent bothered her, she gave no sign of it.

"I'm . . . so sorry about the vial. It's just . . . You startled me." No sooner had the words come out than I instantly regretted them. It certainly wouldn't help matters to blame Lillian for my own clumsiness.

"Nicholas sent me up to ask what you wanted for your breakfast." Lillian spoke without affect, but I felt duly chastised nonetheless.

"Oh . . . It doesn't . . . matter," I replied meekly, glancing at my closed suitcase. I had meant to skip breakfast at Raven's Cove and remain in my room until just after ten. Then my plan was to steal out of the house and meet the cab at the wrought-iron gates to the property.

"Bacon and eggs?" Lillian was dropping the last of the larger shards into the wicker wastebasket beside the dressing table.

"No, thanks. I don't really care for— Just some . . . toast and coffee will be fine."

Lillian glanced up from her task, giving me a curious look. I had the clear impression she'd been testing me; that she knew Deborah didn't care for bacon and eggs and wanted to see what I'd say. Did Lillian, like her cousin, have doubts about my identity? Not that it mattered what either one of them believed at this point, I told myself firmly. Or what I believed, for that matter. Either way, I was leaving.

But then my gaze fell once more on the photo. Was I again acting impulsively? In leaving so precipitously, was I really running away from . . . myself? As I looked at the image of the handsome, adoring man with his arms around the "girl of his dreams," I couldn't help wondering if it would truly be so awful for Nicholas to come to accept me as Deborah; to welcome me back to Raven's Cove? Could this be a chance at a new beginning, not just for me, but for him, as well? For the two of us together? What if he were to once again look at me with that same heartfelt love . . . ?

Just as I was having these thoughts, I heard an audible gasp escape Lillian's lips. For a moment, I believed that she had cut herself on a piece of glass. But she'd already completed the clean-up—at least as much as could be done without vacuuming the invisible shards. Her gasp was the result of noticing the photo on the dressing table.

"What's that doing out?" she demanded. "He didn't leave it there."

I didn't miss the stinging accusation in her words, nor the implied message that Nicholas didn't want the photo on display.

I could feel my indignation begin to surface. But I knew that neither displaying my anger nor allowing myself to be so thoroughly intimidated would serve any purpose other than to alienate Lillian further. I decided to try a new tack. Instead of being defensive and paranoid, I would try to en-

list her sympathies—though I admittedly had my doubts
about whether that was possible.

"Do you know where the photo was taken?" I asked in a
soft-spoken voice.

"St. Martin." Lillian's tone was dull and toneless.

"Before we were married, then," I mused.

Lillian just stood there saying nothing.

"Is this . . . the master bedroom? The room I shared with
Nicholas?"

"Which question do you want me to answer?"

Lillian's question was answer enough.

I felt I had to go on despite the total lack of encouragement I received from this positively chilling woman. I had
to ask the question that hung between us like a sizzling live
wire. "I don't have any idea what our relationship was before . . . before I left, but I'd like us to be friends now, Lillian. You could tell me so much, help me. . . ."

The gaunt older woman continued staring at me. Still not
a word. And not a flicker of sympathy in those dark eyes,
that pale, somber face. Again, I was flooded with a sinking
sensation of foreboding.

I kept talking, hoping the feeling would pass. "Nicholas
says . . . he doesn't know yet . . . if I really am Deborah.
He . . . he isn't sure."

"Isn't he?"

I struggled to make sense of this ambiguous response.
Was Lillian implying that Nicholas really was sure? And
sure of what? Sure that I was Deborah? Or that I wasn't?

My head was spinning.

Lillian's next remark was totally distressing. "You'd better be careful not to get yourself hurt here." With those
measured words of hers went a darkly threatening look.

"What do you mean?" I asked, unable to disguise my
fear.

A sardonic smile curved the older woman's grim lips. "The shards of glass. You could cut yourself if you walked about the room barefoot."

I was certain Lillian had meant her remark to be misunderstood. She had intended to frighten me. Well, she'd done a good job of it.

Meeting the hostile woman's gaze, I replied with saccharine sweetness, "It's very kind of you to be so concerned about my welfare, Lillian, but believe me, you don't have to worry." I had no intention of ever again walking about this room, *barefoot or otherwise*.

CHAPTER FIVE

I found my buttered toast and coffee waiting for me in the sunny breakfast room with its bright southern exposure. Lillian didn't make an appearance. I suppose I should have been grateful, but even though she wasn't physically there, I could feel her presence about me as if her very aura hovered in the air. As for Nicholas, I hadn't seen any sign of him since our strained and disturbing encounter in my bedroom. I assumed he was already in his den, busy at work on another ghoulish tale. I shivered at the thought of it.

Although I had no appetite at all, despite having missed dinner last night, I managed to swallow my buttered toast with some strong black coffee. Then I checked my watch. It was ten minutes to ten. If I left now, I estimated that I could be past the gate to the property and a good quarter of a mile from Raven's Cove by ten-fifteen. I'd flag the cab down there and be on my merry way. Well, I suppose *merry* wasn't the right word. *Frightened, nervous*—any of those adjectives would have better suited my mood at the time.

From where I was sitting, I could see a garden path that curved down to the paved drive. A perfect route for my escape. Yes, I did think of it as an escape, even though I was not being held at Raven's Cove against my will. Far from it. I believed there were forces inside that house of gale-wind proportions pushing me right out the door. And yet, at the same time, something held me there. I knew that something was *me*. The *me* I was just beginning to learn about. The *me* I wasn't at all sure I wanted to know.

My suitcase was still upstairs. Did I dare take the time to fetch it? And what if either Lillian or Nicholas spotted me making my exit, suitcase in hand? It wasn't that either of them would mourn my departure. Certainly Lillian wouldn't. She clearly resented my presence. And Nicholas? He was an enigma. I couldn't fathom what his feelings were for me now. If they were anything like mine, they were a jumble. But then, he knew so much more than I did—about both of us.

Though I might get to understand him better if I stayed. And myself. While I couldn't shake the belief that the key to the mystery about my past lay in Raven's Cove, it was my future that preoccupied me at the moment. What kind of future would I have if I stayed? Even that question filled me with a sense of dread.

Forget the suitcase! I wanted no awkward confrontations or questions. Besides, I owned nothing of any consequence. A visit to a thrift shop would be all that was required to refurbish my meager wardrobe. Unlike Deborah, I had no interest at all in expensive designer clothes or in my personal appearance in general. The blue-and-white flowered sundress I wore was still somewhat creased from being packed, and was probably a size or two too large. Over it, I'd tossed on a red cardigan—the only sweater I'd brought along. Beyond brushing my hair, I'd merely tucked it behind my ears, letting it tumble any which way around my shoulders.

During my whole stay at the hospital I'd never thought anything about what I wore, nor bothered with makeup or gone out of my way to style my hair. Most of the time I'd pulled it back in a ponytail to get it off my face and away from paint splatterings. As for my clothing, I saw it as nothing more than covering for my body. Style wasn't even a consideration. I had discussed this on occasion with Dr. Royce, long before I knew of the existence of Deborah

Steele. His theory was that with no inward identity, I had unconsciously chosen to present a nondescript outward appearance. Not knowing who I was, I had no idea how I wanted to present myself. I'm sure he was right, although it left me feeling melancholy. I admit there were times when I'd seen myself as a rather tragic figure. Dr. Royce perceptively picked up on that mood, invariably chided me for feeling sorry for myself. Then I'd get angry. After which I'd feel enormously better!

I realized as I sat there in that beautifully appointed, glass-enclosed breakfast room at Raven's Cove that I was once again feeling sorry for myself. Hearing Dr. Royce in my head, I could feel the despair giving way to anger. I was not a prisoner. I was free to come and go as I pleased. And I was pleased to be going!

My anger propelled me to take action. I would return directly to the hospital. To Dr. Royce. I would tell him that he was right about the impulsiveness of my departure—which I absolutely believed—and that I needed more time in a *safe, secure* environment before I was ready to assume any identity at all. If I was Deborah, eventually I would remember. And when I did, I would be able to decide what steps I wanted to take as the wife of Nicholas Steele. I would be in charge of my own fate.

I exited the breakfast room through the French doors that led to a flagstone terrace bordered by aromatic flowering azalea bushes. Yesterday's rainstorm, coupled with the bright morning sun, had spread a glistening sheen over the whole landscape. The mountains seemed outlined in light. The air had a rich, fresh tang. I took in gulping breaths, aware of the beauty around me but not fully able to appreciate it. Any other time, my first impulse would have been to grab my paints and try to capture the splendor of it all on canvas. But now, with each step I took, I kept imagining that Lillian and Nicholas were both watching me from the windows at Raven's Cove. I could visualize the look of victory in Lillian's hostile eyes. I imagined Nicholas's expression would be guarded, his dark visage giving nothing away. But what he was thinking—that was the mystery…and, try as I might to deny it, the fascination.

Suddenly that candid shot of him on the beach, the adulation on his face as he smiled down at his young bride, came to mind. A sharp pang of longing and loss shot through me. I forced the image from my mind. Water over the bridge—a bridge I wouldn't be crossing again; a bridge I wasn't even certain I had ever crossed in the first place.

I made my way around to the drive. Relief washed over me as I stepped past the open gates a few minutes later. I picked up my pace. I had to hold myself back from actually breaking into a run. If the taxi driver were to see me breathlessly flagging him down, he might presume that something awful had happened to me. I might have been feeling pretty awful, but I most definitely didn't want to be the cause of any more rumors about Nicholas Steele floating around Sinclair. He didn't deserve that. At least, that's what I told myself at the time.

I had walked far enough along the winding mountain road that when I finally dared to look back, I could see no sign of the vast, imposing house. Which meant to me that I, too, could no longer be seen by either of the house's two occupants. I told myself it was simply suspicion on my part to even be thinking such a thought, but whatever the cause, I still felt that my departure had not gone unnoticed. On the plus side, it had also been unhindered.

A few minutes later, when I picked up the sound of a car approaching on the winding road, I stopped. Until I heard that sound, I had worried that the taxi mightn't show up. There could have been some problem or delay with the last passenger, maybe. Or a breakdown. Something, anything, to keep me from making my escape.

All of that relief drained instantly from me as the car rounded the bend. Not a taxi, but a familiar yellow sports car drew up beside me, the driver giving me a bright, cheerful smile.

"Hop in," Greg said amiably, leaning across and popping the door open for me.

I hesitated, glancing down the road.

He smiled. "I sent it back."

I gave him a look that was a mixture of embarrassment and outrage. What right had he—

"If you wanted a ride to the train station, why didn't you call me, Deb?"

I got in beside him, but he didn't start the car again. Instead, he turned in his seat and examined me with disquietingly close scrutiny. "Did something happen?" His features darkened. "Nick didn't—"

"No," I interrupted sharply, my face no doubt scarlet, as I finished Greg's sentence in my head. "And...and he doesn't like being called Nick, you know."

I didn't think there was anything amusing in what I'd said, but Greg broke out into a spurt of laughter. "Oh, Deb, you're priceless."

"You aren't making any sense," I retorted irritably.

He smiled contritely. "I'm sorry. Poor Deborah. Your lovely head must be spinning. A large part of which I'm willing to bet we owe to Witch Lillian."

I scowled. "Why does she hate me so?"

"Don't you know?" He maintained his fixed gaze on me.

I looked back at him. "She's in love with Nicholas."

"See. I knew coming back was just what you needed."

"That statement has nothing to do with my amnesia lifting, Greg. It's just...obvious. Anyone would be able to see—"

"So, you're letting her scare you off again."

It was the "again" that brought me up short. "I thought when I ran off it was over an argument with Nicholas. What did Lillian have to do with it?"

An odd expression flitted across Greg's features. I couldn't figure out what it meant, which surprised me. Compared to Nicholas's, Greg's face was usually an open book.

"Lillian got on your nerves. You used to storm off sometimes in frustration and drive down to my cottage, complaining that you thought she was off her rocker. You wanted Nicholas to send her away to some sanatorium somewhere. Once, about a year after you were married, you even gave him an ultimatum—her or you."

I stared at Greg. "That's what you meant by saying Lillian drove me off. He refused to do anything about his cousin, so I left." I could see from Greg's smile that he assumed this was another concrete example of my memory starting to come back. It wasn't at all. I had absolutely no recollection of any of that happening. But something was beginning to happen to me. I could sense it, but I couldn't explain it—not to Greg or even to myself.

"Nick's always been very protective of Lillian even though it probably appears to an outsider that the reverse is more the case," Greg commented.

"Maybe they look after each other."

Greg's arm slipped around my seat, but he was careful not to touch me. "Lillian can't meet all of Nick's needs. She knows that, he knows that, and once upon a time, you knew that. I think you still do."

I could feel the heat radiate in my cheeks and I looked away.

"Are you sure you want to leave, Deborah?"

All I had to do was say yes and I knew Greg would take me to the station, help me make my escape, even though it was clear he wanted me to stay. Even a nod would have done. But I couldn't do either. I wanted to, and yet...I couldn't.

As Greg drove me back up to the house, I tried to tell myself that it was only my stubborn pride that was keeping me from running off again. If I was Deborah Steele, I had every right to be at Raven's Cove. Furthermore, I was behaving like a coward, allowing Lillian and Nicholas to drive me away with so little effort on their parts. As for Lillian, it wasn't for her to say at all, whether I stayed or left. And as for Nicholas, if he didn't want me to remain, then he would have to tell me directly, to my face.

So, what was I telling myself? That he wanted me to stay? That my presence at Raven's Cove mattered to him? That I mattered to him?

"What are you thinking?" Greg asked, catching me off guard. I couldn't tell him. I was too embarrassed.

Instead I asked, "What did you tell the taxi driver?"

Greg didn't answer immediately. I think he knew I'd made the question up on the spot. But finally he said, "I told him that you'd changed your mind and decided you'd pick up a few things in town instead of bothering with an all-day shopping trip to New York."

"You always seem so sure of what I'll do."

He gave me a quick smile. "You may not remember me, Deb, but I remember you. I used to know what you were thinking before you did, sometimes. We had a way of reading each other's minds."

"You make it sound like we were...very close." I could feel the tension knotting my muscles. Had there been something between Greg and me? Were those indiscretions Nicholas had alluded to grounded in fact? Was I the kind of woman who would have cheated on her husband? With his close friend, no less?

"Relax, Deb. We were friends. Good friends. That's all."

I saw a shadow of sadness in Greg's face. He was right. We could read each other's thoughts. I knew then that Greg Eastman had wanted to be more than friends. I couldn't help but wonder if I had, too. I had no idea. I could have asked Greg, but I wasn't sure I could handle the answer. I decided that what mattered was that neither of us had acted on those feelings. I don't know why, but I felt an almost-giddy relief at that decision. I guess I didn't want to have been the sort of wife who was unfaithful to my husband, even if my husband was at present a perfect stranger to me—and someone I didn't like in the least.

"He's not working. You scared him."

Greg gestured toward the window at the east corner as he spoke. There was Nicholas, standing by the uncurtained window, looking out with that inscrutable guarded expression as Greg pulled the car around the curved drive.

"What do you mean, I scared him?" I asked Greg as he pulled to a stop. "He doesn't look the least bit scared."

"If you're going to judge Nick by his looks, you won't get anywhere, Deborah."

"How do I judge him?"

Greg didn't exactly give me an answer. Not a direct one, anyway. "Look, Nick's not an easy guy to live with."

"You mean I never found it easy?"

"No, you never did. But you . . . loved him."

"That doesn't mean much—anything—to me now."

"Are you sure about that?"

I didn't answer. I don't think I trusted myself to answer. Because I wasn't sure what I'd say.

"I always used to tell you that if you ever felt like coming down from your mountain, I'd be there at the bottom with open arms." He gave me a tender look. "The offer still stands. Any time. So, don't feel like you've got to run away again, Deborah. I've always been there for you. I always will be. Do you believe me?"

"Yes," I said. And I did.

He smiled, got out of the car and came around to open my door. I stepped out hesitantly, some of my bravery deserting me. My gaze was drawn to the window, but Nicholas was no longer standing there.

"Will you . . . come in for . . . a while?" I asked Greg haltingly.

"Sure. Nick's expecting me."

"Expecting you?" So, that's why Greg was driving up the mountain road to the house just when I was attempting my big escape. I suppose I thought he'd been coming up to see how I was doing. My, my, but I was getting vain.

If Greg saw me blush, he didn't comment on it. Instead, he checked his watch. "And Hal Chapman will be along sometime soon."

"Hal Chapman?"

"Sorry. Of course, you don't remember. Hal's Sinclair's esteemed chief of police."

My mouth went dry. "Police?"

"It's okay, Deb. Relax. No crime's been committed. That's why he's coming over."

I appeared confused.

"He wants to wipe you off the books as a missing person. Can't very well do that until he drops by and sees you've been found."

Missing Person. It had such an ominous tone. And then I thought morosely, wasn't I still missing?

I didn't voice that question. Instead, I said an inane, "Oh," in response, letting Greg guide me up the fan-shaped steps to the front entrance of the house.

The door was unlocked and I tried not to look furtively around as I stepped inside, but I don't think I quite succeeded. In any case, neither Lillian nor Nicholas came into the hallway. I would have to face them at some point, but this was definitely not an instance of "the sooner the better."

"You could do with something to eat," Greg said with gentle authority. "You're not exactly skinny as a rail, but you must have dropped a good fifteen pounds anyway, since..." He led me into a sunny parlor. "Take a load off your feet while I go whip us up a couple of my incredible omelets. You look starved, and I'm starved."

"Won't Lillian mind if you...take over in her kitchen?" I said, anxiously. I was sure Nicholas's cousin felt proprietary about her domain—which I was also sure extended to far more than the kitchen at Raven's Cove.

Greg winked at me. "She'd blow a gasket. But she won't know. I spotted her out on a path near the house as we were pulling up. Her morning constitutional."

I breathed a bit easier knowing Lillian wasn't in the house. But there was still Nicholas. Had he been watching for my return from his window? Had he observed me leaving earlier, as I'd imagined? Was he scared I might not come back, as Greg had said so confidently? I found it difficult to believe, but somehow not impossible. My memory might be gone, but my instincts were intact—and maybe even more acute, now that they were all I could rely on. My instincts told me that Nicholas had a great many feelings that he kept hidden. It was a question of what those feelings were that both unnerved and intrigued me.

I jumped when I heard footsteps on the marble floor. I knew it was Nicholas even before I turned around. He made a distinct sound; but then everything about the man was quite distinctive.

"You have a visitor." He might have been an English butler, his tone and manner were so stiff and formal. I suddenly found myself having to stifle a little giggle. Had I ever giggled in the past when he got so stuffy and off-putting?

Then again, maybe he hadn't had reason to be stuffy with me in the past.

The urge to laugh quickly faded as I considered his message rather than his delivery. A visitor? I hadn't heard a car pull up. But then I realized the room I was in faced the back of the house.

"It's the police chief. His name's Hal Chapman," Nicholas said, waiting for some response from me.

I nodded nervously, wishing Greg weren't off in the kitchen making omelets.

"Would you like to see him in here or outside on the terrace?"

I was surprised that Nicholas would offer me a choice. I expected him to be the one making all the decisions. For some reason, I felt almost ridiculously appreciative of this small courtesy.

"Oh, outside," I muttered. With Nicholas's arrival, the texture of the air within the house seemed to change, becoming more weighty. I would breathe easier outside.

I followed him down the hallway, through the spacious living room to one of the house's several outdoor terraces. This one faced due east, and was the brightest, sunniest spot at this time of day. He pulled the door open, motioning me to go ahead of him.

The police chief rose as I stepped outside. He was a compact man of medium height, just a bit taller than me at five-foot-six. He had amazingly thick mahogany-colored hair and a bushy mustache that was almost the same color except that it was threaded with a few gray strands. He was dressed in casual clothes—a pair of gray trousers and a collared pale blue jersey under a rumpled black golfing jacket. My first impression was that he looked sort of fatherly, not anything like my image of a policeman; but then the only other police I'd encountered—that I recalled—had been the young, earnest, uniformed officer and his older, drawn-looking, partner that night in the hospital after I'd regained consciousness. I also remembered all of their questions and my agony over having no answers. How could I respond when I had absolutely no memory? How could I respond to the questions I imagined Hal Chapman now had for me?

I felt incredibly self-conscious as the policeman's eyes regarded me with riveting interest. I began worrying that he wouldn't believe I was Deborah Steele, thus confirming Nicholas's suspicions. All of a sudden, I felt desperate to have the chief's support. I cursed my appearance, knowing how much it took away from Hal Chapman's image of the glamorous, elegantly attired, provocative Deborah Steele. At that moment, I felt at best like a poor relation.

Nicholas was standing behind me. I hadn't so much heard him follow me out as felt his presence. Was he, too, waiting for the police chief to pass sentence?

"Sit down." It was Nicholas who spoke. For a moment I thought he was addressing Chapman, who was still on his feet. But then I heard the scraping of a patio chair behind me and turned to see Nicholas holding it out for me.

Gratefully, I sank into it. The police chief followed suit. Only Nicholas remained standing. Above it all, I remember thinking at the time. And envying him for it.

After I was seated, I caught Chapman darting a quick glance over my shoulder at Nicholas. In that brief look I saw dismay, pity and shock. But did I see doubt?

It was no picnic—feeling on display, being held up for inspection, having my very identity held in question by some man whom I doubted knew Deborah Steele all that well. My whole posture altered. I sat up straighter, and no longer gazed at him furtively. I regarded the police chief boldly, deciding I'd played the victim long enough, thank you.

"I'm at a terrible disadvantage here, Mr. Chapman," I said in a remarkably steady voice. "I've been through a terrible ordeal, which has had lasting effects, although I fervently hope they don't last forever. For the past couple of months I've lived—or rather, existed—in an awful state of limbo. I can't explain to you—to anyone—what it's been like for me. I lack the words. And you all, fortunately, lack the experience of what I'm going through. Until yesterday, when Greg Eastman showed up at the hospital, I didn't have even an inkling of who I was. And even though Greg was convinced I was Deborah Steele, there was no way *I* could be certain of it. And there's still no way."

I paused. Neither the police chief nor Nicholas said a word. So, I went on, not having the vaguest idea where all this courage was coming from. "But I know one thing. Whoever I am, I am not the same person I was before Greg handed me an identity. Mine or not, it's something I find myself desperate to cling to—at least until I can be convinced it isn't mine." I leaned forward in my chair. "Are you convinced it isn't?"

Hal Chapman's expression went through a complete transformation. The pity, the dismay, even the shock were gone. Instead I saw admiration and even a trace of embarrassment.

He rose from his chair and looked down at me. "Quite the opposite, Mrs. Steele. Quite the opposite."

I caught another glance from the police chief in Nicholas's direction. A seal of approval. However, I had no idea what kind of look Nicholas returned. And, for all the courage I had mustered, I didn't have enough to turn around and see for myself. I consoled myself, instead, with the belief that I would most likely have seen nothing I could interpret.

Just as Hal Chapman was preparing to leave, Greg made his appearance, with a plate of piping-hot omelet in each hand.

"Say, don't tell me I missed the whole third degree?" he said glibly.

I was astounded to hear Nicholas laugh. A rich, hearty laugh, at that. A real tension breaker. Chapman laughed, too. Even I surprised myself by smiling—until I caught Nicholas's eye. It wasn't that I saw dark disapproval in his expression. Quite the contrary. What I saw, what sobered me immediately, was the hint of tenderness and pride I saw as our gazes met. I realized then that it wasn't his disapproval I feared the most, after all. Intimidating though that was, it did engender some healthy anger in me. And anger served as my best defense against being gobbled up. But this other look, this other side of Nicholas Steele, this was what scared me the most. This, I knew, could be my undoing. I could lose myself in his tenderness and approval. I could give myself up completely. The realization stunned me. And it was one that I would find myself struggling against. For there was no escaping the truth: I was wildly, uncontrollably, attracted to Nicholas Steele. Given the slightest encouragement ...

I found myself staring down at the omelet Greg had placed on the glass patio table in front of me. My stomach turned. There was no way I could swallow even one bite. Ignoring the stares of all three men, I jumped up from my seat, fled into the house and back up to my bedroom.

Far from finding sanctuary there, what I found instead rocked me to the core. I heard the scream, but I really didn't know it came from my own lips. As Nicholas, Greg and Hal Chapman burst into the room, they found me staring transfixed with horror at the open armoire.

A brilliant rainbow of reds, smeared and bleeding together, covered every item of apparel inside the closet. Drippings of red paint ran down over the shelves of shoes. From the look of it, no item had been spared. I couldn't pull myself away from the sight. *Licks of blood,* I kept thinking over and over again. *Licks of blood.*

Then I heard Nicholas bark, "Get her out of here."

An instant later Greg was on one side of me, Chapman on the other. Together, they hastily ushered me out of the room, depositing me across the hall in another bedroom, this one far more masculine.

"He's going to have to do something about her," I heard Greg mutter angrily.

I thought he meant me and I gave him a dazed look. But his gaze was fixed on Chapman, whose response was, "You know as well as I do, he's not going to. He'll make excuses for her. He always does."

And then I understood that they were talking about Lillian. They, Nicholas no doubt included, believed that Lillian had destroyed the clothes. Lillian. The woman I'd supposedly pleaded with Nicholas in the past to have put away. Crazy Lillian. Jealous Lillian. Evil Lillian...

"But this is going too far," Greg snapped. "It was downright vicious—"

"I wouldn't go that far. No one was hurt." The police chief's eyes shifted to me. "A stupid, childish prank. That's all it was. Just think now, Mrs. Steele. You'll have the fun of buying yourself a whole new wardrobe. Anyway, you've lost a bit of weight and most of your old stuff probably wouldn't even fit you now."

I smiled weakly, determined to keep myself glued together. Even if it felt like Krazy Glue. "I suppose...that's true."

Chapman rubbed his hands together as he started for the door. "I think I'll have a word with Nicholas before I take off. Maybe a word with Lillian, too."

"Not if Nicholas has his way," Greg said caustically.

As soon as the police chief exited, Greg turned to me, anguish etched into his features. "This is all my fault, Deborah. I should have taken you down to the train station like you wanted. I should have let you go. I should never have brought you back here in the first place. What was I thinking?''

As our gazes met, I made a pretty good guess at what Greg had been thinking—he was in love with me. In bringing me back to Raven's Cove, to Nicholas, he was bringing me close to him once more, as well. Was he willing to settle for only a close friendship again? Or was he hoping, this time around, that I would realize I was with the wrong man?

I always used to tell you that if you ever felt like coming down from your mountain, I'd be there at the bottom with open arms. The offer still stands. Any time. So, don't feel like you've got to run away again, Deborah. I've always been there for you. I always will be. Do you believe me?

Yes, I'd said....

CHAPTER SIX

Twenty minutes after the paint-splattering incident, I found myself in the passenger seat of Nicholas's black BMW sports car. Nicholas was at the wheel. He was driving me into town to purchase a new wardrobe. I had no idea what he'd done with all the damaged items, but later that day, when I returned from shopping and went into the bedroom, the armoire was empty.

I didn't argue with Nicholas when he announced that I'd need some new clothes, especially after he remarked that we were having company for dinner that evening. For one thing, nothing I'd brought with me would have suited such an occasion. For another, I was extremely nervous about meeting new people—new to me now, anyway, although Nicholas implied they were old friends.

I was to find myself on display once again. I would have to face yet more distressed faces, maybe dubious ones. I could already hear them thinking, *Can this really be Deborah?*

As we drove into town, I resolved to make every attempt I could to look more like the Deborah they'd remembered. And, yes, it's true. My attempt wasn't only for the guests. It was for Nicholas, too, although that's an admission I don't know whether I would have been willing to make so openly at the time—a time when I was both acutely aware of and repelled by my burgeoning attraction to my husband.

Transforming myself into the alluring Deborah of old was going to be no easy task. Not only was I lacking a good fifteen pounds, a tan, and a strong self-image, I also had little to go on as far as knowledge of Deborah's style was concerned—which was mainly that photo Greg had shown me at the hospital of a beautiful young golden-skinned woman wearing a skimpy print bikini. Now, if we were giving a beach barbecue...

I wished then that I had taken more notice of the clothes in the armoire, before they'd been destroyed by the paint. Had it just been a malicious prank on Lillian's part? What was the point? Did she think Nicholas would just leave me in *rags?* Did she want me to suffer everyone's pitying looks that evening? It's odd, considering my paranoia, that it didn't enter my mind that there was anything truly ominous about Lillian's act of vandalism.

I glanced surreptitiously over at Nicholas. He hadn't uttered a word since we'd gotten into the car. I suspected he wouldn't bring up the clothing incident, or Lillian's part in it, or even Greg's counteroffer to take me to town for the shopping trip so that he wouldn't be thrown off his writing schedule. For some reason, Nicholas was surprisingly adamant about being the one to take me shopping. I couldn't believe it was my company he sought, since he was treating me as if I were invisible.

My best guess was that he wanted to have some say— probably a complete say—in what I purchased. This didn't please me in the least. For all I'd been through, my spirit of independence and freedom to choose was surfacing, and I resented the idea that someone else would dictate to me what I should wear. But then, the clothes were being bought with Nicholas's money. Or so I presumed at the time.

The lesson I learned that day was that my insight into what was really going on was sorely limited, and grounded in pure fantasy. Contrary to my suspicions that Nicholas would select my outfits, he refused to make absolutely any comment at all about my choices. Ironically, I found myself completely at sea as to what to buy, longing for just a bit of guidance. Was he testing me, I began to wonder? Did he want to see if my taste in clothing had changed since the amnesia? And if it had, what conclusion would he draw?

While it had certainly helped that both Greg and Hal Chapman had seemed fully satisfied that I was Deborah Steele, no one could know Deborah like her own husband. Before I could fully accept that I was Deborah Steele, I needed Nicholas's confirmation. Of course, the return of my memory would have been greatly welcomed, as well.

As I surveyed the clothing in the small, upscale boutique on Main Street, the young, attractive, dark-haired saleswoman was bending over backward to help me. But, she, too, made no suggestions and offered no guidance. Indeed, she went out of her way not to offer a word of advice, which led me to believe that I had strongly discouraged offers of the kind in the past. A woman with definite tastes and her own mind—this Deborah I couldn't remember.

Nervous and unsure of myself at first, I felt much as I had the day before at Gus's, when I'd been overwhelmed by the vast assortment of cosmetics. Cosmetics. I would need some of those, too, for the dinner party. I was uncomfortably conscious of Nicholas a few yards away, sitting on a small cream-colored leather settee skimming idly through a magazine and sipping some complimentary coffee. How strange it was to see him making himself so at home in a ladies' boutique. I would have thought he'd be as uncomfortable as I was. Even more so. I was so suspicious of him then, that I thought he was behaving that way deliberately, to intimidate me. Fortunately, that thought made me angry. I was damned if I was going to give him the satisfaction of accomplishing his goal.

Setting my eyes on an elegantly simple, black silk bare-shouldered cocktail dress on a rack of designer clothes, I held it up for inspection. I was immediately taken with the style and the cut of the dress, and thought the wide canary-yellow satin cummerbund added an attractive splash of color. Coming into the shop, I had spotted a pair of earrings and bead necklace that were a perfect match to the sash. With my blond hair and fair skin, I thought the outfit would be quite becoming.

Holding the dress up in front of me at a three-way mirror, I could see Nicholas clearly. He didn't even look up from his magazine, so I had absolutely no reading as to what he thought of my selection. The saleswoman, however, smiled approvingly, which gave me a bit of a lift. Until I checked the price tag and realized that might be the reason for her delight. The dress was outrageously expensive. The idea of spending all that money—Nicholas's money—made me very uneasy.

I turned to the saleswoman. "Could you get me a cup of coffee?"

"Certainly," she said, hurrying off to the tiny kitchen in the back room of the shop. I didn't want the coffee. I simply wanted to get rid of her for a minute. It was difficult enough for me to engage Nicholas in conversation, and almost impossible around other people.

"Nicholas."

He glanced up as I spoke his name, giving me a distracted look.

I held up the dress. "What do you think?"

He stared at the dress for only an instant, his gaze lifting to my face. I guessed then that the Deborah of old wouldn't have asked for his opinion. The strong-willed, self-assured Deborah might not even have cared whether he liked her selections or not. But then I remembered Greg's comment as I'd studied her photo at the hospital. *She wasn't as sure of herself as she looked.*

"It's very expensive," I said after receiving no decipherable response from him in answer to my question.

There was silence again, two long beats of it, and a sardonic smile on his face. But finally he spoke, knocking down another of my assumptions—that of being a kept woman. "You can afford it, darling. You're loaded," he said airily.

I do believe my mouth literally dropped open. *Loaded?* I had money of my own? Where did it come from? I almost cried then, realizing how little I knew about—about anything. Why hadn't Greg told me I was a woman of means? Maybe he thought if I knew that I was independently wealthy, I mightn't have chosen to come back with him to Raven's Cove. I could simply have taken my money and started over again on my own.

The saleswoman came back with my coffee. I never took even a sip of it. In quick order, I bought the black dress and the accessories to go with it. I also picked out, almost at random, some jerseys, slacks and a few daytime dresses. I didn't ask Nicholas his opinion again and after I was done, the saleswoman handed me my boxed purchases without even asking me to sign anything. As we started out the door, Nicholas took the boxes from me and carried them to the car. I started to step in on the passenger side.

"You'll need shoes." His gaze dropped to my sad excuse for foot covering as he spoke.

Another remark of Greg's echoed in my mind. *There must be thousands of women out there who'd give anything to be in your shoes.*

I meekly let Nicholas lead me off to a shoe store a block down from the boutique.

As we walked, I couldn't help but be conscious of people on the street and even in some of the shop windows staring at us, some discreetly, some quite openly. I was growing to detest being on display, and while Nicholas seemed quite detached and unconcerned about our being the center of the townsfolk's attention, I suspected he didn't care for it any more than I did. However, he was a celebrity, and as such, he was probably used to being in the limelight whenever he was out in public. I was far from used to it and doubted I ever could be.

When we got to the shoe store I was dismayed to find that Nicholas opted not to come inside with me. He chose instead to take a seat on a bench on the street corner outside the shop.

As I stepped inside, the shoe salesman, a lanky, middle-aged man with graying hair, his white shirt unbuttoned at the collar, a tie hanging loosely around his neck, smiled brightly at me.

"Mrs. Steele, how nice to see you again. We've all heard— Well, I just hope you'll be back in—back in step soon."

I was sure he meant to say, *back in shape,* given the way he couldn't seem to avoid staring at my oversize dress and, most especially, my worn, scuffed shoes. I was sure he was thinking that I was in terrible shape, and that the Deborah Steele he knew wouldn't have been caught dead in such pathetic garb. Yet, despite this, he seemed to recognize me instantly, which gave my spirits a boost.

"So, what can I do you for, today, Mrs. Steele?" he asked amiably.

I didn't waste any time setting about my purchases, selecting a pair of black shantung high-heeled sandals to go with my new cocktail dress, leather walking shoes for hiking the mountain trails, and a couple of pairs of attractive everyday shoes—one pair of which I decided to wear out of the shop. The salesman took my old shoes, and after a faint nod from me, discarded them in the trash. With quick efficiency and delight, he then set about boxing my purchases and tucking them into a shopping bag, with no exchange of money or even a signature on a slip required. And taking Nicholas at his word about my financial picture, I confess I didn't even pay attention to the total. How quickly money can turn our heads!

When I stepped back outside, I saw that Nicholas wasn't alone. Sitting beside him on the bench was a very attractive brunette in her late twenties, early thirties at the most. They were so rapt in an animated conversation, Nicholas didn't even notice I was standing outside the door of the shoe store.

A sharp stab of jealousy shot through me. There was my formidable, somber, aloof husband charming the socks off a very lovely looking woman and being clearly charmed by her, as well. This man was closer to the Nicholas I'd glimpsed in that candid shot I'd retrieved from the dressing-table drawer earlier that day. Only now it wasn't his wife that caused his face to light up and make him look so devastatingly appealing, but another woman altogether. A lover? His wife gone only two months and already... But then my spirits sank even lower when I realized that, for all I knew, he could have taken any number of lovers long before I'd disappeared. Retaliation for my alleged deceits? What was good for the goose was good for the gander? Or had the *goose* made the first move?

She spotted me first, just as she'd begun to laugh over something Nicholas was telling her. And what a discovery I must have been, from the stunned expression on her face, her laugh stopping so abruptly it might have been choked off.

Nicholas followed her gaze, his whole demeanor changing, as well. In a second, his amused look was gone, and his mask of arrogant detachment was reinstated.

I had the most desperate urge to flee from both of them. I couldn't stand any more of this. But my legs were so shaky,

I doubted I could take a step—never mind go sprinting off. And then she was coming toward me. I backed into the doorway like a frightened rabbit, at the same time hating myself for my reaction. I don't know what I expected as she approached, but certainly not to find myself wrapped in the arms of this lovely creature.

"Oh, Deborah, you look dreadful. I could cry."

And to my amazement, as I drew my head back there were tears in her aquamarine eyes. Close up, this woman who was embracing me was even more beautiful than from a distance.

I was speechless as she held me clasped against her for another moment, and remained so even after she released me. My eyes shot to Nicholas as he sauntered over. His, in turn, shifted to the beautiful brunette.

"You'd do better to introduce yourself first," he told her dryly. But, unlike when he spoke to me, there was a hint of true affection in his tone. Now, I was the one tempted to weep.

She took my hand, squeezing it gently. "What an idiot I am. Forgive me, Deborah. It was just such a shock seeing you look so...so..."

"Dreadful?" I offered, repeating her own adjective.

She had the good grace to blush. But then she smiled warmly. "On you, even 'dreadful' isn't bad. Besides, you always did go on about wanting to drop a few pounds."

Now it was my turn to flush.

She lightly touched my cheek. "On second glance, you really don't look all that dreadful. It's the clothes, I think. And this is the first time since I've known you that I haven't seen you with a deep tan." She frowned. "Listen to me going on and you truly don't know who I am, right?" There was a hint of hope in her voice that she'd be wrong, that I would recognize her.

I didn't. "Right," I muttered, sneaking another quick glance at Nicholas. There was no change in his expression. He did, however, take my shopping bag from me—whatever else, always the gentleman.

"I'm Julia Ireland, Godfrey's wife." And then, most likely in response to my blank look at receiving this supposedly enlightening information, she added, "Godfrey's Nicholas's editor. Has been for seven years. My dear husband, bless his soul, has amazing fortitude and tolerance. If Nicholas were one of my writers I'd have strung him up by the thumbs long ago. Or socked him one in the jaw, at the very least."

Nicholas laughed. "Fortunately for both of us, Godfrey doesn't have your hostile temperament."

How I envied their easy banter and obvious comfort with each other. Had Nicholas and I ever been this way?

Pushing those troubling thoughts from my mind, I asked Julia if she, too, was an editor.

"Yes. Godfrey and I work for the same publisher. I began there a little over five years ago. And, the minute I saw Godfrey, I set my sights on him. Chased him relentlessly for two years, seven months and four days, however, before I managed to squeeze a marriage proposal out of him. We've been blissfully wed ever since."

Again, Nicholas laughed. A record, as far as I was concerned. "And little did you know that if you'd stopped chasing him so fiercely, you would have caught up to him a good two years earlier. The poor chump was a goner right from the start."

Julia put an arm around my shoulder. I stiffened instinctively, but she seemed not to notice. "You used to think Godfrey was a bit stuffy. He is very British, but then that's what happens to a person when he's born and raised in London," she said with a little laugh. "Perhaps, now that you're starting fresh, in a sense, you'll see us all a bit differently." Her gaze strayed to Nicholas. "As we all, no doubt, will see you."

Within a few minutes, Julia Ireland, with her warmth, humor and good-natured frankness, had won me over entirely. And what was more, she seemed to honestly like me, as well.

"I'm abducting your wife," she announced brightly, taking a firm hold of my hand after Nicholas muttered something about getting back home.

"Julia." He gave her an impatient look.

She, in turn, gave him a no-nonsense look and even lightly pinched his cheek. "We're going to the beauty salon for the full treatment, and there's no point in arguing with me."

"There never is," he said with a faint laugh. "All right. How long will you be?"

"Too long," she replied. "So run along home and whip up some hideous nonsense on your computer. I'll drive Deborah home when we've done."

I had the feeling that "done" meant more than a trip to the beauty salon.

Nicholas gave me an uneasy look, but he didn't ask me if this was what I wanted. Nor, for that matter, did Julia.

A minute later he was heading for the car and Julia was leading me across the street.

As we stepped onto the curb she asked, "Giving you a hard time, is he?"

"Not . . . really." I don't know why, but I felt it was being disloyal to Nicholas to admit the truth.

Julia smiled. She saw right through me. "It's no surprise to me. You did put him through hell, Deborah." She gave me a tender smile. "But then you've been through hell yourself, haven't you?"

I nodded, tears spiking my eyes.

"Come on. We need a stiff drink, the two of us, before tackling your redo."

"I...I don't think I...drink," I stammered as she gestured toward a bar done up to look like a British pub a few doors down. "Did I...before?"

She laughed. "Did you ever."

"I wasn't an...alcoholic?" I asked with alarm.

She squeezed my hand. "No. Alcohol wasn't your problem. You knew your limit when it came to booze."

There was no missing the implication that there were other areas in which I didn't know my limit. I felt the muscles of my stomach constrict.

"Julia. You must tell me...."

She smiled, ushering me inside the cool, wood-paneled pub and over to a quiet corner table. When the waitress came over, Julia ordered us both white wine, then made small, meaningless chitchat until the order was delivered and the waitress went off.

"Shall I give it to you straight?"

I was taken aback by Julia's forthright approach, but I didn't hesitate to say, "Yes."

"Your biggest problem was that you never knew what you wanted. And you won Nicholas far too easily. I always told him he should have put up more of a fight. Like Godfrey did. But the moment Nicholas set eyes on you, he was putty in your lovely hands. The transformation in him was astonishing. Neither Godfrey nor I could believe it. The poor guy was like a lovesick pup."

"I...I saw a photograph of us—"

"The one at the beach on St. Martin?"

"Yes."

"Well, then, memory or not, you know what I mean."

"But, what happened?" I asked her.

A faint frown marred her otherwise-smooth brow. "You never appreciated how good you had it, how lucky you were to have found someone like Nicholas. Although, I thought—"

"What did you think?"

She shrugged. "Before you took off, Godfrey and I both thought the two of you were beginning to work things out."

"You mean, we'd been having...marital problems?"

She laughed, but was then immediately contrite. "I'm sorry. It was just the innocent way you said it." She gave me a long look. "You have changed, Deborah. Not even so much your appearance, but your...manner."

"If Nicholas is the judge, I've changed for the worse. And given what you say, I was pretty awful before."

"I didn't say you were awful. Nor was Nicholas. The two of you were just so different. He's so intense and serious-minded. You were so free-spirited and...well, flighty. And spoiled. All that money. Who wouldn't be?"

"How did I get the money?" I asked.

A flicker of sadness showed in her eyes. "You told Nicholas that your parents were killed in a plane crash when you were sixteen. Your dad had just sold his company—something to do with computers, I think—and between the money from his estate and the huge settlement you received from the crash, you certainly never had to worry your pretty head about having to work for a living."

I stared at Julia, trying to absorb what she was telling me. My parents had died. I'd been left orphaned at sixteen. I was rich, flighty, spoiled. Nicholas had fallen for me hook, line and sinker, the day we met. I'd won him too easily....

Why, I beseeched the heavens, was nothing Julia was saying triggering even the faintest hint of a memory for me? How long would my past remain locked away? Was there no key at all? Was I to be sentenced to this horrible blank screen of a mind for the rest of my life?

"You'd better take a hearty sip of that wine," Julia advised." You look close to passing out."

"I did that already," I muttered, taking a swallow of wine.

"I know."

"Nicholas told you?"

"Don't be angry. I'm one of the few people Nicholas can talk to."

"I envy you." The words came out before I could stop them.

Her hand reached out and pressed mine. "One thing's still the same as before," she said softly. "For it all, you're still in love with him."

I pulled my hand from hers and looked away. "I don't know what I used to feel," I murmured. "And I have even less idea what I feel now toward...Nicholas. And none whatsoever about what...what Nicholas feels toward me." Slowly, my gaze returned to Julia and I gave her a direct, and what I hoped she'd consider an encouraging, look.

She smiled sympathetically. "Come on. Finish up your wine and we'll tackle that mop of hair of yours. A good conditioning treatment, a trim—and maybe a facial..."

I dutifully finished my wine, wondering as I did, if Julia made no response as to Nicholas's feelings for me because she didn't know what they were, or because she knew only too well.

I studied myself in the mirror of my bedroom that evening, quite amazed and pleased by the transformation in my appearance. My hair, though trimmed no more than an inch, now fell in smooth, lustrous waves to my shoulders. And at Julia's suggestion of a side part, one section of it swung seductively, almost covering one eye. My complexion, thanks to the facial, had a fresh, rosy sheen, and even though Julia had helped me select a ridiculously large assortment of cosmetics, I used only a bit of lip gloss and a touch of mascara.

As for my slim figure, I found that I didn't look nearly so waiflike and scrawny in my new black silk dress. Maybe it had to do with the fact that the dress actually fit me, so that the cut even highlighted some curves I hadn't really noticed until then. Would Nicholas notice? I hated myself for having the thought, but I couldn't help it.

I stared at myself in the floor-length mirror for several long moments. I saw that I not only looked very different than I had earlier, I now looked startlingly more like the Deborah in the photo Greg had shown me. This new me looked quite glamorous and self-assured. It was in no way a reflection of how I felt inside, although after learning from Julia that she and her husband, Godfrey, were to be our dinner guests that evening, I felt a bit less nervous about the gathering.

I was having some difficulty fastening the delicate strand of canary-yellow beads around my neck when there was a knock on my bedroom door. I hoped it might be Julia. She'd said she'd try to rouse Godfrey and get to Raven's Cove a bit early.

Beads in hand, I hurried over and unlocked the door only to find Lillian on the other side. She gasped, her whole complexion going ashen. I saw her mouth twitch, but no sound came out. Instead she stepped back as though I might strike her, then turned on her heel and fled without a word.

As I watched Lillian go off down the hall thinking she might have come to apologize about the paint-splattering incident but lost her nerve at the last minute, the door across from me opened. Nicholas stepped out, his look so chilling that I literally shivered under his gaze.

"What's... wrong?" I stammered, thinking my hairstyle displeased him, or the dress wasn't right, or he hated the color yellow, or maybe he thought I'd said something to Lillian about the ruined clothes.

I could see his chest heave under his exquisitely tailored white dinner jacket. "Wrong? Why, nothing's wrong. You look ravishing. As always."

Never had a compliment been delivered with less flattery.

The necklace slipped from my trembling fingers, the beads breaking free and scattering over the floor. I pressed my lips together and bent to pick them up.

"Leave it. Lillian will see to them later. Our guests are due any minute." His voice was a sharp command and I straightened instantly, sliding my hand to my bare neck.

"You don't need the necklace. You never did need much in the way of adornment."

It was only then that it actually hit me that my transformation had been a complete success. Seeing me all fixed up, wearing the right clothes, Nicholas seemed finally convinced I was Deborah. This was what I'd hoped for, what I'd wanted so desperately. But only because I'd foolishly thought it might mean a new beginning for me and Nicholas. Only because I'd thought I might again win his heart. I never dreamed that once he truly believed I was his wife, he would regard me with even more distrust and scorn than before.

CHAPTER SEVEN

Godfrey Ireland looked nothing like I expected. I had imagined that the man—stuffy or not—who had won the heart of the exquisite Julia would have been extraordinarily good-looking in a very distinguished, British sort of way. I'd pictured someone tall, debonair, elegantly built, having dark hair with possibly a sprinkling of gray at the temples. The man that Julia introduced me to as her husband was portly, with salt-and-pepper hair cut almost Marine short. I estimated that he had to be a good twenty years older than Julia, but he wore his age well. He was a man who was quite comfortable with himself.

Once I got over the shock of the disparity between my image of the editor and the real man, it wasn't hard for me to see why a woman like Julia might have fallen head over heels in love with Godfrey Ireland, despite his less-than-glamorous looks. He had an air of generosity and quiet competence about him that inspired both trust and admiration. While he and Julia were a study in contrasts, they seemed to give the best of themselves to each other, creating a vividly appealing combination.

"I'm relieved to have you back," Godfrey said in a genial British accent, slipping my arm through his as he escorted me into the dining room. Unlike my usual reaction to being touched, with Godfrey I felt as though I was being taken under someone's tender wing. "I don't think Nicholas has completed so much as a page of his new book since you disappeared." He leaned a bit closer to me, lowering his voice. "Naturally, you won't mention that to the dear boy."

The dear boy. I had to smile. "No," I assured Godfrey. "I won't breathe a word." Since speaking to Nicholas was so difficult for me, it was a promise I could easily keep.

I would have enjoyed spending more time talking with Godfrey, but Nicholas monopolized him almost entirely during dinner, the two men discussing his last finished book, which was now being readied for the presses. The title alone made me queasy: *Kill Her Gently.*

While the men discussed business, Julia took charge of me, keeping up a steady, friendly banter, telling me amusing tidbits about some of her authors, describing her last trip with Godfrey to Venice, and sprinkling compliments throughout about my improved appearance.

"Doesn't she look absolutely wonderful?" she exclaimed at one point, breaking into a discussion Godfrey was having with Nicholas about the promotion of his book.

Godfrey beamed at me. "I must say, Deborah, that despite your terrible ordeal, you've never looked more... radiant. There's a new softness about you, my dear."

"Yes," Julia agreed immediately. "It's true. I was trying to put my finger on the difference. Oh, I know there are some physical changes, as well. Nicholas told me about the plastic surgery. But, that isn't really the most striking change. Godfrey's right. You do seem... softer." She glanced over at Nicholas, who had stayed removed from the conversation. And, I thought, hoped to remain so.

Which wasn't very likely around someone like Julia, who clearly didn't believe in letting sleeping dogs lie.

Nicholas observed me with a kind of speculation. "I suppose there are some benefits to having amnesia," he said dryly.

Julia scowled at him. "Really, Nicholas, sometimes you can be a perfect bastard."

I couldn't have agreed more with Julia. It was a cruel remark, meant to hurt me. What had I done to this man to make him so bitter?

Nicholas gave Julia a complacent look, ignoring me altogether. "I guess I'm just one of those people who strive for perfection in all things."

Godfrey laughed dryly. "Don't I know that."

I thought Nicholas was going to counter that remark, but just then the kitchen door swung open and Lillian came out with the main course—a tray of roast lamb surrounded with baby carrots and Brussels sprouts.

Lillian, who had cooked and was serving the dinner, didn't join us at the table. Apparently, no one expected her to. Despite my own negative feelings toward Nicholas's cousin, I did feel sorry for her. She seemed so much like one of those poor spinster relatives who are taken in out of pity, women who are little more than servants and yet, who are devoted to their "masters." There was no question in my mind that Lillian was absolutely devoted to Nicholas.

Despite Julia's gaiety and Godfrey's warm, staunch presence, I remained tense and distracted throughout the rest of dinner. I was relieved that Julia did most of the talking, although even so, I found it impossible to concentrate for very long on anything the effortlessly effervescent woman was saying. While I rarely, and then only surreptitiously, glanced over at Nicholas across the long table from me, I was conscious only of him throughout the entire meal. What was especially odd was that even though his dark eyes never once met mine after that one snide remark, I felt like I was under his constant watchful gaze. He seemed to fill all of the space in the room, enveloping me, ensnaring me, even as his gaze focused sharply on his editor.

I couldn't quite hear what Godfrey was saying to him, but whatever it was, Nicholas began to scowl. And then there was a sudden outburst from him that made my breath catch in my throat and even silenced Julia.

"It's lousy. You know it and I know it," he snapped, slamming his palm down hard on the table, his sculptured features freezing in a disdainful grimace.

Godfrey calmly and unconcernedly sliced a piece of his perfectly cooked lamb. "I don't know anything of the sort. I predict *Kill Her Gently* will top *Night Cries* in sales, and be your longest-running bestseller to date."

"That isn't the point and you know it," Nicholas snickered, raking his fingers through his long dark hair.

Godfrey delivered a forkful of lamb to his mouth, chewed, swallowed, and pierced a Brussels sprout before responding. "It's what your readers know that counts."

Nicholas scowled. "Spoken like a true editor."

Godfrey smiled. "I'll take that as a compliment."

"That's your prerogative, old chap," Nicholas countered facetiously.

I thought Nicholas was being incredibly rude, and while I certainly didn't say a word, he must have picked up my expression of distaste. Suddenly I was the focal point of his attention, his dark, brooding eyes boring into me with such intensity that I felt pinioned to my seat.

"You'll have to read the book yourself and tell me what you think." It was the second comment he'd directed at me all evening.

Although I could feel my cheeks reddening, I forced myself to meet his gaze evenly. "I thought you wanted me to read your previous bestseller first. *Night Cries,* I believe it's called." As I spoke, I searched his face for some sign that it was him, indeed, who had put that hideously frightening book in my room that morning. But, as usual, he gave nothing away.

It was Julia who spoke up. "You know Deborah hates horror stories, Nicholas." She looked over at me. "You read only one of his books. It was while the two of you were falling wildly in love on St. Martin. After you read it, you were so spooked you almost turned down his marriage proposal." She grinned. "Well, that's a bit of an exaggeration, isn't it, Nicholas?"

Now it was Julia's turn to get one of his searing looks. It didn't seem to faze her in the least. "Oh, give the girl a break," she told Nicholas blithely. "This isn't very easy for her."

Godfrey dabbed at his mouth with his white linen napkin, his gaze shifting from me to Nicholas. "It's difficult for both of you. Perhaps we should cut the evening short. Julia and I want to get an early start tomorrow. We're driving up to Masquat to do a bit of antiquing and then it's back to the city on Sunday."

"I know," Julia said. "We'll all meet over at the Sinclair Inn for Sunday brunch before we head off. What do you say?"

She looked at me, and I looked at Nicholas. A bit eagerly, I think. I wanted to get together with Godfrey and Julia again. Not only was I already fond of them both, but I was hoping they would dish out a few more tidbits about my past relationship with Nicholas. Which was the precise reason why I thought Nicholas would turn down the offer. I had the feeling he preferred keeping me in the dark. It kept me at a distinct disadvantage and gave him the upper hand—a position I wondered if he and I had battled for in the past. Had that been one of the problems in our marriage? Two strong-willed people constantly battling for control? As far as Nicholas was concerned, I guessed, the battle was still raging. Having no idea what the struggle was about, I couldn't put up much of a fight. For me, it was a case of shadowboxing in the dark.

Given all my ruminations, I was both surprised and pleased when it turned out that Nicholas agreed to the brunch date with the Irelands, although I was sure I wasn't the only one at the table who picked up his momentary hesitation before responding affirmatively.

Twenty minutes later, the Irelands bade us good-night. Julia gave me a warm embrace at the door and told me she'd look forward to seeing me on Sunday. Godfrey took my hand in both of his and kissed me lightly, reassuringly, on the cheek. "Give it time, my dear. I think you'll find it's worth it in the end," he whispered.

I was soothed by Godfrey's words. And I even felt a bit better about Nicholas, thinking he couldn't be all that bad, if someone as nice as Godfrey was fond of him. And I did believe the editor had genuinely warm feelings for Nicholas. As did Julia. Unfortunately, at the time I was hard-pressed to understand why.

"Well, you were certainly a hit," Nicholas said behind me.

Keeping my back to him, I murmured, "You sound surprised. Or is it . . . disappointed?"

There was no answer. Not that I expected one. Nicholas wasn't easily put on the defensive.

Slowly, with some trepidation, I closed the front door. Except for Lillian, who I supposed was in the kitchen busy cleaning up from dinner, Nicholas and I were once again alone. Our first night together in Raven's Cove, considering that the night before I'd conveniently gone unconscious straightaway and thus avoided having to engage in any awkward and strained conversation with my husband.

When I turned, Nicholas was already walking down the hall toward his den. Was he planning to work this late? I thought about Godfrey's comment that Nicholas hadn't written a page while I was gone. It seemed to me he'd certainly been making up for lost time since my return.

I suppose I should have been relieved that Nicholas had no interest in spending any further time with me that evening, but inexplicably, I wasn't. I felt angry at being so thoroughly ignored. How did he expect there to be any hope for us at all if he didn't make the slightest effort to communicate with me? We couldn't go on living like perfect strangers. At least I couldn't. Nor could I force myself on him. The Deborah of old might have been as strong-willed as Nicholas, but I was feeling increasingly vulnerable and unsure of myself with every passing minute.

Although I wasn't tired, there seemed nothing for me to do but head up to bed. I was about to climb the stairs when Nicholas's voice stopped me.

"How about a nightcap?" His tone was so flattened and expressionless as to sound wholly disinterested in my response.

My reaction was surprise, which must have shown on my face.

"It isn't mandatory," he added dryly.

He started toward his den without even waiting for a response.

The man's insufferable manner infuriated me and I was sorely tempted to march right up the stairs. But even as I stood there telling myself it would be the wisest move, I knew—and I was certain Nicholas knew—that I would join him. Had he always drawn me like a magnet? Had my desire for him always superseded my common sense and pride? Or had the latter won out in the end? Had I finally reached my limit two months earlier, leaving him with the intention never to return?

When I entered into his den, Nicholas was already pouring cognac into two crystal brandy snifters. There was a faint smile on his lips as he extended one of the goblets to me. I interpreted the smile as one of victory and almost turned on my heel. But then I saw the painting hanging on the cherry-wood paneled wall over the mantel. I froze in my tracks, my gaze riveted to the large, gilt-framed oil.

It was a full-length portrait of Deborah, looking dramatically beautiful in a white Victorian-style gown, cut wantonly low at the bodice and then sweetened by long puffy lace sleeves. In one hand, she held a floppy sunbonnet, in the other a book. I say *her*, because the woman in the painting looked so ethereally beautiful as to be almost unreal. I couldn't imagine that I had ever looked that way. I took it for an artist's vision.

I stepped closer. The signature in the right-hand corner of the painting was unfamiliar to me. My eyes lifted to the book she was holding in her hand. I could read the name on the cover. It was entitled, *Death's Calling*. The author was Nicholas Steele.

I was so captured by the portrait of this woman—me and yet not me—that I was unaware that Nicholas had come up behind me until I felt his warm breath against the back of my head. I stiffened at his nearness.

"It was painted by an artist in St. Martin. I think he was totally taken with his subject. Men usually were." That flat voice again. "That hasn't changed much. You've got Greg and Godfrey, and even our humble police chief, eating right out of your hand."

I glanced angrily over my shoulder at him. "If you mean they're treating me with kindness and caring, I suppose you're right. And if you want to know how I feel about it, it's a . . . a refreshing change from—" I stopped short, realizing a childish outburst would serve no purpose.

"Go on. Finish what you were going to say." There was a ghost of a smile on his face.

"You're the writer," I said stiffly. "Why don't you supply the missing words?"

His eyes shifted to the painting. "It was an engagement present. I was very touched."

There was nothing in his features to confirm that the feeling had persisted.

"The book's the one Julia mentioned during dinner this evening," he said as an afterthought.

"Did I hate the book?" My voice held a tremor. There was nothing I could do about it.

"I don't really know," he replied bluntly.

"But Julia said—"

"Julia says a lot of things."

"You confide in her."

He handed me my cognac. "It makes her happy to think of it that way. And I like to keep her happy."

"Why?" My voice was a bare whisper. Was he in love with the beautiful, witty Julia? What had I to offer compared to her?

"Why not?" he answered, his mouth twisting in a mocking smile.

He was deliberately baiting me. I had a very strong impulse to toss the glass of fine cognac I was holding, in his face. So strong that my hand must have risen without my being consciously aware of it. Until Nicholas's fingers curled firmly around my wrist.

His touch so startled and aroused me that the snifter dropped from my hand. Cushioned by the thick Persian rug, the expensive glass fortunately didn't break, but the contents spilled, the amber liquid splattering over both our shoes, Nicholas's trouser cuffs and the hem of my dress. First the perfume bottle, then the bead necklace, now a glass of brandy. Had I always been so clumsy?

I bent to attend to the spill, but Nicholas wouldn't release his hold on me.

"Leave it." He drew me away from the wet area of the rug.

I gave him a defiant look. "For Lillian? Does she always clean up all the messes made by others?"

"So, you're feeling sorry for her, are you?" There was a hint of surprise in his voice. And something else. A grudging respect?

His hand was still on my wrist, but lightly now. It would have been easy enough for me to free myself.

Easy? Nothing was *easy* for me where Nicholas was concerned. I could feel the rhythm of my heartbeat speed up. His face was extremely close to mine. I could smell the tangy, citrusy scent of his cologne. There was an utterly sensual smile on his lips now. And a curtain seemed to lift over his dark, brooding eyes, revealing such raw lust that I did almost pass out again.

"Do you want another drink?" he asked, the offhanded tone of his voice completely jarring with the seductive, hungry look he was giving me.

"No. I . . . think I should . . ." But I didn't have the presence of mind to come up with an ending for that sentence, either. This time Nicholas didn't force it. Instead, his fingers slid up from my wrist up to my bare forearm.

A tiny moan escaped my lips. I was mortified by the intense arousal that shot through me at the shifting of his touch. My palms began to sweat and I felt weak with desire. My pulse thudded in my ears.

"I think . . . I will . . . have some . . . cognac. . . ." Anything to steady my nerves. I had to get a grip on myself.

Instead of pouring me a drink of my own, Nicholas touched the rim of his glass to my lips, then tipped the snifter just enough for the cognac to moisten them. Instinctively, my tongue darted out across my lips, tasting the rich, fiery liquid. Nicholas's dark gaze never lifted from my mouth. Then, with infinite delicateness and exquisite sensitivity, he ran his thumb across the same line my tongue had taken.

The feeling was unimaginable; his caress was so electrically tender and erotic that I could feel a sigh escaping from deep within me. My legs, as rigid as pillars, were trembling. I felt so vulnerable, so at risk.

"No." I don't think any sound actually came from my lips. I was only capable of mouthing the word. And I wasn't even sure what I was attaching it to, as Nicholas was no longer even touching me. But I could detect his body heat. And mine. I could hear our ragged breaths.

His midnight eyes were fixed on me. "What is it you want?"

I was braced for his tone to be mocking, but instead, I heard only a hint of desperation in his voice.

"I don't know," I managed to utter weakly.

The dark eyes scrutinized me, impaled me. "You're lying. You do know."

I couldn't meet his gaze. He was right. I was lying. But the truth seemed too embarrassing, humiliating, wanton....

"What... What do you want?" I whispered.

I watched his eyes, their dark pupils growing even darker. "You know that, too."

Without another word, he set his glass down and wrapped me slowly in his arms. For the first time, I saw a truly tender smile on his lips. I cried out—not in alarm, but with sheer relief—as his lips covered mine. My mouth opened under his, and my body moved into him as he tightened his hold on me until we were pressed breathlessly together.

Our kiss deepened, both of us helping it along, our bodies twisting and trembling with anticipation. My hands flew to his hair, snapping the rubber band from his ponytail so that his thick locks fell around his face and mine, his dark strands tangling with my blond ones.

He abandoned my lips, and his mouth and tongue glided down my neck, tracing the curve of my collarbone. Then he was breathing into my ear, his tongue circling the lobe, making darting little thrusts inside.

I clung to him, lost in the erotic sensations sweeping through me. Some small part of me tried to will my body to behave, but my body wouldn't listen.

"Tell me," he whispered hotly into my ear. "Tell me what you're feeling."

"Oh," I cried. "Like I've never felt before." I looked up into his midnight eyes. "Is it true? Have I ever felt this way before?"

The room was bathed in blue light from the full moon outside and just one small lamp on Nicholas's desk. He looked eerily handsome and formidable in that light. And I felt very fragile and weak, the yearning inside me threatening to explode through my very pores.

"You baffle me," he murmured, turning his head slightly so that a shadow fell across half his face, giving him an almost-demonic look. I felt a flurry of fear, but it was minuscule compared to the heat burning inside me.

"I can't help it," I whispered earnestly.

He stood perfectly still, his arms still holding me loosely. "You're quite beautiful."

"It's . . . the dress . . . and the haircut . . . and . . ."

"No."

I swallowed hard. Something inside me seemed to float up and out of me, as if I'd been cut free from some ropes holding me to the earth. I was soaring. "Oh, please—" The words were but a breath on my lips.

He pulled me hard against him then, his lips devouring me with fierce kisses, almost desperate in their urgency. And I kissed him back, just as desperate, just as needy, wanting, wanting to feel whole again, believing that only Nicholas could make this happen for me. He was my lost half as I was his. Together, we'd both be complete.

My desire for Nicholas was like a tangible force, driving me. I could feel the rhythm of our two bodies beat in time with my pulse. I was enveloped in his aura. It had captured me from the first moment I'd set eyes on him. Maybe, I thought, this was the only way for me to break free, to truly understand Nicholas, to find myself.

The room was silent except for the mingling of our shallow breaths that echoed inside my head like the brewing of a storm—an omen that I would not, could not, heed.

I made only the vaguest utterance of protest as he began unzipping the back of my dress. His mouth claimed mine again as my dress swished to the carpet. But this time his kiss was almost ruthless.

A thread of fear curled through my escalating passion. What was I doing? This was crazy.

I felt his hand against the bare flesh of my back, moving slowly, sinuously down over my silk panties. I clutched at his dinner jacket, white-knuckled.

"Oh, Nick, Nick..." The name I'd uttered only in the throes of passion, he'd told me.

His mouth clamped down over mine, cutting off not only my words, but my breath. This kiss was brutal, cruel, and his hands gripped my flesh painfully. Terror infused me. Nicholas was no longer making love to me; he was conquering me, dominating me, assaulting me.... I began to struggle with all my might.

"Don't fight me." His voice was like a cold tendril, biting and caustic.

"No, please—" I cried out, panic overtaking me completely. "No, no, no—"

He shook me almost violently, his eyes bright, hard points, flashing. "Stop it. I said you don't have to fight me. I'm not going to attack you, for heaven's sake. It was what you wanted as much as I did. Obviously, you've changed your mind. Fine." His features were dark and stormy, but I saw that he wasn't only angry as he wanted me to believe. There was a quiver in his lips that he couldn't quite control.

And his eyes held a haunted glint. He, too, was shaken by what had happened between us. I was sure of it.

He let me go then and my legs were so rubbery I sank to the floor, burying my head in my hands as I broke into sobs. Nicholas bent down and scooped up my dress, tossing it carelessly at me.

"I hate you!" I cried out in a small, hollow, childlike voice, clutching the dress against my body covered only in a skimpy black lace bra and black bikini panties. "And you hate me, too."

He ran his fingers through his tangled hair as he glared down at me. "It would be a lot simpler all around if either one of those statements were true." There was anger and frustration in his voice, but also anguish.

He turned while I somehow managed to slip my dress back on. Meanwhile he finished off the cognac in his snifter, then picked up my spilled glass.

Taking a clean snifter from the bar, he poured me a considerable serving.

I shook my head as he brought it to me, wanting only to flee. Flee that room, flee Raven's Cove, flee Nicholas. I never wanted to see him again.

"Drink it," he ordered, his compelling voice willing me to obey.

I took the glass from him. I was shaking so badly I needed to use both my hands to get the drink to my lips. But I took several swallows. The cognac burned going down, but the trembling inside me started to subside a bit.

I finally forced myself to look at him. He was leaning negligently against the back of a brown leather sofa. "We can't do this, Nicholas. At least . . . I can't."

He gave me a jaded look. "So, it's Nicholas again."

It was a cruel, insensitive remark, but one I sensed even
then was calculated to keep my anger toward him fueled—
to protect me from him, and him from me. Only later, did I
understand it was also to protect him from himself.

CHAPTER EIGHT

My sleep that night was fitful at best. If nothing else, I longed for a respite from Nicholas, but his image haunted my dreams. Every time I closed my eyes I would see his taunting, self-satisfied smirk, or his deprecating sneer, or worst of all, that rare, tender smile that had made me dissolve into his arms. We would embrace in my dreams, passion soaring, but soon the passion would edge into violence. Nicholas's caresses would become bruising. I would hear the wind howling, the rain begin. Terrified, I would lie there frozen beneath him, a victim sculptured in ice. . . .

I must finally have fallen into a deep sleep somewhere around dawn, only to be jerked awake close to eleven the next morning by a sound inside my room.

I let out a gasp as I discovered Lillian over by the chaise, gathering up my black silk dress, which I'd carelessly discarded the night before.

"How did you get in here?" I demanded angrily. After yesterday's intrusions, I had made sure to lock my bedroom door before going to bed.

Lillian merely gave me one of her haughty looks. Then I saw the ring of keys she wore around her wrist. Locked doors provided no barrier from the housekeeper. Nor did they seem to indicate to her that she wasn't welcome.

"I'm going into town to do the weekly grocery shopping," she said offhandedly. "I thought you'd want to have your dress taken in to the cleaners, as well. Cognac stains silk, and if it isn't attended to right away, it won't come out."

I stared dazedly at her, my face no doubt scarlet. How could she know that I'd spilled cognac on my dress? There were only two ways. Nicholas had told her. Or . . . she had been spying on us the night before.

The faint smile on her face told me the latter was the more likely. I don't know which emotion was stronger—my fury or my mortification. Lillian, however, seemed quite unconcerned with my emotions.

"I've always selected the meals, but Nicholas wanted me to ask you if there were any special items you wanted."

From the arch tone of her voice, it was obvious that she wasn't at all pleased with having to consult with me, but, as always she would honor her beloved cousin's requests—or orders, depending on how one viewed them. Too upset and distressed to respond, I just shook my head.

She efficiently folded my dress over her arm and briskly strode to my door. "Nicholas is working all day and wanted me to tell you he wasn't to be disturbed."

I gave her an icy look. "I have no intention of disturbing him."

Her twisted and altogether-unbecoming smile made my blood boil.

"Lillian!" I called out to her as she opened my door to leave.

She stopped, but didn't turn her gaze on me, nor did she make any verbal response.

"From now on, please don't come into my room unless I invite you."

She did turn, then. And the look she gave me was so malevolent it made me catch my breath. I could tell from the way her whole face went rigid that it was all she could do to hold back her temper. Even worse, to swiftly cross the room and strike me down. If looks could kill . . .

* * *

After Lillian's departure it took several minutes for me to gather myself together. When I did, I immediately contemplated attempting another flight from Raven's Cove. I could call Greg this time. Not that I would give him any details as to why I was leaving. I couldn't tell him about what had happened between me and Nicholas. But would Greg guess? Did he really know me that well?

I was so ashamed, so humiliated by my wanton behavior with Nicholas the night before. Part of the reason I wanted to flee was that I couldn't imagine how I could ever face him again. Even though I would have liked to put all the blame on him, I couldn't deny, even feeling as awful as I did, that I had wanted him as desperately as he'd seemed to want me. If he hadn't gotten so rough, frightened me so, I don't know if I could have stopped if I had wanted to.

I shivered, thinking again about Lillian. It made my skin crawl to picture her peeking in on us. It was positively perverse. I felt she must be mad. How could Nicholas keep her here? How could I stay on in the house with the two of them?

I strode into the bathroom, my mind made up, already planning my next departure. But as I showered, my indignation and rage began to outweigh my panic. If I did flee, I wouldn't only be running away from Nicholas, Lillian and Raven's Cove. I would be running from myself.

Upset as I was, I knew I couldn't leave. Not yet. Not until I had done my best to reclaim my past.

I dressed hurriedly and with purpose, slipping into a pair of new navy cotton-twill slacks and a white jersey that I'd bought at the boutique the day before. With Lillian gone on her errands for the morning and Nicholas locked away in his den, I realized that this was my first real opportunity to do a bit of exploring around Raven's Cove. Was Nicholas working on his newest horror novel, or just avoiding me?

For I certainly intended to avoid him. I vowed that there would be no repeat of the night before. By the time I was fully dressed, I had even lulled myself into naively believing I was fully in control my emotions, of my own fate.

I left my room, knowing just what it was I needed to find, what I was going to search out. Since my arrival I had been struck by the noticeable absence of any Deborah Steele-signed paintings about the house. Greg had indicated that I'd done a fair bit of painting at Raven's Cove. Had Nicholas stored all of my work away after I'd left? Or Lillian?

During my stay in the hospital, my art had become my whole focus and connection with living. I knew it was possible that the trauma of the assault on me might have changed my style somewhat, but I felt sure that when I saw some of Deborah Steele's earlier paintings, I would not only know immediately if they were mine, but they also might trigger memories for me in a way that nothing else could. What is it they say? A picture can speak a thousand words?

There was a fresh pot of coffee and homemade muffins in the kitchen. With Lillian gone, the spacious room with its honey-oak cabinets and mint-green countertops took on a warm, friendly feel. And I thought to myself: I like to cook.

That simple thought nearly took my breath away. *I like to cook.* It was a revelation. The first real connection with the me I once was. *I like to cook.*

I laughed aloud, tears filling my eyes. For just an instant, I forgot entirely about my resolve to keep my distance from Nicholas. Instead, I felt an overwhelming impulse to race into his den and share my discovery with him. I'm sure he would have thought I'd gone crazy. Besides, he'd given strict orders that he didn't want to be disturbed. Especially by me, I was sure.

Even though there was no one with whom to share my startling discovery, I felt as if the first real chip in the granite that encased me had come loose. This was the start, my first glimpse into my past. And now it was up to me to keep chipping away at the stone, until, at last, I was free.

Still smiling to myself, I noticed a ring of keys hanging on a hook just to the right of the kitchen door. After a moment's hesitation, I crossed the room and slipped the key ring from the hook. Holding the ring against my chest, I could feel my heart start to beat in a guilty but exhilarated fashion. Using a back staircase to avoid having to pass Nicholas's den, I stealthily made my way up to the second floor. My disappointment was palpable as I found that none of the bedroom doors was locked. Nor was there anything of interest or any clues for me in them.

Across from my room was the room I'd been led to the day before by Greg and Hal Chapman while Nicholas was seeing to the paint-splattered clothes in my armoire. As soon as I stepped inside this time, even before my gaze took in the unmade bed and the white dinner jacket draped neatly over the back on an armchair, I knew this was Nicholas's bedroom. It held his scent.

I stood motionless by the door. So this is where he slept, I thought. Just across the hall from me. No more than a few long strides away. I felt a disturbing, unbidden flash of arousal, and found myself having to fight a terrible urge to stretch out on his rumpled bed, breathe in his smell, see if any of his body heat remained. For all that had happened between us last night, for all my resolve of the morning, I was utterly dismayed to realize how much I still desired Nicholas. The feeling raced through my body, out to my extremities, over my flesh. Like a wave rolling in to shore, it crashed against my senses.

I fled the room as if it had been possessed. In a way, I suppose it had.

Standing out in the hallway, I had to struggle to catch my breath. When I got a grip on myself I headed for the stairs and went up to the third floor.

This space was smaller than the other two floors and had a musty, faintly medicinal aroma. There were only three rooms leading off the hallway. I tried each of the doors. They were all locked.

The keys jangled on the ring because my hands were so shaky as I searched for the one that fit the first locked door. After several nerve-racking tries, I got the right key.

I felt an instant stab of guilt as I realized that I'd blithely let myself into Lillian's bedroom, of all rooms. Well, I appeased my guilty conscience, this made up for the times she'd done the same to me. Tit for tat. But I still didn't feel very good about it. Two wrongs didn't make a right.

My breath caught. Somebody had told me that once. *Two wrongs don't make a right.* Before... Before the hospital. Before the assault. One of my parents? A teacher? My heart gave a jerk. My memory was starting to return. Yes—only flashes, it was true. But until that morning, there'd been nothing. This convinced me all the more that being at Raven's Cove was the right place for me to be.

I stared around Lillian's room. Now that I was here, I couldn't just turn around and walk out without giving the space a brief inspection. Besides, as much as the woman repelled me, I was greatly curious about her.

The decor of the room was, like the woman who occupied it, plain and rather grim. A simple bed, a Shaker-style maple bureau, an upholstered gray armchair with a reading lamp beside it, and a maple writing desk. The room was impeccably tidy. A place for everything, and everything in its place. Not that there were many things about. Indeed, the only object that drew my interest was a framed photograph on the bureau.

I drew closer to examine it. It was a picture of a much-younger Nicholas, maybe in his early twenties. Even then, his features were fiercely striking and commanding. He was looking testily but resolutely into the camera. Beside him was a young woman with dark hair. She was smiling brightly, giving her plain face an almost-pretty look. It took a few moments of study for me to see that this was Lillian. A younger, gayer Lillian. A Lillian in happier times. Again, despite everything, I felt a wave of pity for her, and thought to myself, she hadn't aged well.

My gaze fell on the drawers, my temptation to explore the secrets inside warring with my sense of what was right. I confess I went so far as to start to slide the top drawer open, only to shut it quickly, sorely ashamed of myself.

I hurried out of the room, feeling very much the voyeur now. Once out in the hall, with Lillian's door again locked, I hesitated as I regarded the other two doors, debating whether or not to go on. Realizing I mightn't have this golden opportunity again, I forced myself to continue.

The room beside Lillian's proved to be a storage area for some bulky pieces of furniture and several huge stacks of books. I thought at first they were copies of Nicholas's dreadful horror novels, but as I took a closer look, I was surprised to find, instead, a number of the great classics, many volumes of poetry, even the complete works of Shakespeare. I opened a few books at random. Nicholas's name appeared on a nameplate in each of them.

The last room on the third floor was dark and stuffy. I flicked on a light switch. This space turned out to be a pleasant sitting room, but one that had been gathering dust for a while. Two months' worth?

The room itself didn't elicit any memories for me, but I felt certain this had served as a kind of getaway space. I thought it made a perfect studio, with its skylit northern exposure. But if it had once been used for this purpose there was no sign of it now. I saw no easel, canvas or paints. Not even paint drippings on the oak floor. And no paintings on the walls.

I felt sorely disappointed and confused. Surely, if any painting had gone on at Raven's Cove, there had to be a studio. And this seemed like the ideal space for one. After a brief survey of the room, I crossed to what I took to be a closet only to discover, upon opening the door, a small anteroom beyond which was a narrow flight of stairs that led up to the attic.

As I stood in the tiny vestibule, the air took on a new texture—thicker, almost shroudlike. A compelling force seemed to tug me up these stairs, and yet I felt a sense of dread with each step I took. At the top I was confronted with yet another locked door. Was it only luck that the first key I tried opened it? Bad luck, then . . .

The image haunts me still. It always will. But that first sight— Oh, that first sight made the bile rise in my throat and I clutched myself as if I had been physically violated.

There it was. What I'd been searching for. The artist's studio, brilliant northern light streaming into the room, the smell of oils and turpentine in the air. And here were the paintings, more than a dozen of them. But whatever secrets they might have held for me, whatever clues or memories they might have stirred, I would never discover. Each and every canvas had been slashed to shreds, savagely, viciously mutilated, the paintings themselves made unrecognizable. The paint-stained clothes in the armoire had been one thing—a spiteful prank. But this was no prank. This was something altogether different. There was a violence and hatred in this vandalism. Who had done this? The first name that came to my mind was . . . Lillian. How much she must have hated me. I could even picture her slashing the paintings, her cruel, exultant face triumphant. She would wipe out all memory of me. There would be nothing of me left—

"They weren't all that good."

I spun around at the sound of Nicholas's voice, the ring of keys falling from my hand, both hands then flying to my gaping mouth. My eyes were wide with shock. And fear.

I shall never forget the look on Nicholas's face that day. It was filled with such loathing and bitterness.

I stared at him in horror. No, I thought. Not Lillian. She hadn't been the one who had wanted to destroy all memory of me.

"You . . . did this?"

He regarded me with that infuriating arrogance, saying nothing. But his silence was answer enough for me. I wanted to charge at him, strike him, demand he admit the truth. The whole truth. Nothing but the truth.

But was I strong enough for the truth? At that moment, no. At that moment, I wanted only to get out of that dreadful room.

Only then was I aware that Nicholas was standing in the narrow doorway, blocking my exit. Panic flooded me. I felt trapped, cornered. Afraid to step forward, unwilling to stay put like the frozen statue in my dreams, I backed up, tripping over a leg of the easel.

"No!" I screamed as Nicholas started toward me, quickly righting myself. He stopped dead in his tracks, throwing up his hands. In surrender? Frustration? I wasn't sure.

He let his hands drop, shoving them into his pockets, his voice rough as he muttered, "This is impossible." He gave me one last inscrutable look, then spun on his heel and descended the stairs.

Eager as I was to leave that awful room, too, I wanted to give Nicholas a good head-start.

"So, there you are. I've been looking all over the place for you."

Greg came and took a place beside me on the grassy knoll at the back of the house. I set aside my magazine.

The instant he set eyes on me, his brows knitted together. "What happened? What's the matter?"

I cursed the fact that my face read like such an open book. I needed lessons from the master himself—the impenetrable Nicholas Steele.

Greg's eyes bored into me. "Deborah."

I hesitated, but when I saw the sincere concern etched in his features, I whispered, "Greg, you must tell me. Is there really no doubt in your mind that I am . . . Deborah?"

He gave me a long, intent look before answering. "No doubt at all. I've covered every avenue possible to try to trace any alternative leads to your existence prior to that assault. I came up completely empty-handed. I even went so far as to check on whether Deborah had any relatives, cousins and the like, around her age." He shook his head, then gave me a questioning study. "Does it make you feel better or worse to know you're Deborah?"

"I found . . . my paintings."

Greg regarded me silently. "Did you?"

I felt as if he were playing for time. Did he know, then? I believed he did.

"Why?" I cried out in anguish. "Why would he do such a savage thing? Why did he destroy what had to be such an important part of me?"

I tried to fight back the tears, but I couldn't. Greg reached into his pocket and pulled out a handkerchief. Very gently, even cautiously, he dabbed at my eyes.

"You have to understand, Deb. After you left, Nicholas was . . . beside himself. He . . . lost control. Despair can drive people to do hideous, senseless acts. He went on a rampage. I suppose it was the very fact that your paintings meant so much to you that made him want to destroy them. He wanted to get back at you."

I looked away. "He did."

"Have you spoken to him about it?" Greg asked gently.

I laughed harshly. "Spoken to him? Hardly. One doesn't speak to Nicholas. At least, I don't seem to have the knack for it. I think he...hates me. And so does that dreadful cousin of his."

"Deborah..."

"Do you know? I don't think either of them was all that sure I was Deborah. Until...last night. I had on a decent dress, had my hair fixed up, looked...more like myself...for the first time. I realize—now—that was why Lillian had such a shocked look on her face when she saw me last night. She looked like she was seeing a...ghost. I think she hoped...I was dead." I took a breath. "And maybe Nicholas hoped so, too." I heard my voice break in spite of myself, and I couldn't hold back the tears. They streamed down my cheeks.

Greg seemed beside himself. His face was so anxious, so worried for me.

"Oh, Deborah, I'm so sorry. I never thought...I never dreamed it would be this way for the two of you. I honestly believed Nick's love for you would win out over his bitterness and sense of betrayal in the end. And I...I thought being home, being with Nick...would help you recover your memory."

I gripped his hand. "That much is true, Greg. I am. Did you know...I love to cook?" I laughed—a bit hysterically, I think. I was close to the edge, but didn't know it. "It came to me, Greg. Quite out of the blue. A fragment of my past. It just flashed in my mind while I was alone in the kitchen this morning. All of a sudden, like a whisper in my head, came the realization that I love to cook. That's not something I ever thought about in the hospital. It's not something I...knew. It's true, Greg, isn't it? I do like to cook."

He gave me a quirky smile. "Yes, it's...true. Only, Lillian—"

"Never gave me a chance to do much cooking," I finished excitedly for him.

His eyes narrowed. "You remember that, too?" His tone was incredulous.

I pursed my lips. "No. But that's true, too, isn't it? The kitchen at Raven's Cove is strictly Lillian's turf."

Greg nodded, continuing his close scrutiny. "What else do you remember?"

I smiled ruefully. "That two wrongs don't make a right."

He looked puzzled.

"I remember someone telling me that once. Maybe one of my parents. When I was growing up. Before...before they died."

I looked eagerly over at Greg, but he seemed less than astonished by my flashes of memory. "I know it isn't very much. But...it's a matter of a chip here, a chip there."

"Chip?"

I stared dejectedly down at my lap, realizing how long a way I had to go.

"It's okay, Deborah. I think I understand. Don't look so sad. It breaks my heart."

I felt such tenderness toward him at that moment. He was being so sweet, so caring, so kind to me. I don't think, until that moment, I realized how little kindness I'd received since coming to Raven's Cove. None at all from Lillian. And only a brief moment or two from Nicholas the evening before.

I felt my face heat up with the shame of those moments. Now there was one memory I would have given anything to be able to forget.

I forced myself not to think about them for the time being, at least, concentrating instead on Julia and Godfrey Ireland. They, too, had been kind to me. I was truly grateful to them for that. But my gratitude toward Greg was different. I felt that Greg not only saw a truer side of me, but a truer side of Nicholas, as well: the dark side of him.

Greg looked across the terraced lawn to the neighboring mountain crest. "Deborah, I think you know that I would do anything for you." He shot me a quick look. "Anything."

I believed him. "There's nothing you can do...just yet," I murmured.

He turned to me then, grasping my hands. "Leave with me, Deborah. Leave with me now. This minute. You can stay with me. For as long as you like. I won't make any demands. I promise you. I just want to...look after you. I was wrong. Wrong to have brought you back in the first place. Wrong to have talked you into coming back here yesterday. Let me do the right thing now, Deborah."

I was tempted to take Greg up on his offer. I'd be lying shamelessly if I said I wasn't. Here was this kind, caring, tender man willing to give me shelter, look after me, protect me. But I couldn't leave. I tried to make him understand.

"If I go now, I'm afraid I'll be doomed to this...shadow world. My past is like a jigsaw puzzle, Greg. And I snatched up a couple of tiny pieces of it today. Maybe tomorrow, I'll snatch a bigger piece, several of them. Maybe, before long, my life will begin to take on shape and substance. It's here that I'll find those pieces. I can't leave until I've got enough of them to form a real picture in my mind. Then ... Then, hopefully I'll be able to gather the rest of them elsewhere, away from Raven's Cove, and put the whole puzzle that's me all together."

A sharp scowl etched Greg's features. "What if no other pieces come to you tomorrow? Or the next day? How long are you willing to stay here? How long are you willing to take...the risk?"

I stared at him. "Risk? What do you mean?"

He couldn't quite meet my gaze. "I just...worry about

you, that's all. Your slashed paintings, your old clothes destroyed..."

"You... You don't think...?" I couldn't finish the sentence. Nor did I need to. We both knew what I was asking. Just as we both knew what Greg was implying.

How far would Lillian go—or Nicholas—if their tempers got fully out of hand? I had seen loathing on both their faces. But I had also seen tenderness and longing on my husband's face. A part of him might have hated me, but there was another part....

Greg's hand fell lightly on mine. I didn't pull away from his touch this time. "Listen to me, Deborah. Promise me one thing."

I opened my eyes and met his tender gaze. "Yes?"

"Promise me that the very first moment you feel you're... in any kind of danger... you'll call me immediately. It doesn't matter if it's only your imagination. I don't want anything to happen to you, Deborah. I don't think I could live with myself if... if..."

I pressed my fingers to his lips. "Don't say it."

He took my face between his hands. "Do you promise?"

I looked into his warm hazel eyes, my heart beating strangely. "Yes," I whispered. "I promise."

His gaze drifted from mine, then he dropped his hands as though my skin had scalded him.

"What's wrong?" I asked with alarm.

"It's that bitch," he bit out acidly.

I was so startled by his coarse outburst, that it took a moment for me to direct my gaze where he had glanced.

And that's when I saw her at the window. The vile Lillian. Spying on me. Again.

CHAPTER NINE

I didn't see Nicholas for the rest of that day. When I came down to the dining room for dinner at seven in the evening, only one place was set on the long, gleaming mahogany table. Was this to be the way it would be from now on? I wondered. Would Nicholas and I be strangers in our own home? Was he still avoiding me because of the fiasco of the night before, or was he now punishing me for having "trespassed" and uncovered my ravaged paintings?

But I wasn't trespassing. This was my house, too. By all accounts, save my own, I was Nicholas's wife. Those paintings were mine. He'd had no right at all to destroy them. Nor did he have the right to keep me from having access to the studio I had once used. If I chose to resume using the studio to paint again, I saw no reason why I couldn't.

Actually, that was the first real impulse I'd had to take up a paintbrush since I'd arrived at Raven's Cove. I'd been in too constant a state of turmoil to even consider it. I felt as if all my creative juices had been drained out of me. Yet, I knew I needed to get back to painting. It would be good for me, provide a real escape from my misery. I remembered how good I'd felt at the hospital when I painted. It had been my sanctuary. It would be—again.

Yes. I'll begin tomorrow. And then I thought of that attic studio and shivered. I couldn't paint up there, the scene of such violation. I would never be able to get the image of those slashed paintings out of my mind. I would have to find some other place in the house. There were certainly plenty enough unused rooms for only two people. No, I reminded myself. Not two. Three. Lillian might only occupy a tiny bedroom on the third floor and preside over the kitchen, but I could feel her haunting presence throughout the house. She was always watching me. Like the night before, in the den with Nicholas. And again this afternoon with Greg. I wondered if she reported my meeting with Greg to Nicholas. She must have seen him comforting me. Would she distort the encounter into some romantic liaison, hoping to turn Nicholas against me even more? Was that another reason why he hadn't joined me for dinner? How could I have forgotten about Lillian, even for an instant? Wishful thinking, I supposed.

I forced her from my mind once more, concentrating on what would be a good spot for a new studio. One of the north-facing bedrooms on the second floor. Yes. That would do nicely. It would mean moving out some of the furniture, or at least reorganizing the pieces so there'd be room for me to set up an easel by the window. I could clear off a bookshelf and line it with some vinyl shelving paper to store my paints.

I supposed I would have to ask Nicholas if he minded. Would he mind? I wondered. Again, those mutilated canvases flashed before me eyes. But he'd been angry, then. Or as Greg had said, in despair over my leaving. Well, I was back now. And he hadn't tossed me out. So, he might feel perfectly fine about my taking up painting again. It would keep me occupied. Keep me out of his hair. Not that I intended to get in his hair, mind you. I told myself quite firmly that my only reason for remaining at Raven's Cove had to do with regaining my memory. Nothing else.

I resolved that I would discuss my plan for the new studio with Nicholas the following day—if he didn't again issue orders that he wasn't to be disturbed. But then I remembered that the next day was Sunday. We had plans to join Godfrey and Julia for brunch in town. I would bring up my request to convert one of the bedrooms to a studio while we drove together to Sinclair.

Lillian strode into the dining room with my dinner—a plate of roast chicken seasoned with rosemary, new potatoes sprinkled with butter and dill, and fresh-cooked baby peas. It all smelled quite good. I told Lillian so, curious to how she'd receive a compliment from me.

She merely shrugged. "Nicholas is fond of chicken."

"Is he?"

She gave me a wary look, as if I were prying. Didn't I have a right to know my husband's preferences?

"What are his other favorite foods?" I prodded.

Her odd expression made me feel as though she were laughing at me. A private joke. And a cruel one, I thought.

"I don't see how it matters," she muttered.

"I just thought...on occasion...I might like to do some...cooking myself for Nicholas." I knew, even as I said the words, that in Lillian's mind I'd be speaking what amounted to blasphemy. I could practically read her mind. Cook for Nicholas! In her kitchen! The audacity! Not only had I come back home to reclaim my husband, but now she would think that I was trying to take over in the one domain that had always been hers alone. No doubt she was clinging to the old axiom—The Way To A Man's Heart Is Through His Stomach. And Lillian had the direct line.

I don't think she would have answered me at all if I hadn't stared her down. I was quite proud of myself, refusing to let her get away with giving me the evil eye.

Finally she said in a huff, "I doubt Nicholas would be pleased. He's used to my cooking. And he doesn't like change very much. He doesn't like it at all."

"Sometimes," I countered, quite courageously I thought, "change is important, whether we like it or not."

She glared at me.

"I've changed, Lillian. I'm not the woman you once knew. I don't think I ever will be, again." I hesitated. "Tell me about the Deborah you knew, Lillian. Please."

She gave a sinister laugh. "The Deborah I knew," she echoed darkly. Then her dull, malevolent eyes bore into me and she gripped my forearm. "The Deborah I knew was a vain, self-absorbed woman. Greedy, demanding, deceitful. She always did as she liked. Never thinking of anyone but herself. Never caring who she hurt. Nicholas made a fool of himself over her and he paid the price."

She leaned so close to me I could smell her breath. It smelled of whiskey and peppermint. I nearly gagged. "He won't be fool enough to pay it again. You won't get what you want here, missy. Not from Nicholas. You think being all sweetness and innocence is going to win him over, but you're wrong. If there's any price to be paid this time around, the one who'll be paying it will be you," she whispered ominously into my face.

Her fingers tightened on my flesh. The combination of her bruising grip, her foul breath, and her dreadful words made me positively ill. I could feel the color drain from my face. I knew she meant to frighten me, and she was doing a damn good job of it, but I could feel a stirring of anger, as well. *You won't scare me off this time, you witch. You won't get him that way. Or any way. Nicholas could never be yours Lillian. Not in the way you want. Not in the way he could be mine. . . .*

Releasing her hold on me, she straightened and wiped her palm on the front of her apron as if my skin had contaminated her. Let me tell you, I felt it was quite the other way around.

Her gaze dropped to my plate. "Your dinner's getting cold," she said with bland indifference.

But she didn't fool me this time. She was far from indifferent. It was just another one of her ploys. I was sure she wanted me to jump up from my chair and race from the room. I could even picture her gloating as she gathered up my untouched plate of food. Nauseated as I was by my encounter with her, I wasn't going to give her that satisfaction.

"You're right," I said evenly, even though my throat was raw and constricted. Taking up my fork and knife, I cut into the chicken.

She hovered there, watching me place a morsel in my mouth. Was she hoping I'd choke on it? If she couldn't starve me to death...

I admit it wasn't easy to swallow that bite, but I did. After she left, I forced myself to eat every last bite on my plate.

A clean plate. That's a good girl....

My mouth went dry. Those words had just sprung up in my mind. Out of nowhere. A voice in my head. A woman's voice. Sweet, proud, loving. My mother?

I smiled tremulously. Another little piece of the puzzle. Greg needn't have been so pessimistic. It was happening just as I'd thought, just as Dr. Royce had suggested to me back in the hospital.

I closed my eyes, trying to dredge up another memory or expand on that one, but my mind drew a blank. I couldn't even recreate that sweet, melodic voice. I felt frustrated, but refused to give in to it. Be patient, I counseled myself. It's coming back, slowly but surely.

I considered bringing my empty plate into the kitchen, but I didn't want another encounter with Lillian. She had made her position quite clear. Whether or not she believed I had changed was of no concern to her. I could be a bitch or an angel and she'd feel the same way toward me. She wanted no part of me. And she most definitely wanted me to have no part of Nicholas.

Was that why I hesitated as I passed the closed door of his den? Was I out to spite Lillian? Make her jealous? Or was it something else? Was I at the mercy of my feelings for Nicholas? Had he cast some sort of spell on me? No matter how frightened or upset I was, no matter how much I fought against it, I was compellingly drawn to him.

And there was one more reason I stopped at that closed door. Because of the amnesia, I was forced, through no fault of my own, to live behind enough closed doors. Here, at least, was one that could be opened. All it took was courage.

My hand trembled as I rapped lightly on the door. I could hear Lillian's grating voice in my head: *Nicholas is working all day and wanted me to tell you he wasn't to be disturbed.*

There was no response, and my courage was fast disappearing. I couldn't bring myself to knock again and I certainly wasn't brave enough to boldly try the door. I decided it was most likely locked, anyway. Dropping my hand to my side, I turned away just as the door opened.

Nicholas stood there, filling the doorframe. He looked pale and tired, his hair all ruffled. "Yes," he said so gruffly I nearly started to flee down the hall. Somehow, though, I managed to hold my ground. "I wasn't sure . . . if we were still . . . going tomorrow."

He stared blankly at me for a moment. "Going where?" His voice was a touch less curt.

So, he hadn't even remembered. I supposed my reclusive husband had little interest in a get-together with friends in town.

"We made plans to meet Julia and Godfrey—"

"Oh, right," he said offhandedly.

"Well?"

He surprised me with a half smile. "You're looking forward to it, aren't you?"

"I like them both. And it would be fun to—"

"To get away from here for a while?"

My eyes skidded off his face. "If you're too busy, I could go alone." I cursed myself as soon as I'd made the offer. Now, he'd think that, as before, I'd be just as happy to go off without him. Really, I think I would have been justified at that point in having such feelings. Nicholas had certainly done his best to foster them. But, inexplicably, I had no desire to go alone. I wanted Nicholas to join me.

Before he could toss off what I was sure would be an insinuating comeback, I quickly said, "I'd much rather we went together." I knew my face must have flooded with color. What an idiot I was. What a stupid fool I was making of myself. Why hadn't I left well enough alone and just walked right on past his den?

"All right," he said so quietly, for a moment I wasn't sure I'd actually heard him.

Finally I nodded, not knowing what else to say.

"How was your dinner?" he asked as I started to step away.

I stopped. His question brought Lillian's outburst in the dining room rushing back into my mind.

"Don't you care for chicken?" he asked.

I nodded. "Chicken's fine. The dinner was...very good. Lillian's an excellent cook."

"Yes," he agreed amiably. "There's not very much in her life she can take pride and pleasure in, besides cooking."

I was tempted to tell him that she took equal if not greater pride and pleasure in tormenting me. But I didn't. Instead, I said something inane like, "I hope your work is going well."

"As well as can be expected," he said, a hint of exasperation in his voice. "One of these days I swear I'll give it up." He eyed me sardonically. "Don't go blabbing that to Godfrey now, or he'll have one of his famous attacks of indigestion. And then I'll have Julia to answer to. She watches over him like a mother hen."

"I . . . I won't say anything—to either one of them," I stammered.

He smiled condescendingly and I realized only then that his admonishment had been purely rhetorical. Had I always been this naive? Not from any of the pictures that had been painted of me.

"About that encounter in the studio . . ." he began cautiously.

I gave him a startled look. "Let's not . . . talk about it." I desperately wanted to forget all about that encounter. I knew if I brought up what Greg had told me about why he'd destroyed the paintings, Nicholas would most likely deny it. Or get angry at Greg for revealing a confidence to me. And then I remembered Lillian standing at that window, watching me and Greg this afternoon. If she'd told Nicholas, as I suspected she had, then he might not be very pleased at my mentioning Greg at all.

Surprisingly, it was Nicholas who brought him up.

"Greg told me you'd done quite a bit of painting at the hospital. I noticed you didn't bring any of your work back with you."

I felt like saying, *Why should I have? So you could mutilate those, as well?*

But I didn't. Like so many other things I wanted to say to Nicholas, I censored it, afraid to incur his wrath or go looking for trouble. Instead I said blandly, "I donated them to the hospital."

"I see," he said, his tone equally bland. Was he doing some censoring of his own?

I thought to bring up a discussion of a new studio space, but decided I'd tackled enough for one night. These brief encounters with Nicholas were invariably draining and emotion-laden.

"Well, I'll say good-night, then," I ventured after he'd held my gaze for an overly long moment.

He didn't respond immediately. I found myself wondering if he was debating whether to invite me into his den again. Another nightcap? And then . . .

If he were to extend another invitation into his "lair," I knew I'd have had to be crazy to accept his offer after what had transpired there between us only twenty-four hours earlier. But, I was feeling a little bit crazy . . .

Nicholas merely nodded, muttered, "Good night," and had the door closed before I'd even finished my thought.

We were to meet the Irelands at the inn at noon. I was dressed and ready by eleven, having chosen a soft cotton, peasant-style peach blouse and a swingy peach-and-dusty-rose cotton-print skirt. Finding a silver comb in one of the dressing-table drawers, I brushed one side of my hair back, intending to hold it in place with the comb. But first I spent a few minutes examining it. I kept hoping that objects such as the comb—things that had once been mine—would give off some special vibes, jarring my memory. But the comb lay in the palm of my hand like a foreign object—just as everything else in this room that had been mine—mine and Nicholas's—felt alien, unknown. It didn't make sense to me. I replaced the comb in the drawer, letting my hair fall loosely around my shoulders, and, on impulse, decided I would phone Dr. Royce at the hospital and discuss the phenomenon with him.

I forgot while I was dialing that it was Sunday, but as it turned out, Dr. Royce had come into the hospital for the morning to catch up on some paperwork. When he came on the phone he sounded truly happy to be hearing from me. The feeling was mutual. I even felt a momentary longing to be back in the safety and security of his office. . . .

"How are you doing?" he asked right off the bat.

I hesitated. "That's not an easy question to answer."

I could picture his warm smile. "No, but I never required easy answers from you in the past."

Now it was my turn to smile. "You certainly didn't."

"So, tell me."

"I...I don't have much time. Nicholas and I are... meeting friends for brunch."

"That sounds nice," he said pleasantly.

"Yes. Yes, they're very nice people. The Irelands. Godfrey Ireland is Nicholas's publisher. And Julia—"

"If you don't have much time, Katherine... Or should I say Deborah?" The question was pointed.

"Another tough question," I replied. "I suppose it is... That is...I suppose I am...Deborah." I told him about the few flashes of memory that had come to me since being at Raven's Cove.

Dr. Royce was delighted. He saw this as real progress.

"But it's not very much. It's not as much as I'd hoped I'd remember...being home. What's especially confusing to me, Dr. Royce, is that none of the things that were Deborah's— mine—ring a bell. I don't really feel any connection with...with this woman who I was supposed to be."

There was a brief pause. "Maybe your mind is doing this deliberately."

"I don't understand," I said.

"Perhaps there are things about yourself, about the way you were, that you don't like. Things you might even prefer never to remember."

Tears started to slide down my cheeks.

"Deborah? Are you there?" he asked, his voice concerned.

"I'm...here. And I think...maybe you're right," I murmured. "I...wasn't very...nice." After a brief debate with myself, I went on to tell him some of the things I'd learned about the Deborah of old.

"Not that everyone sees me in exactly the same way. But the picture as a whole is less than . . . angelic," I finished.

"Ah. So now your goal is to be an angel," he teased lightly.

"Hardly," I said with a dry laugh. "I'm no angel, Dr. Royce. Not by a long shot." I almost told him then about my intimate encounter with Nicholas, but before I gathered up the courage there was a knock on my door.

"I . . . I have to go, Dr. Royce. May I . . . call you again?"

"If you really need to, Deborah," he said gently. "But I don't think it would be in your best interests, psychologically, to use me as a crutch. You're doing better than you think, you know."

I didn't agree, but neither did I argue with him. As I hung up, I felt as though a lifeline had been severed. How could I call Dr. Royce in the future when he'd made it clear I needed to learn to stand on my own two feet?

I was surprised to find Nicholas at the door. I thought he'd send Lillian up to fetch me while he waited in the car. I almost felt as if I were being picked up for a date. My depression over the end of my phone call with Dr. Royce ebbed.

Nicholas looked very arresting in a dark tweed jacket, black shirt and black pants. Instead of a traditional necktie, he'd chosen to wear a string tie held closed by an intricately carved silver-and-turquoise Indian clasp at the collar.

As I stood on my side of the door observing him, he was doing the same to me. From the faintly sardonic glint in his dark eyes, I made the assumption that my own appearance was lacking in both drama and appeal.

I felt immediately self-conscious, deciding the outfit was inappropriate, too flashy, the colors all wrong, and I should have put that silver comb in my hair, after all. Once upon a time, I would have known the right things to wear and the right hairstyle to please Nicholas.

"Are you ready?" he asked brusquely.

"I'll ... just grab ... a sweater," I stammered.

"You won't need it. It's warm out." A ghost of a smile curved his lips. "Besides, it would be a shame to cover up such a pretty blouse."

I'm embarrassed to say I blushed like a schoolgirl at his compliment. To give Nicholas his due, he didn't rub it in.

Once we were settled in his sports car, I began debating at which point to bring up my desire to convert one of the north-facing bedrooms into a studio. Confined together in that tight space, I felt particularly constricted. And Nicholas, silent and subdued behind the wheel, hardly invited conversation.

Finally, three-quarters of the way down the hill, I just blurted it out. I will never forget how exceedingly grateful I was to him for not questioning me as to why I didn't want to use the studio that had already been set up on the third floor.

"Which room would you like to use?"

I told him.

He didn't respond immediately and I took it to mean he wasn't pleased with my choice.

"It would only mean a bit of rearranging...."

"It wouldn't be ideal," he muttered.

"That's all right," I started.

"Give me some time to think about it. For now, it's so lovely out, you can set up an easel outside."

"Yes. Of course. I just thought—"

"You're eager to get back to painting, then." The remark came across as half question, half statement.

"Well ... yes. My painting is very important to me." I hesitated, gathering up nerve. "Wasn't it ... before?"

He gave me a quick glance. "In a way, I suppose it was," he replied in a flattened voice.

"I don't understand," I said.

"No, I suppose you wouldn't."

Is it any wonder why my conversations with Nicholas were so excruciatingly frustrating? The man gave nothing away. I felt that there were so many doors he could open for me, but he stubbornly refused. At the time, it was beyond me to understand why. Only later...

"I invited Greg to join us for brunch."

His sudden shift startled me.

"I thought you'd be pleased," he said languidly. "You seem to have been enjoying his company so far," he added insinuatingly.

I was sure, then, that Lillian had told Nicholas about my *tryst* with Greg out behind the house the day before. Anger surged in me. What right had Nicholas to turn an altogether innocent and friendly encounter into something tawdry?

Giving him a defiant look, I said, "I am pleased. Greg's been very kind to me. It's very nice of him to stop by and chat with me when he has the chance. There really hasn't been anyone else—"

"You've made your point," he said stiffly.

And so I had.

We drove in grim silence the rest of the way into town. I was no longer looking forward to this brunch. Nor was I now the least bit pleased that I'd practically begged Nicholas to join me. I was sure his somber presence would cast a pall over the gathering. I wished we weren't even going.

To add to my discontent, I hadn't even won Nicholas's permission to convert one of the spare bedrooms into a studio for myself.

CHAPTER TEN

All heads turned in our direction as Nicholas and I were led by an ingratiating maître d' to our table at the Sinclair Inn's cozy but crowded dining room. How rude people were, I thought. I supposed Nicholas's celebrity status made them feel they had the right to gawk. Glancing at Nicholas, I saw that his jaw was set, his dark eyes directed straight ahead, ignoring all the looks. His stride was so long, he passed the maître d', leaving me to tag along after the two of them. I felt as though everyone in the room was whispering, "She's certainly taken a turn for the worse since she's come back. Looks like a scared rabbit."

Godfrey and Greg both rose as I reached the table. Nicholas, however, had already slid into a seat beside Julia. He gave her an affectionate kiss on the cheek. How I envied her that friendly little gesture he bestowed on her. Yet, when Greg greeted me with an innocuous peck, I stiffened, my gaze darting to Nicholas. Would he take this as yet another sign of something brewing between me and his friend?

Nicholas met my glance with a twisted smile, increasing my discomfort.

"You look pale," Julia commented, observing me closely. Then she turned to Nicholas with a scolding expression. "You need to get your wife out in the sunshine more. Maybe a second honeymoon is even in order. A idyllic revisit to St. Martin?"

Nicholas laughed dryly. "You know why you could never edit horror stories, Julia? You're too much of a romantic."

"Besides, who goes to the Caribbean at this time of year?" Greg offered.

Godfrey smiled at me. "Do you good, Deborah. Oh, not St. Martin. But, some sunshine."

"Well, actually, I will be getting some more...sun," I muttered. "I'm going to take up painting again. Landscapes."

For some reason I couldn't fathom, my remark brought the table to silence. Greg came to the rescue. "Deborah did some lovely landscapes at the hospital. Mostly mountain settings," he added, with a warm smile in my direction.

Julia and Godfrey nodded, their smiles muted. Nicholas made no comment, nor did his grim expression change. Instead, he glanced over at the buffet table. "Well, shall we go fill up our plates?" Before anyone replied, he was out of his chair and heading for the food.

Julia gave my hand a little pat. "Odds are he's having problems with his new book. He's always surly and impatient when he comes to an impasse."

Godfrey quickly seconded his wife's opinion.

I couldn't agree with them more about my husband's mood. Only I didn't think it was his new novel that was causing Nicholas problems. I was sure it was me.

Godfrey and Julia went over to the buffet, and Greg pulled my chair out for me. He gave me a worried look as I started to rise." What's wrong, Deb?"

I gave him a winsome smile. "Wouldn't it be nice if, one day, you didn't need to ask me that?"

"It isn't like you to hold back on me," he murmured as I stepped away from the table.

I paused for a moment, my gaze meeting his. "Isn't it?"

When I arrived at the buffet table, I was surprised to find that Nicholas had filled a plate for me as well as himself. He'd selected some fresh ripe melon and a blueberry waffle hot off the griddle drizzled with butter and fresh maple syrup.

"This was always your favorite," he remarked idly as he handed me the plate, but I could feel his eyes watching me closely, testing me still. "Tell me, do tastes change with amnesia?"

I gave him a testy look. "I wouldn't know that, would I?"

His expression softened a fraction. "No, I suppose you wouldn't." He looked down at the plate. "If you'd prefer something else..."

I found myself smiling. "Actually, the waffle smells wonderful. Thanks."

Greg and the Irelands, who were all close by, smiled approvingly at me. Or maybe they were just relieved, since I'm sure it was obvious to all of them that Nicholas still had residual doubts about my identity.

The only one who didn't smile was Nicholas. How was I ever to win his approval or pass his tests, I wondered? I suppose a healthier question for me to have asked myself would have been, Why did I want to win his approval in the first place? I suppose because I felt my whole identity hung on his acceptance. And because, against all reason, I wanted to see him look at me just once the way he'd looked at me in that photo.

The brunch itself turned out to be much more pleasant than I'd anticipated. Nicholas was rather withdrawn, but the Irelands kept up a bright steady conversation, offering amusing and delightful stories. I found myself laughing and was grateful to them once more for perking up my spirits. Greg Eastman was another matter. I felt exceedingly self-conscious whenever he spoke to me directly and, anxious, each time, that Nicholas would misinterpret every word or gesture on either of our parts. What made it worse was that I knew that Greg had strong feelings for me. I believed Nicholas knew that, too—and, no doubt, suspected that I felt the same way toward Greg. But while I was certainly fond of Greg then, it was vastly different from the way I felt about Nicholas. Love, hate, fear, longing—that vast spectrum of intense emotions were all jumbled together in my mind where he was concerned. As tumultuous as my feelings were for Nicholas, they had certainly revived my interest in life as nothing else had since the assault and my memory loss.

The gathering drew to an end long before I would have liked, but Julia and Godfrey were eager to get on the road so that they'd miss some of the weekend traffic back to the city. Before they left, they both encouraged Nicholas in turn to bring me in to New York for a visit.

"We can go shopping," Julia said to me. "And I'll pick up tickets for some shows."

"Get Nick to the city?" Greg quipped. "He hates everything about it. The noise, the crowds, the traffic. Give the guy a break." He turned to me. "I drive into Manhattan for a few days every couple of weeks while I'm vacationing up here. Just to check in at the office and make sure things are running smoothly. If you feel like coming in with me anytime, just say the word."

From the corner of my eye, I could see Nicholas's mouth harden. I smiled pleasantly at Greg and then at the Irelands. "I'm afraid I feel much the same way about the city as Nicholas does."

Godfrey eyed me curiously. "Well, that's certainly a change."

Julia nudged her husband. "Naturally, after what Deborah went through, she'd feel differently about Manhattan. I'm the first one to say that crime is completely out of hand in the city." She pressed my hand gently. "You have my word, though, Deborah. If and when you want to come into town, Godfrey and I will watch over you as if you were the Hope diamond."

"Ditto for me," Greg added. "We all want to make sure nothing ever harms you again, Deborah."

Although Greg included the others, I knew he was speaking for himself. And I was sure that Nicholas knew that, too.

In the car, driving back to Raven's Cove, Nicholas was grimmer than ever. After about ten minutes of the silent treatment, I couldn't stand it anymore.

"There's nothing going on between me and Greg," I blurted out. "I don't know what went on in the past between us—Greg's assured me we were just good friends— but whether or not he's telling me the truth, I just want you to know that my loss of memory has in no way affected my ability to know what I feel now. I am not romantically interested in Greg. Whatever Lillian's told you—"

"Lillian's very protective of me," he muttered.

"And she hates me," I snapped. "I'm sure she'd like nothing more than to stir up trouble between us. As if there isn't enough stirred up." Now that I had gotten going, I found that I couldn't stop. "It isn't fair, Nicholas. You always have me at a disadvantage. You know so much and I don't know anything at all. I feel like I'm holding on by a thread—and that any minute you might come along and snip it. And I don't even know why. You toss a few innuendoes at me and then turn your back on me. You've been cutting, insinuating, distrustful, insufferably rude. If you hate me so, why— Why don't you just tell me you want me out of your life?"

I was shaking with emotion by the time I finished. And it didn't help matters any that Nicholas said not one word in reply to my tirade. Which, I admit, was better than hearing him tell me that he did want me out of his life. Because the truth was, I didn't want him to banish me.

I sank back wearily in my seat and shut my eyes. How much more of this could I take? My mental state was precarious at best.

We were a good two-thirds of the way up the mountain road to Raven's Cove when out of the tense silence, Nicholas said, "You do look pale."

The next thing I knew, we had pulled over to the side of the mountain. Nicholas switched off the ignition. "Well?"

I gave him a blank look.

He opened the car door. "Everyone seems to think I've been depriving you of sunshine. I may be all you say, but I've never intentionally deprived someone of something they needed, if I was capable of giving it to them."

It was an odd speech and I sensed some hidden meaning behind his words, but it would be a while before I'd grasp the meaning fully.

"There's a particularly sunny path along the cliff just off to the right. Shall we?"

I didn't know what to say. Nicholas wanted to take a leisurely walk with me? After I'd hurled abuse after abuse on him? It didn't make any sense. Unless his sudden pleasantness disguised a fiendish scheme to toss me off the mountain. After all, I already had proof of Nicholas's volatile temper. The image of those slashed paintings continued to haunt me.

Still, as he came around to my side of the car and opened the door for me, I stepped out without so much as a word of protest. Also, not without a sizable degree of trepidation. Not that I seriously considered that he wanted to do away with me. Not then, anyway...

The dirt path was narrow and winding, but a relatively easy hike. Nicholas walked on my right, closer to the cliff edge. I relaxed a bit. He seemed in a harmless-enough mood as we ambled along at a leisurely pace, the sun warming us, neither of us saying anything. Unlike the other silences I'd shared with Nicholas, this was the first one, surprisingly, that wasn't laden with tension. I didn't really know why this was, but I sensed a distinct change in Nicholas's mood. Maybe I'd gotten through to him with my outburst. Maybe he was regretting having treated me so badly. And I felt better, too, having gotten so much off my chest. Maybe it would clear the air for both of us.

From the distance, a train whistled. It must have been pulling out of town. Two days ago, I had come so close to being on that train, heading away from Sinclair, Raven's Cove, Nicholas. Now, here we were, Nicholas and I, walking side by side, basking in the warmth of the sun and the beauty of the setting. I felt oddly content, and when I dared a peek over at Nicholas, his features seemed more relaxed, as well.

"Are you serious about one day giving it up?" I asked timidly. "Your horror novels, I mean?"

Nicholas shrugged his shoulders. "It's a threat I hold over Godfrey. Keeps his blood circulating."

I still can't imagine what made me so bold, but I shook my head. "That's not the only reason. I think you have a . . . a longing to write something . . . else. Something altogether different."

He gave me an edgy look. I immediately regretted my words. Things had been going so well. Comparatively speaking.

After a prolonged silence, he responded, "I did start a different sort of book once. One of those ludicrous flights of fancy we writers all have at one time or another to write 'the great American novel.' No ghouls, no witches, no monsters—at least not the supernatural kind. Regular, everyday people can be plenty monstrous enough."

"Yes, that's true," I whispered. "We all have the capacity to be cruel as well as kind, to hate as well as love, to be violent as well as gentle." I stopped, pressing my lips together, fearing Nicholas would take what I'd said as a direct attack. I hadn't meant it that way.

Surprisingly, he smiled at me. "Maybe you ought to be writing instead of painting."

I thought he might be making fun of me, but there was no sign of it in his expression. I was disconcerted. "Did I ever...write?"

He came to an abrupt stop. I froze, not knowing what to expect. I rarely did, where Nicholas was concerned.

He didn't say anything right away. He seemed to be choosing his words. "I know that you're desperate to fill in all the blanks. It must be quite dreadful, living in a dark void. But, for now, for today, anyway, let's not talk about the past. Let's just experience whatever is happening right at this moment."

I was struck by his sympathy and earnestness. It was in such sharp contrast to the biting, sardonic manner he assumed so often. Strangely enough, I didn't think either attitude was bogus. And this realization made me feel closer to Nicholas than I ever had before. Because, like him, I, too, felt as if I were a study in emotional contrasts.

We continued strolling along the ribbony path, breathing in the fresh piney air, a surprising ease settling about us. I know it sounds silly and very schoolgirlish to say, but that was the most peacefully happy stroll I ever took. It felt like a beginning. A new beginning for me and Nicholas.

We must have walked a good mile before he suggested we sit for a while and rest.

"I should have thought to bring along something for us to drink," he said.

I smiled. "It was rather spur-of-the-moment."

He smiled back, almost boyishly, gallantly dusting off a small boulder before I settled on it. My heart felt a stirring, different from anything before. I liked this new Nicholas. His warmth and gentleness were a welcome relief from the sullen, withdrawn, suspicious, almost demonic man I had known thus far.

He made himself comfortable on a nearby rock, giving me a thoughtful, measured study.

"Your skin is very fair."

I had to bite back the question on the tip of my tongue— *Wasn't it fair before?*

"I don't think I'll burn," I said instead. "And the sun does feel wonderful." I looked out over the broad Catskill mountain range. One peak in the far-off distance looked whitecapped still. "I'd like to paint all this."

He stared at me for a long moment, his expression unreadable. And then he said, "There's another path closer to the house that has a similar view. I'll show you tomorrow if you like." He hesitated. "We can go into town in the morning and you can pick up whatever supplies you need. There's a halfway-decent art shop in town. Whatever you don't find there you can order through the mail."

"Oh, I'm sure I'll be able to find most of what I need in town," I quickly said, almost giddy with his kind offer. After a pause, I murmured, "Thanks, Nicholas."

He seemed embarrassed by my gratitude, but also, I suspected, touched.

He stretched out his long limbs and closed his eyes, tilting his face up to the sun. It was as though he were willing me to study him. Or at least it felt that way. The impulse, for whatever reason, was too strong to resist.

I observed him in much the way I'd taken to studying a still life or landscape before I painted it, trying to see the lines and shadows, the structure and texture, the nuances and the emotional draw. In Nicholas's face, I could see the arrogance and self-assurance, even the ruthlessness, in the strong lines of his striking profile; but now I saw that those very qualities seemed at war with that other, more tender, giving side of his nature. It served to create an arresting turbulence in his features. It helped explain why there was such a searing passion about him.

I was so engrossed in my study of him—my own emotions admittedly were running a bit wild—that it took a moment or two for me to realize he'd opened his eyes.

I flushed.

He smiled. "You're getting some color already." He was teasing me, but there was nothing cruel or condescending in his tone.

"I haven't done any portraits—at least not that I can remember." I didn't want him to think I was prodding him for information. Taking time out from searching for clues to my past was good for me for a change, just as it seemed to be for Nicholas. So I hurried on. "I would like to paint you, though."

I expected to see him frown and then turn me down cold. Didn't he suffer enough people staring at him wherever he went? Why should he want to subject himself to my close scrutiny, as well?

I should have known it was pointless to second-guess him.

He tilted his head toward me, so that the right side of his face fell in shadow. "Why is that?" he asked, curious.

I didn't know how to answer him. I struggled for the words. "Because you're so... complex," I finished inadequately.

He laughed dryly. "You don't throw your compliments around, do you?"

I grinned. "Will it soothe your ego if I tell you I find you very striking—that you have a strong physical magnetism, a powerful presence?"

"You aren't going to stop there, are you?" he prodded lightly.

I laughed. "If I go on, will you let me paint you?" The hint of coyness in my voice surprised me even more than it surprised Nicholas.

Wonderful, unexpectedly joyful days followed. A whole week of them. As if my happiness had some magical powers over the weather, each day was sunnier and more radiant than the day before. Never had I seen the sky bluer, the sun brighter, the greenery more vibrant. Never had the air been richer. And never had I been more bewildered. Or happier.

Nicholas squired me to town the following day as he'd promised, and then insisted on carrying my easel and paints out to an exquisite promontory up a path about a quarter of a mile from the house. The spot provided an even more spectacular vista of the mountains and village below than the one we'd stopped at the day before. I was delighted. And better still, my delight seemed to please Nicholas enormously.

I didn't understand what had caused such a complete transformation in Nicholas, but I wasn't about to question it too deeply, for fear it would just disappear in a puff of smoke. It's funny having had that thought, knowing what I know now. But during those pleasure-filled days, I truly had no presentiment of sinister undercurrents; I heard no distressing echoes; I was completely unaware of encroaching danger. Even the ominous Lillian seemed no threat to me during that golden week. She kept her distance from me as much as possible. I suspected that Nicholas had either spoken to her or that she had simply been forced to accept that I had won my husband back after all her efforts to drive me off. I didn't gloat. Once my fear of her had subsided and my relationship with Nicholas seemed to be blossoming, I was again filled with pity for her. Was she to blame for loving Nicholas so? Any more than I was to blame?

Yes, I believed I was falling in love with him. Before there had been fierce attraction, though that feeling certainly warred with my fear of him and my own common sense. But this feeling was something different. Nicholas's tender care moved me. He was so changed. Gone completely during those splendid days was that arrogant man who had so easily seduced me and then treated me with such rough, selfish abandon. To my consternation, Nicholas was now far more a gentleman than I would have liked him to be. I kept thinking, I am his wife. He has every right— And so do I....

Each day our routine would be the same. We'd have breakfast together at nine each morning, then Nicholas would gather up the tools of my trade and carry them out for me to the bluff. Once he'd helped me set up, he'd give me a quiet smile, then go off to his study to work. At noon, he'd arrive with a picnic lunch. We'd eat together under the blue skies, then both return to our respective work until dusk, at which time we'd take a leisurely stroll along one of the many mountain paths. In the evenings, after dinner, he'd invite me into his den. While I read a magazine or a popular novel— though never one of Nicholas's horror stories—he would edit and revise the writing that he'd completed that day.

We didn't talk very much, but I didn't mind. Once or twice I did try to bring up our past together, but Nicholas still seemed intent on barring any discussion of our yesterdays. I interpreted this to mean that he wanted us to have a fresh start. At the time, as much as I wanted to reclaim my memory, I believe I wanted a fresh start with Nicholas even more.

On the following Sunday, a week to the day our relationship had begun its transformation for the better, he appeared, as usual, punctually at noon with a well-stocked picnic basket. Immediately I noticed that he was in a particularly festive mood. He kept smiling and whistling, like a little boy very pleased with himself. I thought him adorable—certainly not a word I would have used to describe him before.

"What is it?" I coaxed as he laid out a blanket and unloaded the basket, placing cold chicken and dilled potato salad on our plates, then pouring us both some wine.

"You'll see," he said mysteriously. "In time."

Knowing it was impossible to budge Nicholas once he'd made up his mind, I dutifully sat down to eat. He glanced over at my easel, the back of my canvas facing him.

"When are you going to show me your painting?" he asked. I'd been very circumspect about my work. Nicholas had never seen any of my new stuff and I was nervous about his reaction. Would he still think I wasn't very good? I decided I wouldn't show it to him until it was completed, and then, only if I was fully satisfied.

I smiled coquettishly. "You'll see. In time."

He laughed. He had a wonderful laugh. The sound excited me, made me feel buoyant. There was a dreamlike quality about his laugh. But then there was a dreamlike quality about everything, those days.

After he took a few bites of food he stretched out across the blanket and looked up at the sky.

"I think it might rain tomorrow," he mused.

The sky was as clear as it had been for the past six days. "There's no sign of rain." He must have picked up a hint of anxiety in my voice.

"Does the rain still . . . bother you?" he asked gently.

"Even the thought of it," I confessed.

He gave me a look that was so tender I believed that if he had the power, he'd keep the rain from falling for me.

I nibbled on my chicken for a few more minutes, but I had no appetite. Not for food, anyway. I gave him a tentative look, but his eyes were now closed. Had he fallen asleep? After a moment's nervous hesitation, I stretched out beside him.

Immediately, he glanced over at me. I blushed like a schoolgirl. But I didn't jump up. I continued to lie there beside him, our shoulders just barely touching, our eyes locked.

"You never call me Deborah," I murmured. "Have I... changed so much?"

He gave me a strained look. "Yes. More than I can grasp, sometimes."

I think he suspected that I might take this as an opening to question him again about the Deborah of old. He silenced me quite effectively. And delightfully. With a tender kiss on my lips.

Even as my lips parted to deepen the kiss I'd been craving for days, he was already drawing away. Next thing I knew, he was gathering up the food and dishes and stowing everything back in the picnic basket.

"Nicholas." Could he hear the expectation and desire in my voice?

He must have, because he shook his head, giving me that solemn look of his that I clearly saw was returning full force. "I took advantage of you once. I'm not going to do that again," he muttered.

How could I tell him that it wasn't the same this time? We had both changed. Or, at least, we were both now daring to show those parts of ourselves that we'd kept under wraps because they made us feel so vulnerable.

"Come on. There's something I want to show you," he said, his manner subdued.

I gave him a beseeching look and he smiled at me again, some of the boyishness returning to his features. My heart soared.

He reached out his hand to help me up. His grasp was firm. I felt comfort in that grasp. I felt a kind of security I hadn't known before. Oh, if only it could have gone on forever like that, without interruption ...

"Where are we going? What's this about?" I asked excitedly. Instead of following the same path that led back toward Raven's Cove, he was leading me on a detour.

"Did anyone ever tell you you're an impatient young woman?" he teased.

I smiled. "It must run in the family," I said flippantly.

He didn't smile back. Instead he gave me one of those damnable inscrutable looks of his. I was afraid I'd insulted him. I even started to apologize when he squeezed my hand.

"So, what do you think?" he asked brightly, whatever having caused his momentary upset gone.

I followed his gaze and saw a small gazebo-shaped gingerbread cottage in a clearing not very far from the main house. I hadn't noticed it from Raven's Cove because of the thick stand of fir and oak that kept most of it from view. The cottage looked like it had been plucked right out of a fairy tale.

"Why, it's charming," I murmured. "What's it used for?"

"I used to write out here sometimes," he said lightly. "Come take a look. I've had a bit of work done on it."

He still had hold of my hand and he was walking so fast, his strides so long, that I had to run to keep up with him, arriving a bit breathless at the doorway.

I lost my breath completely when he opened the door. He'd converted his former writing space into an artist's studio that even Rembrandt would have envied. A vast skylight had been cut into the roof on the north side of the main room, which was much larger than it seemed from the outside. Every possible item an artist could need was there, including a magnificent antique easel, which, for all I knew, could have once been Rembrandt's. The floor of the studio was a rich terra-cotta stone, with several colorful handwoven Native American rugs scattered about. A large adobe wood stove sat in the center of the room, ideal for cold winter days. In a little nook off to the right was a completely outfitted kitchenette. In another nook, this one larger, was a teal-blue velvet chaise. There were vases of fresh flowers everywhere, their scent so heady I felt a bit dizzy. Nicholas crossed the room, opening the doors to an antique wardrobe that revealed a state-of-the-art stereo system. He switched it on, and a Beethoven piano concerto filled the room.

"The bathroom's over here." He opened a door to the right of the wardrobe, beckoning me over. My legs were a little wobbly as I crossed the room.

The bathroom, like everything else, was top of the line. There was even a huge Jacuzzi tub, and because the room faced the privacy of the woods, one entire wall was glass. I could recline in that marvelous bathtub and feel like I was in the middle of a forest.

I stepped back into the center of the studio, slowly pivoting, trying to take it all in. Nicholas stood a few feet from me, observing me intently.

"You're pleased," he said finally.

I laughed and cried at the same time.

What I did next, I did purely on impulse. I ran to him and threw my arms around his neck, kissing him with ardor. As I pressed against him, I could feel him trying desperately to hold back.

I lifted my face to him, tears blurring my vision. "Don't think of me as Deborah, Nicholas. I'm not her. Not anymore. Not the woman you remember. The woman who brought you...pain. Whatever happened between us in the past no longer exists for me. If only I could wipe out *your* memory, as well..."

I saw the anguish and the desire etched so deeply into his features. I lifted a brand-new sable paintbrush from a new copper holder. Slowly, gently, I began stroking the brush along his face—across his forehead, his eyebrows, his nose, his sensual lips.

"If I could paint you," I murmured, "I would erase all the lines of suffering. I would paint you smiling." I looked into his shimmering dark eyes. "I would paint you smiling and naked."

He smiled, then. There was only one thing missing. With a newfound brazenness, I began unbuttoning his shirt.

He touched my cheek and ran his hand lightly down my hair. "If only I'm naked, I'll be at a distinct disadvantage. Don't you believe in equality between artist and model?"

Our gazes locked. "Absolutely," I whispered, feeling my whole body come to life.

His hand moved to the zipper of my sundress. But he hesitated. "Are you sure about this? It isn't just...gratitude or something like that?"

I drew the brush lightly down his chest, circling in a feathery stroke around his nipples, watching them harden, mine hardening just at the sight. "Nothing like that. This is nothing like anything that's ever happened before."

His lips moved to mine. Even our mingled breaths seemed charged with an erotic current.

CHAPTER ELEVEN

We undressed each other slowly, savoring the wondrous texture of flesh, the strength of muscle, the marvelous curves and angles of our bodies. Oh, how can I describe those incredible moments? The excitement, the fever racing in my veins, the blotting out of everything from my mind— every fear, every inhibition, every doubt.

Tears still come to my eyes when I think of Nicholas's gentleness that golden afternoon. He touched my body as if I were both the most fragile and the most precious jewel on earth. The initial anguish that had been an ache etched in his features vanished, to be replaced by wonder, amazement, even.

"This isn't real," he kept murmuring. "This is like a dream."

It was a dream for me, too. A dream come true. If no past had ever existed for us, it wouldn't have mattered. That day in my beautiful new studio, Nicholas claimed me as his own. As I claimed him. No boundaries existed between us.

I lay stretched out on the chaise, Nicholas on his knees beside me, the sable paintbrush in his hand.

"Let me be an artist now," he whispered, as he glided the tip of the brush sinuously down between my breasts. "Let me paint you here—" the brush slid around one nipple "—and here—" around my other nipple "—and now here—" across my belly, my jutting hip bone. "And we must remember to keep the painting balanced—" There was a soft feathery stroke up my inner thigh. Only it wasn't the sable brush stroking me now; it was Nicholas's tongue.

A low, broken moan escaped my lips as he gently coaxed my thighs farther apart.

"What a work of art you are," he murmured against my burning flesh, then nibbled gently, seductively until my legs were splayed apart, my body writhing uncontrollably under his skilled, erotic ministrations. I felt a strong hand slide under my buttocks, arching me up. I could feel his warm breath, then the caress of his tongue, circling, then stroking in a slow, steady rhythm. My body began to quiver violently, my fingers digging into his scalp, driving him on. As if he needed encouragement. I felt that any second I would explode into a million pieces. And then I did—a divine, exquisite explosion, with Nicholas there to gather up all the pieces and put me back together again.

Had I ever experienced such ecstasy before? There was no way I could know then. And it didn't matter. I almost wanted it to be the first time.

I told him as much.

"It isn't over yet," he whispered huskily, moving over me, smiling down at me. Oh, how I'd dreamed of that radiant, adoring smile. Was I still dreaming? Could this really be happening to me?

My arms wrapped around him and I clung to him, our bodies aligned on that wide velvety chaise, flesh against flesh. His weight took my breath away, but I wanted to feel that weight. It made it all real. I longed to tell him I never wanted to let him go, I never wanted this time to end, but I didn't trust myself to speak. I didn't want to break the spell, so I just held him tightly, wordlessly. As he held me.

It must have been torture for him to hold back his own climax, but he seemed determined to make this experience utterly different from our encounter in his study. He began caressing me with infinite tenderness and patience. Far sooner than he seemed to expect, I was again ablaze with longing. My palms stroked down his back and over his buttocks, marveling at his long, lean, rippling muscles. There was an innate animal quality about Nicholas that was breathtaking. I'd felt it the first moment I'd set eyes on him as he moved toward me in the hallway of Raven's Cove, like a specter, a dancer, a predator—all grace and power.

The strains of the Beethoven concerto filled the room, mingling with our panting breaths. The feel of him, the scent of him, the sight of him all combined to intensify my ribboning desire. There was nothing I would have denied him. He had only to ask. But he caressed me in silence, asking me nothing, telling me nothing, our bodies speaking a language uniquely their own.

Yes, yes, my body crooned silently, the muscles in my thighs trembling, my heart fluttering as he filled me at last. *So good... You feel so good, so right.*

Nicholas could hold back no longer, no more than I could. He threw his head back, the cords at the sides of his neck sharply defined, his lips parted in a soundless cry of release that mingled with mine. Then his head dropped and he buried his face in my hair, his breath coming in short, ragged pants.

It wasn't only the fiercely exhilarating physical connection that I experienced with Nicholas that day; I felt as if his very essence had become a part of me. At that moment of union, I allowed myself to believe I truly understood this powerful and complex man—as if this most intimate of acts made everything simple. But it didn't. Later, I would discover that it was just the opposite; it made everything so much more complicated.

Even as we were both still catching our breaths, his lips glided over my eyelids, my cheeks, my nose, the line of my jaw. Was he noting the differences in his mind? Thanks to a faceless madman smashing me senseless in the night, this wasn't the same nose Nicholas once loved. Not the same jaw his lips had once caressed. I wasn't the Deborah he had once adored. But then I reminded myself that I also wasn't the Deborah he had come to mistrust, maybe even to hate.

There was no hate in his eyes that afternoon. It was almost impossible for me to imagine it ever being there again. I was blinded by passion, I suppose many would say.

In the late afternoon, I returned to the promontory to gather up my paints, easel and canvas and move it all to my new studio. Nicholas had wanted to come out with me, but I gently discouraged him. I needed some time alone, to absorb what had happened, let it sink in. And I kept waiting for memory to flood me as sensation had flooded me while Nicholas and I had made love. Wishful thinking, I suppose. But even though there were no flashbacks, it didn't mar my happiness. I thought nothing would ever mar it again.

"Well, don't you make a pretty sight."

I let out a little gasp of surprise—Greg Eastman seemed to have sprung up out of nowhere.

A giddy smile curved my lips of their own accord. "Do I?"

He scrutinized me more closely. I could feel my face redden.

"What's this?" he asked, cocking his head. "A bright smile when only hours ago, you looked so sad you as much as broke my heart."

I almost blurted out that my husband and I had become lovers. But I held back, sensing that it might upset Greg, even though I felt certain he'd understand—and be happy for me, if disappointed for himself. It had become obvious to me by then that, at the back of Greg's mind, was the hope that if things didn't work out for me and Nicholas, he might stand a chance.

"Painting out here on this glorious bluff. Who wouldn't be happy?" I murmured softly, not quite able to look him straight in the eye.

He saw that I was packing up and came around to have a look at the canvas. This made him my first viewer and I felt a bit nervous.

"What do you think?" I asked when Greg made no comment.

"Has Nick seen it yet?"

"You don't like it." My voice was heavy with disappointment.

He gave me a chastising look. "Are you nuts? It's great. Better than anything you did in the hospital."

I let out a sigh of relief. "I haven't shown it to Nicholas yet. He— He wasn't all that enthusiastic about my... my earlier works." For an instant, my mind flashed to those mutilated canvases, but I quickly willed the image to disappear. No more hateful visions, I vowed. Whatever Nicholas had done in the past was of no consequence now. We had begun anew.

"Nick's not an art critic, Deb. What do you expect from a guy who spends most of his time conjuring up ghoulish creatures dripping with blood and gore?"

I shivered.

Greg immediately apologized. "I'm sure he's going to love this painting. I don't suppose you'd consider selling it."

I gave him a baffled look. "Selling it?"

He blushed. "To me. I'd love to have it. But, I suppose... Well, I just thought..." He grinned. "You've got me stammering like a schoolboy."

I smiled at him. "You're very sweet, Greg. I'm touched that you'd want to buy the painting. But I couldn't—"

"No. No, of course. I understand."

"I couldn't sell it to you. Not after all you've done for me. But I'd be delighted to make you a present of the landscape. It's the very least—"

"It would mean a lot to me, Deb. More than... More than I can say."

I nodded—my way of telling him I understood.

"First, though, I've got a few finishing touches to add. I'll do it tomorrow morning in my new studio." Just thinking of the studio, of the unique way Nicholas and I had christened it, made my cheeks heat up.

"New studio?"

"A little cottage near the house. Nicholas converted it into a studio for me. As a surprise." *And what a surprise. What an incredible surprise!*

"I'd love to see it," Greg said enthusiastically.

But I couldn't show it to him then. For that day, anyway, I wanted to keep the studio just Nicholas's and mine.

"Come by tomorrow afternoon. And you can pick up the painting. After I bite the bullet and show it to Nicholas. He's been badgering me all week to let him have a look."

A shadow fell across Greg's face.

"What is it?" I asked with concern.

"Nothing. It's just, maybe you shouldn't give me the painting, Deb. I don't want Nick to misconstrue..." He let the sentence trail off, looking away.

"We've straightened that all out, Greg," I said soothingly.

He turned back to me. "Have you?"

"Nicholas knows there's nothing *to* misconstrue between us."

"That wasn't the feeling I got at the inn," he countered. "Every time I so much as said a word to you, he was giving me the evil eye. Believe it or not, Nick and I used to be close friends."

"And you will be again," I assured him, squeezing his hand. "Nicholas and I had a talk after we left the inn. We've...sorted things out." Smiling, I added that I was very proud of myself for confronting the matter head-on.

Greg smiled back. "Good. That's good, Deb. You've got to stand up to him, you know. Not let him intimidate you. In the past, he—" Again, he stopped short of a finish.

"Tell me," I insisted.

He kept his face averted.

"Please, Greg. I want to know. I need to know."

He gave me an uneasy look. "He had his way of keeping you...under his thumb."

"What way?" I demanded.

Greg's face reddened. "He would...seduce you. It was the one hold he always had over you, Deb. You never could resist that sexual magnetism of his." He hesitated. "Whenever things got uncomfortable for Nick, or when he felt you were pushing too hard, or demanding too much from him, or if you got angry or frustrated with him, he could always appease you. With sex." He let out a whoosh of air from his lungs. "It was something you told me once, in confidence. It wasn't easy for you to tell me. Or easy for me to hear. You cried, getting yourself into quite a state, going on about Nick having cast a spell on you."

I looked away, my mind whirling, my thoughts inchoate. Greg wasn't describing the tender man who'd made love to me less than an hour ago. Nicholas hadn't "appeased" me. Nor could I picture him ever being so manipulative. Not where our sex life was concerned.

Yet, it was certainly true that I found Nicholas sexually irresistible. As much, if not more so, than I had in the past, I imagined. And now that we'd finally consummated the passion that had been building all week, I wanted him more than ever. That he had a piercing sexual magnetism was unassailable. He ignited passion in me that I sensed could override any other feelings.

Greg was implying that Nicholas had seduced me in the past as a way of keeping a distance between us. That didn't make any sense to me at first. I had felt such an intense closeness while we'd made love. But then, as I thought about it, I couldn't help remembering that Nicholas had whispered no words of love to me during our passion. Nor had he either spoken my name or even murmured any endearments. The whole time we'd made love, the whole time I'd thought I was absorbing his very essence, had he been holding back a part of himself?

"Damn it," Greg muttered hotly under his breath. "I've upset you. And here I came over to cheer you up." One of his hands floated to my chin. He cupped it gently. "Don't be blue, Deb. What can I do to make it up? I'll do anything. Anything," he murmured earnestly. "You mean the world to me."

And then, before I knew what was happening, his lips were on mine. A terrible stab of conscience shot through me as I drew back. Had I unthinkingly led Greg on? I really did feel very fond of him—but not in a romantic way. I couldn't let him think that we could ever be anything more than friends. The time had come to tell him the truth: that Nicholas and I had become husband and wife again in the truest sense. But even as I opened my mouth to speak, a shadow drew my eye.

Nicholas stood on the path that led to the promontory, motionless as a deer caught in a car's headlights. But his expression was neither startled nor frightened as a deer's might have been. There was almost no expression on his face at all, save for the tight line of his mouth and the narrow slant of his dark eyes.

Those eyes fixed on me and I felt wretched. And, yes, a little afraid.

A moment later, he spun around and took off up the path. I turned to Greg, feeling helpless, devastated. Unlike Nicholas's masklike expression, Greg's face radiated distress and embarrassment.

"I'll go after him, Deb. I'll explain."

But something hard settled in my heart. "No," I said so sharply, Greg jumped. "No explanation is needed. If there isn't trust between a husband and wife, what is there?"

As Greg tried to soothe me, telling me to just give Nicholas a little time and space to calm down, I felt a dark void closing in on me. I welcomed it now, embraced it, wanting all my memories to be swallowed up in the blackness, wanting to remember none of it. I had foolishly thought my loss of memory the cause of my greatest anguish. It was proving, instead, to be love.

I carried my canvas and paints back to my new studio. As I stepped inside, Nicholas's scent still lingered. Exhaustion and despair swept over me. Was it possible that only a couple of hours ago I had known such happiness? Now I envisioned more strain than ever between myself and Nicholas. He was a proud man. But I, too, was discovering my pride. I sank down wearily on the chaise, trying to tell myself that Nicholas would come to his senses shortly. Greg was right. I just needed to give him a chance to cool off. One day soon we'd laugh about it. But even as I told this to myself, I didn't really believe it.

For one glorious week, I'd floated on cloud nine, but now it was as if that cloud had burst open in a clap of thunder, sending me hurtling to the earth below. That unyielding expression on Nicholas's face had chilled me to the bone. I could feel it as a physical wrenching.

The studio seemed to close in on me. I squeezed my eyes shut, praying things would work out. I would swallow my pride. I would talk with Nicholas. I would make him see that he could trust me completely.

The sound of footsteps made me jump from the chaise. I flew to the door, a smile on my face, thinking Nicholas had come to talk things out.

I flung the door open and gasped. It wasn't Nicholas, but Lillian. Her dark eyes fixed on me with a mix of triumph and hatred.

"What do you want?" I demanded.

"I thought you'd like to know that Nicholas has gone off for the evening."

"Gone where?"

She smiled slyly. "I wouldn't know."

I didn't believe her.

"I wouldn't wait up for him," she added. "When he goes off like this, he sometimes doesn't return for days."

How did she know in what state he'd gone off? Had she been spying again? I didn't doubt it. She probably knew every move both Nicholas and I made. A shiver raced down my spine. Had she spied on us here in the studio earlier this afternoon?

She gave me a pitying look. "Your kind never learns."

I glared at her, my fury barely contained. "And just what kind am I?"

"Greedy," she bit out acidly.

"You don't know anything about me," I snapped. "And less about Nicholas than you think."

She laughed in that hard, mechanical way of hers and turned her back to me, shutting the door. As if my declaration didn't even merit one of her typically cutting remarks.

It was after midnight when I finally crawled into bed that night. Nicholas hadn't returned. The thought of him spending the whole night out, perhaps even longer, made me feel miserable.

A wind kicked up. The windows rattled. I pulled the covers up under my chin. A rainstorm was brewing. Perfect timing, I thought morbidly.

I dozed off, only to be awakened by the sound of a car pulling up. I glanced at the clock. Two-fifteen. Tossing off the covers, I leaped out of bed and ran to the window to see Nicholas's BMW pulling into the drive. Observing him step out of the car made me feel giddy with relief. I even raced across my bedroom and unlocked my door.

Come to me, my darling!

I ran a comb through my hair and dabbed a bit of perfume behind my ears. As I heard his footsteps on the stairs, I flicked on my bedside lamp. He would see the strip of light beneath my door and know I was awake, that I was waiting for him. I held my breath in nervous anticipation as I heard him start down the hall.

But he didn't so much as pause at my door. He went straight on to his bedroom. I heard his door slam shut. In the silence, I could even hear the bolt being thrown in the lock. Not only did he have no intention of coming to me, he was ensuring that I wouldn't be able to come to him.

The full import of his action brought me to tears, shattering my illusions about living happily ever after with Nicholas. I felt lost and hopeless—more so than at any other time since I'd awakened in the hospital. Climbing back into bed, I resolved that we would have it out in the morning, Nicholas and I. We couldn't go back to living here in two armed camps. I couldn't remain in the house without his tenderness, his passion, his gentleness. I could bear anything as long as he didn't deprive me of that endearing part of himself.

The only way I managed any sleep at all that night was by clinging to the illusion that the next day we would work things out. I awoke late the following morning with eyes red from crying and a splitting headache. In no mood for a face-off with Nicholas just yet, I decided to go to my studio, put the finishing touches on my landscape. And I thought to telephone Greg at some point before noon, suggesting that it might be best if he didn't come for the painting that day.

Nicholas's bedroom door was ajar as I stepped into the hall. I spotted Lillian inside, making up his bed. Yes, she was always there to tidy up after him, I thought scornfully. Tiptoeing past the room so as to avoid another possible run-in with her, I hurried to the backstairs that led to the kitchen. I grabbed a thermos off the shelf, poured some coffee into it and wrapped a corn muffin in a paper napkin. I glanced out the window. It wasn't raining yet, but it was overcast, the sky was gray, the landscape still wind-swept and blanketed in a murky fog.

I tried to shake off the terror that always engulfed me in weather like this—and the sense of foreboding that always accompanied it. I envisioned Dr. Royce standing beside me, a comforting arm around my shoulders. *Don't close yourself off to the storm, Deborah,* I could imagine him saying. *You must get past the terror to find yourself.* But, more than ever, the terror seemed to have a steely grip on me.

I braced myself as I opened the kitchen door and stepped outside, the wind whipping my hair every which way, its chilling tentacles seeping through my thin sweater and slacks. Breaking into a run as I caught sight of the studio through the trees, I stumbled over a fallen limb and went crashing to the ground. The air was momentarily knocked out of my lungs and it took me a few moments to sit up and survey the damage. For one thing, I'd broken the thermos. And the muffin, which I extracted from my pocket and un-wrapped, now resembled a pancake. There was a nick on my knee and my palms were rubbed raw from having used them to brace my fall, but otherwise I was unscathed. I counted myself lucky.

Scrambling to my feet, I hurried on my way, being more careful where I walked. The wind howled through the trees as I made my way to the studio. The sound was so eerie, it made the hairs rise along my arms. I was glad when I got to the studio door and found it open. I'd had an awful panic that Nicholas, out of anger, might have locked it up.

Stepping inside the lush space, I quickly shut the door. The wind didn't rattle these newly hung windows. The studio felt solid, sound and safe. My private haven. I would paint for a while and it would calm me, soothe my aching head, provide me with the courage to have another heart-to-heart with Nicholas later on.

I slipped off my sweater and hung it on a hook near the door. Nibbling on my squashed muffin, I started for the kitchenette to see if there was any instant coffee in the cupboards. Finding a jar, I smiled, realizing Nicholas's thoughtfulness. That little discovery boosted my spirits a bit. He cared. And then I remembered his excitement and pleasure in showing me the studio. He'd done all this for me. Surely, I thought, he wouldn't let everything between us be ruined because of one innocent kiss from a friend that I had neither encouraged nor enjoyed.

I heated up the water and made my cup of instant coffee. It was only when I was carrying it across the room that my gaze finally came to rest on the easel where my canvas was still perched.

I stopped short. That's odd, I thought, seeing that a white cloth had been draped over the canvas. I hadn't covered it. Some of the paint was still wet when I'd left it the afternoon before.

My mouth went dry. I began to tremble, and the hot coffee splattered over the rim of the mug, scorching my hand. I hardly noticed. My mind was racing. Someone had been in my studio, either the night before or earlier that morning. Someone had covered up my painting. But why?

I forced myself toward the canvas, my heart pounding with dread. The silence spun in the room, making me dizzy and nauseous, and my head throbbed so much now that it almost blinded me. How I wish it had!

Throwing the cloth back, I looked at the canvas. The coffee mug dropped from my hand, and my mouth opened in a wordless wail of horror.

This canvas, like those in the attic, had been slashed and mangled beyond recognition. I nearly collapsed by the brutality of the sight. This mutilation was even worse than those others. I hadn't really been able to identify with the paintings in the attic. They weren't mine in the same way. I'd had no recollection of having painted them. But the savage destruction of this landscape felt like an assault on me personally.

I started to weave and willed myself not to pass out. Forcing in deep breaths, my fury slowly began to overtake my revulsion and horror. Nicholas had done this. Just like before. In a fit of unfounded jealousy, he had struck out at something dear to me. For all I knew, he'd even overheard my offer to give Greg the painting. Well, Nicholas had taken care of that token of gratitude.

I flew out of the studio, mindless of the inclement weather. How could Nicholas have done such a grisly thing? How could he have misjudged me so utterly after what we'd shared together? And then an echo of those words I'd overheard that first day at Gus's hissed through the wind. *What person in his right mind could even come up with such gruesome, morbid ideas? He must be warped. He must be warped. He must be warped.*

CHAPTER TWELVE

The storm broke when I was in sight of the house. By the time I burst through the kitchen door, I was soaking wet and shivering. My eyes skirted the kitchen. Lillian wasn't in sight. Just as well, for both of us. I was nearly crazy with rage and anguish at that point. I might have said things I'd later regret. And she might have said things that would only exacerbate my fury.

The glint of a bread knife on the kitchen table caught my eye as I started across the room. I stopped short, my gaze fixing on the sharp stainless-steel blade. I stood there, motionless, staring at it.

Wait, I thought. What if I was on the wrong track? What if I'd jumped to the wrong conclusion? What if it wasn't Nicholas who'd slashed my landscape? Why not Lillian? She would have known about the other paintings that Nicholas had destroyed. She would know he'd be the first one I'd think of when I saw my latest painting destroyed in the same way.

What if this was Lillian's way of breaking us up? If she had spied on us in the studio yesterday, she'd know that Nicholas and I had recaptured the love we'd once known together. I could imagine the jealousy, the hatred and, yes, the pain, of what she must have felt.

I recalled her visit to my studio late yesterday afternoon, when she'd gloatingly told me Nicholas had gone off and I shouldn't bother waiting up for him. How lucky for her that Nicholas had witnessed that kiss Greg gave me. But would she think it enough to drive a permanent wedge between me and my husband? I might be able to explain the kiss to him, win back his trust, his love. Lillian couldn't have that.

How easy it would have been for her to slip back to my studio last night or early this morning and do her dark deed. I could almost picture the crazed look of satisfaction on her face as she slashed into the canvas—again and again and again.

In the silence, the wind began to whine and the rain beat against the kitchen windows. I found myself moving toward the knife. Were there telltale signs of paint on it? Oh, how I wanted it to be Lillian and not Nicholas! If it was her, I could talk to Nicholas, make him see that his cousin was a very sick woman—possibly, even . . . dangerous.

But he'd heard all that from me before. From a me I didn't remember. Would he treat my concerns about Lillian as he'd treated them before? Dismiss them as childish, spiteful, uncaring? But it wasn't that. I did care. If only because I loved Nicholas and Lillian was his cousin. And because I knew that she loved him. And that her sickness had twisted her reason. I'd seen enough sickness in the hospital to recognize it. Lillian needed help.

I walked over to the knife and picked it up. Save for a few bread crumbs clinging to the jagged teeth, the blade was clean. Of course, if she had used this knife or any other on my canvas, she would have been smart enough to clean it thoroughly afterward. She wouldn't want a finger to point to her. She'd want me to blame Nicholas, see him as some sort of depraved monster, get scared and leave. Then she would once again have Nicholas all to herself.

I sat down at the kitchen table, resting my forehead in the palms of my hands, my damp hair falling about my face. Was it Lillian? Or was it Nicholas? How could I accuse either one unless I knew for certain? If Lillian was mad, how did I know that it didn't run in the family? Nicholas could be just as mad. The way things were going, I wasn't any too sure of my own sanity.

It took all my courage to get up and go down the hall to Nicholas's den. I realized that the only solution was for me to ask him straight out if he had destroyed my painting. Odd, that for all the brutality, rage, and seething passion that I attributed to him, I didn't think he would lie to me.

I knocked on his door. There was no answer. Was he so deeply absorbed in his writing that he hadn't heard? I knocked again, a little harder. The door gave way, inching open.

"Nicholas?"

No answer. I gingerly pushed the door open wider.

The room was empty. Where was he?

I started to turn away, but something made me stop. A strange pulsing in the room. A shudder went through me, so swift and sharp that it was as if I'd suffered a fierce blow. I couldn't understand it. Not then, or even now. But a whispering voice in my head willed me to shut the door and cross the Oriental-carpeted room to Nicholas's desk.

The top of his desk was very tidy, his computer monitor was turned off. On the printer beside the monitor was a single printed-out page. It lay there facedown. I stared at it as if it were some live, threatening being. Temptation to see what was on that page warred with my fear. In the end, temptation won out.

My lips compressed, my heart pounding, I lifted the page and turned it over. There was only one line written on it. A few words. Just words. Never before had I imagined how powerful and terrifying words could be.

He was filled with such hate and jealousy that he had to destroy everything that was a part of her....

I read the words over and over, my heart twisting in my chest. Tears fell on the page. And when my eyes were too blurry to see, I opened the top drawer of his desk to shove the paper inside.

And that was when I saw it. Glinting up at me from atop some blank sheets of stationery in the drawer. An exquisite silver letter-opener, the hilt encrusted with jade stones. But it wasn't the jeweled handle that drew my attention. It was the sharp, shimmering silver blade sprinkled with spots of oil paint.

I felt faint. First the line of writing, now this. So, it was Nicholas. He had destroyed my painting. *He was filled with such hate and jealousy that he had to destroy everything... everything... everything... that was a part of her..... And what would he destroy next?

"What are you doing, snooping around in here? Nicholas doesn't like anyone coming into his den just as brazen as they please."

Lillian's scolding voice brought me up short. I turned on her, almost fiercely. "I'm not just anyone. I'm Nicholas's wife."

She laughed shrilly, her gaze flicking contemptuously over me. "He sees what's going on. Right under his nose again. Just like before. Well, he's no more a fool now than he was in the past, you little tramp. He won't let you get away with it. You'll be the sorry one in the end. Oh, yes. Good and sorry."

I glared at her, beside myself with anger and misery. "You're sick. The two of you. You're both sick. You deserve each other."

"Then why don't you just leave. Right now. Get out before you destroy him," she hissed. "He doesn't love you. He'll never love you. You bring him nothing but grief."

I was livid. How could she accuse me of bringing him grief. I was the one who was suffering. I was the one who was being torn apart, broken, destroyed.

I saw her hand slip into her apron pocket. I half expected her to withdraw a gun and just shoot me dead on the spot. But instead, she pulled out a pair of keys on a metal ring and flung them at me.

"Go on. Here are the car keys."

They sailed right on top of Nicholas's desk. I stared down at them. When I looked back over at the door, Lillian was gone.

I could feel a fever raging in me. I looked again at the keys. My way out. My source of escape.

God, I didn't even know if I could drive. I snatched up the keys. On a leather tab attached to the ring were the carved initials, D.S.

D.S. Deborah Steele. My own keys. I guessed they were for the silver sports car that was always parked in the garage beside Nicholas's BMW. My keys. My car. My chance.

Taking nothing with me, I raced down the corridor for the front door. Yet, even as I fled, there was a small part of me hoping Nicholas would spring out of nowhere, call me back, plead with me not to leave him, beg me to forgive him.

Would I have given him a second chance? Or did I just want the satisfaction of seeing him suffer my loss? I don't know. I was in a pretty bad state at that point.

Anyway, he didn't appear. He didn't call out to me. My steps tapped hollowly on the marble floor, an empty, echoing sound.

I had no idea where Nicholas was. Locked away somewhere waiting for me to leave? Knowing that he had given me no alternative? Wanting me out of his life? I hated him then for not having the courage to tell me straight to my face. I added "coward" to my list of charges against him.

It was raining hard as I raced from the house to the garage. Thanks to the storm, a preternatural darkness blanketed the daylight. I was gasping for breath as I got to the silver Corvette convertible, my hand trembling so badly as

I tried to fit the key into the door lock that I had to use my other hand to steady it.

My soaked clothes clung to my skin as I slid behind the wheel. I sat there for a few moments, brushing my wet hair back from my face, trying to dredge up a memory of myself driving this car. How often did I use it? Was I a competent driver? Reckless?

Nothing came to me, but I found myself turning the key in the ignition and shifting quite naturally into reverse. If only it wasn't raining. I was overwrought enough without it. And now, to compound my terror, I had the prospect of navigating the car down the winding mountain in the storm after not having driven in at least two months.

As I started down the road, my hands clutching the steering wheel, I tried to imagine Dr. Royce sitting beside me in the empty passenger seat.

Thatta girl. Take it nice and easy. You can do it. You can do anything you set your mind to. There's nothing to be afraid of. You know what you have to do now. I imagined his voice rising and falling to the steady rhythm of the windshield wipers.

The road seemed much narrower, now that I was driving. And the oaks and fir trees towered grotesquely along the left-hand side of the road, looming down on me, while the jagged cliffs seemed to close in on my right. Every time I rounded a bend, the wind leaped at my car like a springing panther. One careless turn of the wheel and I could go careening over the cliff and down the mountain. It was the very stuff of horror. I might have been the doomed heroine in one of Nicholas's dreadful books.

But I didn't want to think about Nicholas or his tales of horror. Or, indeed, his acts of horror. I was getting out, getting away. It was over for us. I willed my mind to numbness, focusing every ounce of my concentration on making it safely down the mountain road.

I must have been about two-thirds of the way down, feeling a bit better and more confident, knowing I was almost home free, when I heard an odd pinging sound. At first I thought it was nothing. I was just pulling out of an S curve and saw a reverse one just ahead, this one much sharper, and my foot shifted to the brake to lower my speed.

The car started to slow just as it had each time I'd braked before, when suddenly there was a second pinging sound. The next thing I knew, the brake pedal lost all its tension and slammed to the floor under the light pressure of my foot. I don't know how many fractions of a second it took for my brain to make the connection between the dysfunctional pedal and the reality that my brakes were gone, but when the realization struck, there was some small blessing in the fact that there was no time for me to panic. I was heading downhill, coming up on another hairpin turn, and the line on my speedometer was steadily edging up to fifty.

Instinctively, I grabbed for the emergency brake and yanked with all my might. Nothing happened. I was coming into the turn. Both hands on the steering wheel now, the speed uncontrollable, I fought with all I had in me to keep the little car on course.

My tires shrieked with a kind of mechanical anguish on the wet pavement as I came around the first part of the curve. I took my eyes off the road for only an instant to check my speedometer. The line wavered around sixty-five. Only a reckless race-car driver would take a curve at this kind of speed. And I was far from feeling like a race-car driver. Terror began to swamp me and I didn't know if I would survive the rest of the turn.

As I felt the car start to skid on the slick pavement, I didn't even have the pitiful satisfaction of seeing my whole life flash before my eyes. The only vision I had was of Nicholas—Nicholas and I, entwined in each other's arms on that velvet chaise. At least I'd leave this earth with a pleasant image.

Even as I felt myself giving in to fate, another part of me rebelled against it. I wouldn't give in. I still had a whole life ahead of me. And a life behind me yet to discover. I couldn't let it all end there, in a storm on that desolate road.

Fighting for control as I came around the second part of the curve, my tires must have come within inches of the edge of the cliff. Had the shoulder been soft, it would have been curtains for me. I knew there were any number of curves still ahead of me. With my speed steadily escalating, could I really manage all of them?

And then, as if fate had decided to take pity on me, I rounded the last of the curve and saw a wide, flat grassy pull-off on my left, beyond which was a hilly embankment. I had no time to think or consider the merits of my decision. It was a case of now or never—never in the all-too-literal sense.

Yanking the wheel sharply to my left, I skidded into the pull-off. Holding on for dear life, praying my seat belt would keep me from flying right through the windshield, I steered the car straight for the embankment. Like a bucking bronco, it bolted up the hill, whined loudly, then ground to a dead stop as the engine went dead. And like an amateur rodeo rider, I did nothing but hold on for dear life as I was jolted back and forth, my chest smashing against the steering wheel, then my back slamming into the seat.

It took me some time to realize I had come through the harrowing experience physically uninjured except for some sore ribs. A wave of exquisite relief washed over me and that was when I allowed myself to break down and cry. I must have sat there bawling, tilted up at a forty-degree angle, for a good ten minutes before I heard the sound of a car approaching.

Rubbing my eyes with the heels of my hands, I managed to kick the door open and scramble out. My legs were so rubbery, I crumpled to the ground. I just sat there, helpless, the rain pouring down on me, as the car came around the bend and swerved sharply into the pull-off.

As soon as I saw the flash of yellow I started to cry again with relief. Greg squealed to a stop and came flying out of his car. I was laughing and crying at the same time as he ran to me and gathered me up in his arms.

"Oh, Greg, Greg... I didn't think... I almost didn't... How did you know...?" A rush of words came stammering out of me.

He held me close, gently rubbing my back. "Are you okay?" he asked anxiously.

I nodded, my head pressed against his chest. "Yes. Yes, I'm fine. Just a little...car trouble." I broke into a laugh again. And even I knew I was on the edge of hysteria.

"Come on, you're getting soaked. I'll take you—"

Before he could finish the sentence, I clutched at his raincoat, frantically shaking my head. "Not back to Raven's Cove. I can't go back there, Greg. Please, please..."

"It's okay, baby. I wasn't going to take you there. I'm taking you to my cottage. We'll get some brandy down you, get you into some dry clothes, and then you can tell your good buddy, Greg, all about it."

His voice was warm and strong and comforting. Willingly, I let him lift me in his arms and carry me back to his car. He set me gently in the passenger seat and raced around to the driver's side. As he slid in he gave me a closer look.

"Are you sure you haven't broken any bones? Did you pass out at all? Are you in pain anywhere?"

I managed a weak smile. "I'm fine. Really. I don't know how that's possible, but I really am."

Despite the pallor on his usually tanned complexion, he smiled back. "You always were one heck of a wild driver, Deb."

I stared at him. "It wasn't me, Greg. It was the brakes. They... They just went on me. I heard...this ping, and..."

Greg's gaze flickered over to my semivertical silver sports car, then back to me. Something struggled in his eyes. Was it fear, anger, despair? I couldn't tell, but I suspected that he was questioning the same thing I'd begun to question. Was it an accident that the brakes had given way? Or had someone deliberately arranged for them to fail? That pinging sound echoed in my head. And the vision of Lillian tossing me my keys and telling me to get out, flashed before my eyes. Had she intended to make certain that once I left I'd never be able to return?

I felt Greg's arm sweep around my shoulders.

"You're shivering," he said softly.

"Let's go. Please."

He pulled out and started down the mountain, one hand on the wheel, the other remaining around my shoulder. I found his touch comforting now, and even let my head drop against the damp sleeve of his raincoat.

"Where were you heading?" he asked after a few minutes.

"I'm not sure," I admitted. "I think I might have been ... heading to your place."

Out of the corner of my eye, I saw a faint smile curve his lips.

"Were you coming up to Raven's Cove to see me?" I asked.

He didn't answer right away. "I wanted to have a talk with Nicholas. I felt real lousy after I left you yesterday. I shouldn't have kissed you, Deb. I didn't want to stir up any trouble for you and Nick. Especially after I got the feeling from you that the two of you were...starting to work things out. *Were you?*"

I didn't trust myself to speak, so I just nodded.

"If I hadn't been such a jerk and kissed you—"

"No," I said, cutting him off. "It was more than that. I...don't want to talk about it now. Later, okay?"

"Sure," he said gently. "Whatever you say, Deb. Whatever you want."

I reached up and squeezed his hand. "You really are a good friend, Greg. I hope I realized I was so lucky... before."

Greg insisted on carrying me into his cottage. I didn't put up much of a fight, because for one thing I still felt very shaky, and for another, it just felt good to have two strong male arms around me at that particular time. I did protest when he started to set me down on his gray tweed sofa, which matched the two swivel armchairs facing it.

"Don't. I'm soaked."

He smiled. "Right. The first order of business is to get you out of those wet clothes. How does a nice hot shower sound?"

"Make that a bath." I wasn't sure my legs would hold me up.

He winked, carrying me straight through his cozy, masculine living room that ran the length of his house, its windows looking out over the road and beyond to the mountains. I noticed a telescope set up by the far window and I wondered if Greg could see right up to Raven's Cove with it.

Edging a paneled oak door open with his shoulder, he carried me into his bedroom, a pleasant, roomy space with a brass double bed, plain oak furniture that was too new to be called antique, and a large, colorful rag rug on the floor. Windows facing both the north and the back, looked out over an untended lawn and an old storage shed. Through an open door, I saw a small, tidy, white-tiled bathroom.

He set me down on a wooden chair near one of the windows and dropped to his knees to take off my shoes.

I stiffened. Did he think I was in such a state of shock that he would need to completely undress me? I pressed a hand lightly to his shoulder. "Why don't you find me some things to change into and then I'll . . . take care of the rest."

His cheeks reddened. "Good idea. How does a flannel shirt sound? And you can roll up a pair of my jeans and I'll find you a belt."

I smiled. "Thanks."

He was on his feet now, rushing over to the closet. "And I'll start your tub going. I'm afraid I don't have bubble bath or anything. This is strictly a bachelor pad."

"Plain old hot water sounds perfect," I said appreciatively, although I do remember wondering if Greg ever entertained women in his cottage. Did he date much? Had he ever been seriously involved with a woman? Was there a woman in his life even then? Maybe back in Manhattan? This wasn't the time for a discussion of Greg's love life. Another time, though, I decided.

After he'd seen to everything in quick order, Greg stood at his bedroom door and looked back at me, not saying a word.

"What is it?" I asked uncertainly.

He smiled rather boyishly. "I'm just glad you're all right. Really glad, Deb. And . . ." He hesitated. "And glad you were on your way here. I guess, for a while, I was worried that you wouldn't feel you could turn to me." There was a wistful expression on his face. "This feels a little like old times."

His eyes fixed on me and I felt a flurry of discomfort. I didn't know about the "old times."

I wasn't sure I wanted to. And I wasn't sure that Greg might not be misconstruing my presence in his house.

"Hurry up and get out of those wet things and into the tub," he said brightly. "I'll go make us some tea and start a fire. What with the storm, it feels more like late fall than spring."

He started out the door, but glanced back at me one more time. "Oh, and I'll call over to the garage and have your car towed in and... checked over."

His expression was grim now, no doubt matching my own.

After taking a quick soak in the tub just to get the chill out of my body, I dried off and was hurriedly putting on the dry clothing that Greg had lent me, when I heard Greg and another man arguing beyond the closed bedroom door. Even as I recognized Nicholas's voice, the door burst open and there he stood, wet and windswept, looking like a man possessed.

I was stunned more than frightened by his appearance. In the few short hours since I'd last seem him, he seemed to have aged five years. His face was drawn, sharp crease lines cut into the corners of his mouth, and there were large, dark shadows under his eyes.

"I was driving down the mountain, looking for you. I saw the car." Sheer pain flashed across his features. "I went straight to the hospital. Then the police. I thought—" He didn't go on. I saw that he couldn't.

"I'm all right," I said gently. "The brakes failed."

His eyes looked tortured. "No one's used that car in months. I should have had it serviced before—" He gave me a heartfelt study. "It must have been harrowing for you."

There was no point in minimizing what I'd been through. I simply nodded.

Nicholas let out a ragged sigh. "Is it too late for us?"

I don't know what I expected him to say, but certainly not that. I was at a loss how to answer him. And then I saw Greg come up behind Nicholas. He, too, looked suddenly more haggard. And worried.

"She's been through enough for one day, Nick," he said tightly.

Nicholas seemed not to hear Greg. His gaze remained riveted on me. I imagined I must have looked quite a sight, in my borrowed, oversize clothes, my hair still damp and hanging limply to my shoulders. Was it too late for us? I could feel my heart beating strangely, a warmth suffusing me. A longing.

I could feel Greg's eyes on me, too. And I knew what he was thinking—that once again Nicholas was seducing me, just as he'd always done in the past. I could hear Greg's voice in my head. *Don't let him win out again, Deb. There's too much at stake. It's too dangerous. Give in now and you're lost.*

I wanted to shout at them both to go away and leave me alone. I couldn't think straight. My temples were throbbing, my thoughts in chaos. Somewhere in the room a clock was ticking. *Tick, tick, tick.*

And then Nicholas was walking toward me. Slowly, very slowly. I could have bolted. I could have shouted out to Greg to stop him, knowing Greg would have done as I asked, guessing he would have liked nothing better. But I remained silent and didn't move a muscle.

I knew Greg was still at the open door, watching us both, but as Nicholas stood facing me, only inches away, everything else was blocked out for me. I remember telling myself I should be afraid, I should be wary. But I felt no fear then, no alarm.

"It was the painting, wasn't it?" There was desperation in his hoarse voice.

My lips compressed. I fought back the tears.

"It won't happen again," he murmured.

My eyes searched his. Was this an admission of guilt? As was always true of Nicholas, everything about him remained ambiguous. I could never quite sort him out. Everything he said, everything about his appearance and his actions, hinted of deeper meanings. Meanings I longed to comprehend.

"Please come home."

Home. The way Nicholas whispered the word made me feel like it really *was* home for me. The way he was looking at me made me feel like that was where I belonged. More important, where he wanted me to be.

I closed my eyes, trying to achieve a modicum of common sense and not just let my heart run riot. Was I solely at the mercy of Nicholas's expert, enticing seductions as Greg had said? And why did Nicholas want me back? To torture me with his constant ambiguities? Or was it merely male ego? Did Nicholas believe he and Greg were locked in a competition for me and he was damned if he was going to be the loser?

Those questions all flew through my mind in a matter of seconds. Then my eyes opened. Nicholas and I looked at each other in silence. Then his hand tentatively reached out to mine. Our fingers barely touched, but the sensation was dazzling. And I knew then, that no matter how unwise, how dangerous, even, it was not over for me and Nicholas. Not over by far.

"I'm ready." The words tumbled from my lips.

Nicholas nodded, his expression unchanged. He showed no relief, no pleasure, no joy, not even victory. But he did slip his hand in mine, entwining our fingers.

As we started past the door, I smiled weakly at Greg, silently begging for his understanding. But he looked openly distraught and angry, gripping my arm as I started by him.

"Deb," he said hoarsely. But then his eyes met Nicholas's and they stared each other down.

Neither man said a word. My breath held. I could still hear the steady tick of that clock. Only now it sounded like the ticking of a time bomb. My hand, still entwined in Nicholas's, gripped tightly.

"Please," I murmured to both of them.

Greg reluctantly drew his gaze back to me, faintly shaking his head. But then he relinquished his hold on my arm and stepped back.

"If you need me, Deb, you know where to find me." He looked from me to Nicholas. "Next time, though, phone me to come get you in my car, or call for a cab," he added acerbically.

Nicholas shot him a look that was both savage and weary, then he tugged me gently and we headed for the door. Headed back for Raven's Cove. Headed *home*.

CHAPTER THIRTEEN

When Nicholas brought me home from Greg's, neither of us seemed ready for penetrating conversation. The car crash may not have taken a great physical toll on me, but emotionally I was completely spent. All I wanted to do, which I told Nicholas as soon as he pulled into the drive at Raven's Cove, was crawl into bed and go to sleep.

He nodded, mumbling something about getting back to work. Immediately, those words I'd read on that sheet of paper only a short while before, sprang into my mind: *He was filled with such hate and jealousy that he had to destroy everything that was a part of her...*

I quickly told myself that it was important that I learn to separate out fact from fiction. The question was, how much of the fiction Nicholas wrote was based on fact? Or, at least, on his own deep-seated emotions?

I stayed in bed until close to dinnertime. I might have stayed there later still, maybe till the next morning, if Nicholas hadn't knocked on my door and asked if I wanted to join him downstairs for dinner.

I hesitated—not so much because I didn't want to spend the time with him as because I didn't want to see Lillian. I gave a little start when Nicholas filled in the pause by telling me that his cousin had gone out for the evening, and we'd have to fend for ourselves. Had he read my mind?

I opened the door.

He smiled roguishly and my heart leaped. "I'm a rotten cook," he said.

"I think I'm pretty good," I countered shyly.

"That's settled, then. You're hired."

It was the closest to a bit of bantering exchange as we'
ever had, and it did wonders for my mood. I smiled up a
him, feeling lighthearted and somewhat light-headed, a
well. "Only if you'll pitch in."

His dark eyes sparkled. He looked young again. Almos
boyish now. And so, so handsome. Seeing him look tha
way almost made it seem that everything that had hap
pened to me that morning had been a bad dream. Of course
I had only to return to my studio and see that ravaged can
vas to know it wasn't. But I pushed the painting from m
mind—and that harrowing roller-coaster ride down th
mountain. I desperately needed a respite from all the fea
and grief. I sensed that Nicholas felt the same way. In tha
brief exchange at my bedroom door, I felt that he was set
ting the tone for the evening. Nothing too intense. We woul
keep it light and friendly. Which was fine with me. There'
be time, I thought optimistically, for sorting out the heav
stuff later.

Without Lillian about, the whole house took on a new
lighter feel. Even with the storm still raging outside, I felt
warmth and security inside the house that I'd never befor
experienced in Raven's Cove. I even thought to myself, thi
could be a wonderful home to raise a family. All those un
used, spare bedrooms filled with children.

I must have blushed, because Nicholas gave me a curiou
smile.

"How about if we start off with a big salad?" I said in
anely.

Nicholas's smile deepened, as if he knew I was thinkin
about something altogether different.

How amazing, I thought, that I would be back at Ra
ven's Cove, never mind contemplating making beautifu

babies with Nicholas, when only hours before, I had both hated and feared him. Had he cast a spell on me?

Whatever the cause, the effect was like a dose of curative medicine. We banged happily about the kitchen, Nicholas at the cupboards, pulling out various canned goods, me at the refrigerator, gathering up lettuce, tomatoes, a nice green cucumber and some endive for salad. In the meat bin, I came upon two lamb chops. I held them up for inspection.

"Will these do?" I asked.

"Perfect," he said, then added teasingly, "But what will you eat?"

A short while later as I hovered by the stove browning the lamb, I glanced over at Nicholas as he stood at the kitchen sink peeling the cucumber. I smiled to myself. Wasn't this the picture of ordinary, everyday happy domesticity? Oh, if only there had been any real truth to that picture. How wonderful if we could just be an uncomplicated, contented married couple, I thought wistfully.

When everything was ready, we both agreed it would be nice to eat at the kitchen table, which was smaller and had a cozier feeling than the long formal dining-room table that could easily have accommodated a dozen people.

Nicholas did run off to the dining room for a moment and came back with a pair of candles in beautiful silver candlesticks. He lit them and set them on the kitchen table while I went to turn off the light.

We sat across from each other. Nicholas poured a chilled white wine into both our goblets. We tapped glasses, not saying anything, then each of us took a sip.

"Everything smells wonderful," he said, setting down his glass and admiring the fresh salad with vinaigrette dressing and the lamb chop topped with a béarnaise sauce. His voice was subdued, but he smiled at me.

"Let's dig in," I said, my bright tone slightly forced. There was something about the two of us sitting alone in our kitchen, our faces lit by the soft glow of candlelight, eating a meal we had prepared together, that unnerved me a bit. In the strangest way, it seemed more intimate than our making love the day before.

I suspected Nicholas, too, felt uneasy. We both concentrated intently on our food, mumbling little compliments back and forth every few bites, but neither of us made any effort at real conversation.

When we'd finished, I was quick to gather up the dishes and carry them to the sink.

"Do you want to wash or dry?" he asked.

"Oh," I said hurriedly as he approached the sink, "I'll clean up on my own." Somehow, the thought of the two of us, standing side by side at the sink, attending to the dishes like a typical married pair, felt like too much for me. I was afraid I might actually break down and cry. Nicholas wouldn't know what to make of my outburst and I felt there was no way I could explain it to him. I could hardly understand it myself.

Was that relief in his face when I offered to take on the task alone? He stopped short, at a loss for a moment, then nodded. "If the rain lets up, we could take a walk after..." He let the sentence trail off.

"I don't think it will let up. Anyway, I should turn in early," I mumbled, turning on the tap, my back to him.

"You're right." There was a pause. "I'll say good-night, then." His voice had turned sober. I strained to pick up some hint of disappointment beneath the surface of his tone, but if it was there, I couldn't detect it.

I nodded, keeping my back to him, for fear my face would give away the truth of my desire for him to rush over, sweep me into his arms and up the stairs to our bedroom, me a willing Scarlett to his Rhett.

Instead, I heard the faint groan of the hinges as the kitchen door swung open and then closed again. Telling myself it was for the best and knowing as I said it that I was a terrible liar, I began washing the dishes with a vengeance.

That night I awoke to thick darkness. Groggy at first, I wondered vaguely where I was. Then I remembered. My bedroom at Raven's Cove. What was it that woke me? The storm? The rain and wind had kept up throughout the evening, coming down with added fury when before I'd turned in for the night.

No, it wasn't the storm that had woken me. It was the opening and then the closing of my door. I heard a floorboard creak, and a cry of alarm escaped my lips.

"It's me. Nicholas."

I sat up in bed, my eyes slowly getting used to the darkness. His form began to emerge out of the shadows as he approached my bed.

"I didn't mean to frighten you," he said softly.

"I'm not frightened," I replied, not fully sure I meant it. "You just startled me."

"There's something I want to say to you." His voice was somber and resonant.

I waited tensely.

"I just want you to know that you're not a prisoner here. If you're unhappy, or...whatever, you're free to leave." He sounded so grave and distant that I wanted to cry. How stupid of me to think that a few hours of conviviality would alter the formidable Nicholas Steele. He probably regretted our brief interlude of playfulness, whereas it had meant so very much to me.

He sat down on the edge of my bed. He was close enough and my eyes had adjusted well enough now to see his face. "Do you want to leave?" he asked me directly, but there was a slight softening of his tone.

I gave him a bleak look. "Do you want me to leave, Nicholas?"

Was that a smile on his face or just the shifting of shadows? "Would I have carted you off from Greg's place if I wanted you to leave?"

"I wasn't planning to stay there. Greg found me on the mountain. He brought—"

Nicholas pressed a finger to my lips. "You don't have to explain anything."

"But there's so much…" I started to protest, but this time he silenced me with a light brush stroke of a kiss.

I felt the incredible pull of desire. "Oh, Nicholas," I cried, then flung my arms around him.

He gathered me fiercely to him. "I have never wanted anyone the way I want you," he murmured against my ear. "It's driving me a little mad."

This admission, far from troubling me as it might have, filled me with even more desperate longing. "Let's be mad together," I whispered, drawing him down with me onto the bed as his mouth moved over mine, hard and demanding now.

I don't even recall him removing my nightgown. It just seemed to float off me. My senses were all fully drawn to his hands running over my bare skin, cupping my breasts, my nipples hard as first his fingers and then his mouth captured them.

My flesh was on fire—an exhilarating and erotic contrast to Nicholas's marble-cool skin as he pressed himself down on me, planting small kisses over my face, down my throat, in the hollow between my breasts. When he began to lift himself away, I cried out in protest.

"I want to see you," he whispered.

Even as I shut my eyes against the soft lamplight that filled the room, I could feel Nicholas's piercing gaze surveying me. I couldn't help thinking he must be making comparisons between the voluptuous Deborah he'd first fallen in love with, and the pale, thin woman lying there now. I was sure I came up wanting.

"You're so lovely," he murmured. "And you don't even have any idea of it."

I opened my eyes and looked over at him as he lay stretched out alongside me. "Do you really think I'm...lovely?" I asked incredulous.

His palm slid lightly down the curve of my hip. "More than lovely," he said huskily as his hand dipped down between my thighs.

I smiled tremulously. "Not as lovely as you, Nicholas. You really are breathtakingly..." I searched for the right word and finally settled on, "Male."

He pulled me against him, but after a moment I drew back. I saw anxiety flicker across his face.

I smiled more boldly now. "I want to look at you."

He looked a bit surprised, but pleased. "Tell me what takes your breath away," he said in a teasing voice.

I felt my cheeks warm. "How about if I...show you?"

I'm not sure who was more startled by my suggestion, Nicholas or me. But he said with a soft and yearning tenderness, "Nothing would please me more."

As my hands and mouth began to rove over his body, I could feel a heat emanating from his marble coolness. At first I couldn't help wishing that I could remember how it had been when we'd made love in the past. I so didn't want to disappoint Nicholas. More than that, I wanted to give him as much pleasure— No, more pleasure than he had ever known. It was as if the old Deborah wasn't a part of me; that this was an altogether-new me. I realized then that I wasn't out to win back Nicholas's love. In some strange way, I felt in competition with the woman I had been in the past. I wanted to win Nicholas away from her.

He really was magnificently male, his body smooth and muscular, his scent earthy. As I slid my tongue down over his firm, flat stomach, Nicholas moaned softly. A flood of desire beat through me like a tide, radiating down my limbs. I loved the feel and taste of him. Delicately, the tip of my tongue cruised along his body, an inordinate pleasure filling me. As my tongue dipped lower, my fingers curving around that part of him that was most ultimately male, he emitted an involuntary groan. My lips parted and as I drew him slowly inside my mouth, I experienced an exquisite euphoria and closed my eyes in rapture, every fiber of my being caught up in my sensual ministrations.

With a low growl, Nicholas gripped my shoulders, pulling me roughly up to him, capturing my mouth, his kisses hard and demanding. I cried out in delight as he claimed me, my whole body pulsing in delicious surrender.

Only when Nicholas felt the ultimate vibrations beginning inside me, did he, too, let go in a rhythm that took both our breaths away. And then we were both melting, all of our energy, all our reserves of strength flowing out of us and we just held on to each other, trembling, smiling, as tears edged from the corners of both his eyes and mine.

I fell asleep in Nicholas's arms. It was the first blissful, contented night of sleep I was able to remember having. Even though Nicholas was gone from the bed when I awoke the next morning, the scent of him remained. I hugged his pillow against my bare breasts and smiled. I still felt a bit giddy.

My upbeat mood lasted until I ran into Lillian in the kitchen as I was pouring myself some coffee. My back was to the door as she came in, but I could tell it was her. There was always a heavy aura about her.

Slowly, I turned to face her. She just stood there staring at me, her features hard and unyielding.

"Did Nicholas tell you that I had a car accident?" I asked, closely watching her face for any sign of culpability.

"He told me," she said blandly as she crossed the room and took some potatoes from a bin under one of the cupboards.

I went on watching her as she selected a half-dozen potatoes and began to scrub them clean at the sink. "It was the brakes," I told her.

She didn't look up from her task. "Was it?"

I said nothing more, realizing I had no right to convict her of tampering with the brakes when I still had no proof they had been meddled with. I resolved to phone Greg and find out to which garage he'd had the car towed. Then I'd call them and question the mechanic.

I left Lillian to her potatoes and went into a small sitting room on the main floor, closed the door, then headed to the telephone on a Queen Anne desk.

Greg picked up on the second ring. He sounded relieved that I'd called.

"Are you okay?" he asked anxiously.

I smiled. After last night, "okay" was an understatement. "Yes," I said quietly.

I heard his breath whoosh through the earpiece. "What's the matter?" I asked.

"It's about your car," Greg said soberly.

"Yes, that's why I was calling. I didn't know which garage had picked it up and I wanted to find out—"

"I just got finished speaking with Len over at the garage," Greg cut me off.

I knew before he said another word that our suspicions had been justified. And then he confirmed it. "Someone messed with the brakes."

"Oh, Greg," I gasped.

"Deb, you're not safe there. Listen, I'm going to leave this very minute and I'll pick you up by eleven."

"No," I cried. "I can't. I can't leave, Greg."

"Deb, don't you see what's happening to you? You're getting sucked in, just like before. He knows exactly which strings to pull—"

"You can't think it was Nicholas who... Oh, Greg, he wouldn't. He... loves me. I know he does." I surreptitiously looked around the room, then lowered my voice. "It's got to be Lillian. Greg, she hates me so. She was the one who gave me the car keys yesterday. And kept goading me to leave."

I heard a long sigh at the other end of the receiver. "You don't know Lillian, Deb. She would never take any action without Nicholas's approval. Whatever she's done, whatever she plans to do in the future, it's only with Nick's blessing."

"No," I said sharply. "I don't believe you. Why would he...?"

"His jealousy and paranoia are getting twisted into a dark sickness, Deb. Oh, he wants you, but that's not love. He's beyond loving. He wants to possess you completely and utterly. And when he thinks he'll fail, he strikes out. Or gets that warped cousin of his to strike out for him. The point is, you're the one receiving all the blows."

"No. No." I wouldn't listen to him. I couldn't.

"Something terrible happened to you yesterday, that made you leave Raven's Cove. You hinted at it, but you never told me what."

My head began to pound. I wished I'd never phoned Greg. I couldn't bear to hear what he was saying to me. He was wrong. He *had* to be wrong. Surely Nicholas couldn't have been behind Lillian's vile and demonic acts?

"It was the landscape you'd promised me. He destroyed it. Right? Just like he did all of your other paintings," Greg said when I made no response.

"How did you know?"

He laughed harshly. "I'm a detective, remember? And even if I weren't, I could add two and two. He saw me kiss you. Maybe he was lurking about for a while before we spotted him and heard you offer me the painting as a gift. Come on, Deb. The minute you saw it slashed to shreds you thought it was Nicholas."

"Please stop, Greg." But even as I pleaded, I recalled that sharp silver letter-opener I'd found in Nicholas's desk drawer, the blade spotted with paint.

"Deb, I can't just sit back and let something happen to you. Please let me come and get you."

I shook my head. I couldn't leave. It was as if some powerful force held me. "No. No, listen, Greg. I'll promise you this. If there's another...incident, or anything that gives me the slightest reason to be afraid, I promise I'll call you." I laughed weakly. "You can come racing up here on your yellow charger and whisk me off."

Greg made some response, but I wasn't listening. The door to the sitting room had begun to open slowly, riveting all my attention. When I saw Nicholas step inside, my heart gave an instinctive leap of panic. If he knew I was speaking to Greg, would his jealousy again be inflamed?

"Thank you very much for the information," I said, mustering an impersonal tone. Before Greg could reply, I dropped the receiver into the cradle.

"That was the garage," I explained, hating myself for lying, but feeling that I had no alternative. "They seem to think there's some possibility the brakes were...tampered with on the Corvette."

"Who did you speak to? Len?"

"I... I'm not sure. I didn't get his name." I couldn't meet Nicholas's steady gaze.

"You're pale."

I smiled weakly. "I didn't get much sleep." My gaze skidded over Nicholas's face, but he was wearing one of his unreadable expressions. Did he know I was lying?

I gave him a beseeching look. "Lillian gave me the keys to the Corvette, Nicholas."

He didn't respond.

Anger and hysteria welled up in me. "Damn it, the woman clearly hates me. I felt it from the first moment I saw her. And, if anything, she hates me more now than before. I think she's insane, Nicholas. I think she'd like nothing better than to see me dead. Don't you see? You're only making it worse, covering up for her. Don't you see—?"

Suddenly, Nicholas grabbed hold of my wrists. Only then did I realize that, in my outburst, I'd stormed over to him and was beating my fists against his chest.

"Stop it," he demanded sharply. "You're letting your imagination run away with you. As for the car, Len said there was a small possibility the brakes could have been tampered with, but there was an equal if not greater possibility that the brake linings could just have worn through."

I stared blankly up at him. Was he telling me the truth? Had the mechanic really said that? But Greg had made it sound so certain.

I shut my eyes and started to sway. Nicholas guided me over to the sofa. I sank into it. "She does hate me. You can't deny that," I said hoarsely.

"Lillian hates everyone," he countered flippantly.

My eyes popped open. "Not you. She loves you."

He smiled. "Yes, you're right. She loves me. And I'm damn grateful for that."

I gave him a baffled look. "What do you mean?"

"When I was a wild and reckless teenager, she saved my life. Nearly losing her own in the process. It happened not far from here. My folks had a summer place and Lillian was staying with us. I decided to do some rock climbing. Lillian hated heights, but I goaded her into coming along with me. I felt so invincible, until I lost my footing and found myself dangling precariously over a precipice. Lillian had to scramble up a treacherous section of rock above me, throw me a rope and literally pull me up to safety. To this day, I don't know where her strength came from. I must have weighed a good forty pounds more than her at the time. At any point, she might have gone toppling right over the side of the mountain with me. I kept yelling at her to leave me and go get help, but she knew as well as I did, that I wouldn't be able to hold on that long.''

When he finished, I didn't know what to say. Certainly, he owed his cousin an incredible debt of gratitude, but did this cloud his ability to see that she was a seriously and possibly a dangerously disturbed woman? I had no doubt that Lillian would always come to Nicholas's rescue, even if it meant risking her own life. The question that haunted me was, Did that also include risking my life, too?

Nicholas gently stroked my cheek. ''Don't spoil things with unnecessary worry, darling,'' he murmured.

I felt a little rush of delight at the endearment. Pressing my head to his shoulder, I found myself wanting to push all worry aside as much as Nicholas wanted me to. ''Yes, you're right. It's too lovely a day to be worrying.''

He smoothed my hair from my face. ''Why didn't you tell me it was Greg and not the garage you were speaking to when I came in?''

I sat up abruptly, my face flushed. ''How did you know?''

He smiled complacently. ''You're a lousy liar.''

''I hate it, besides,'' I confessed. ''It's just that I thought you'd be upset.''

He turned his face from me, shrugging his shoulders. ''Because he's putting the make on you?''

''Nicholas.''

He turned back to me. "Are you going to deny it?" His dark eyes bore into me and I felt a shiver of fear.

"I don't have any romantic interest in Greg, Nicholas. I refuse to believe after last night there could be the slightest doubt in your mind of that. And other than that one innocent kiss you saw, whatever Greg's feelings, he's behaved at all times like a perfect gentleman."

"A perfect gentleman biding his time. And filling your head with fears while he waits."

I hated the insinuating, harsh tone in Nicholas's voice. I longed for his lover's voice, for his sweetness, his tenderness.

He rose abruptly. "I've got to get back to work. Will you be painting today?"

I almost said, "What's the point?" but held my tongue.

"I think I'll have a cup of tea and read outside for a while on the terrace," I said hollowly, gesturing toward the French doors leading from the sitting room.

"I'll make it up for you and bring it out," he offered pleasantly. "Two sugars, right?"

I nodded.

"You're the only one in the house with a sweet tooth," he said with a smile. "But then, everything about you is sweet."

Was he mocking me? Or making up to me? It was impossible to tell. As always, with Nicholas, I was left to fill in the blanks. As if I didn't have enough of my own blanks that needed filling in.

CHAPTER FOURTEEN

As I sat on the terrace near the bluff, reading a biography of Rembrandt and sipping my tea, my mind started to drift off. I lay the book facedown on my lap and closed my eyes. Vague visions danced across my lids, but they were fleeting and elusive, like shadows racing past a car's headlights.

I felt myself being drawn into a strange sort of netherworld where everything was gray and shadowy. A feeling of menace began to creep into my bones. I told myself I was just overwrought. A brief nap, that's what I needed. It was such a lovely day. After my stormy yesterday, I welcomed the sunshine and the cool, refreshing mountain air. Yes, I thought, I'd just rest out here for a while.

I kept thinking I was dozing off, and yet, oddly enough, a part of my brain seemed so awake and alert. Out of the murky grayness, images slowly began to form. A dark, narrow staircase, like the one leading to the attic studio at Raven's Cove. Only this staircase seemed to go on forever. And then I began to make out a figure climbing the stairs. I gave a little start as I recognized the figure. It was me. I was wearing a long, flowing dress. Like the one in the portrait over the mantel in Nicholas's den. I was even holding a bonnet in one hand, a book in the other. Nicholas's book. Not the one in the portrait, but the one I'd found on my bed that first day, the one with the awful shrieking woman. I was clutching this book against my breast as I climbed the stairs. Only I wasn't just climbing. I was running. Breathless, frightened, I raced up the stairs, seeing no end in sight. I kept glancing back over my shoulder. But I could see no one chasing me. Still, I could feel the danger. The me who was witnessing all this began to urge myself on. *Hurry, hurry. Don't stop now. You've got to make it to the top. You've got to....*

But the stairs seemed never to end. My steps were beginning to falter. I had to stop to catch my breath. I still could see no one pursuing me. Yet I could hear someone now. Yes, footsteps. Footsteps on the stairs. Not racing; slow, steady, confident. My pursuer knew there was no escape for me. Just as I knew it.

There was a painful stitch in my side. My hand pressed against it, trying to stem the ache.

My book toppled from my lap. The thudding sound it made as it landed shook me from my reverie. I realized I was clutching my side just as I had in the vision. I could feel a real ache. And, I, too, was a little breathless. How strange.

My eyes opened—not easily. My lids felt so heavy. Blurrily I stared down at my book that had landed splayed open on the grass, the covers facing up. I leaned over in my lounge chair to reach for it, my elbow bumping into the table beside me, toppling my cup of tea. Some of the amber liquid splattered on my beige trousers.

I frowned as I watched the stains forming. Or, at least I tried to frown, but the muscles in my face appeared to be in rebellion. They weren't cooperating. My face felt numb. And something else was odd. I couldn't seem to reach the damn book. I watched with strange fascination as my arm took on an elastic quality, stretching toward the fallen book. But no matter how much it stretched, the book remained inches out of my grasp.

I stared at the elusive biography of Rembrandt. Only, as I kept looking at the back cover, the photo of the distinguished gray-haired author began to transform before my eyes into a photo of Nicholas. And the front cover—

I let out a weak cry. It was that awful horror novel of his, the one I'd been holding in my vision, the one with the screaming woman, her mouth gaping open in terror. No, no, no. It couldn't be. I wasn't reading that book. I would never have selected it. I needed no fictional horrors.

Repulsed though I was, I strained harder to grab hold of the book. I almost felt as if my life depended on reaching that hateful tome and tossing it over the cliff. I wanted it gone forever. I never wanted to see that terrified woman again.

I stretched out my arm, my fingers almost touching a corner of the book. Just another inch. I could do it. I could do anything when I set my mind to it....

I fell out of the lounge chair onto the ground. And then I was crawling—no, dragging myself along the grass. Like a soldier under fire. *Stay low. Keep your head down. One false move and it's curtains....*

I remember telling myself that what was happening wasn't real. That it was crazy, even. But I kept on kneeing and elbowing my way toward that ever-elusive book. The landscape around me blurred as I drew nearer to the book, which seemed to be moving closer to the edge of the bluff. I dragged myself on, closer and closer—as if I were being lured by a siren.

No, not lured, I thought, my head clearing for an instant. I wasn't dragging myself. I was being dragged. Someone was tugging at me. Pushing me. And the cliff was coming up on me, the book now nowhere in sight.

Terror gripped me. My mouth formed the shape of a scream, but no sound came out—just like the woman on the cover of Nicholas's book. Only now I was the woman on that cover....

I tried with all my might to pull myself away from the dragging darkness, but a wall of cold, black dread washed over me, flowing into my flesh. I could hear the echo of a scream. The woman on the staircase?

"No, no!" It was me. It was me screaming. Hands were grabbing at me. My eyes opened only to find myself staring straight down the jagged mountainside. The air was rushing at me and I felt like it was going to sweep me over the edge.

Desperately, I fought against the hands that were tugging at me. I struggled wildly, only to realize if I wasn't careful I could end up hurling myself over the cliff unassisted. I felt doomed. Lost.

And then strong hands dug hard into my shoulders and as I twisted my neck to confront my attacker, I saw Nicholas. He was giving me his dark, foreboding look. I began to shriek hysterically.

"Stop it. Stop it, you little fool," he shouted over my screams. "What are you trying to do? Kill yourself?"

The next thing I knew, I was in his arms.

"You look awful," he said, his voice low and toneless.

I held my breath. It would be so easy for him to toss me right over the bluff. I would scream, but no one would hear me. No one but Lillian. And she was the last person to care.

He stared down at me. "You must have passed out. You might have fallen right off this cliff if I hadn't come out to check on you." His expression still dark and somber, he carried me, not closer to the edge of the bluff, but into the house and up to my room. Neither of us spoke. Only after he deposited me rather unceremoniously on my bed, did he say anything.

"You'd better spend the rest of the day in bed. I'll bring you up a fresh cup of tea and some scones Lillian made this morning."

I tried to tell him I didn't want anything, but my voice was little more than a hoarse, incoherent croak.

I watched him cross to the door. He stood there for several moments, his back to me. I saw his shoulders heave. And then he glanced back at me. Last night he'd been my lover. Last night I'd known that I truly loved him. And yet, as I looked back at Nicholas today I didn't know whether he was my attacker or my savior. He stared at me in silence and I frantically searched his face for the true answer. If only, this one time more than any other, his features could have mirrored the inner truth that was Nicholas Steele. No such luck. As always, whatever he was feeling and thinking was locked away in some private place that I couldn't reach. Just like that elusive book of his I'd been trying to grab hold of before.

"The book," I mumbled.

He gave me a perplexed look. "What book?"

"That I...was reading. Outside." It took all my strength to lift my head from the pillow. I wanted that book. I felt desperate to know if it was the biography or Nicholas's horror novel that was lying out there on the terrace so close to that cliff.

He scowled. "I don't think you ought to do any more reading today. And if you aren't feeling better by tomorrow, I'm going to have one of the doctors in town come up and have a look at you."

My head sank wearily into the pillows. I felt cold despite the warm sunshine flooding in through the windows. It might as well have been storming. Maybe, I thought, the storm had entered me, just as Nicholas had entered me last night—both of them locked inside me, raging, seething, giving me no peace.

My head began to swim as I tried to focus on Nicholas's face. Like that first time I laid eyes on him, his face became a kaleidoscope of faces, spinning, spinning. I squeezed my eyes shut. When I opened them again, he was gone.

I kept fighting off the drowsiness that was tugging at me, trying to claim me. I told myself I had to stay alert. It was the only way I could protect myself. I knew that I was wildly in love with Nicholas, but I had no great confidence in my ability to trust him. As for Lillian, I thought her capable of any nefarious deed my mind could conjure up. I was certain Nicholas's cousin was quite mad.

Greg's words to me on the phone that morning popped into mind, even as I tried to shut them out.

You don't know Lillian, Deb. She would never take any action without Nicholas's approval. Whatever she's done, whatever she plans to do in the future, it's only with Nick's blessing. With his blessing. With his blessing . . .

I pressed my clenched fists against my ears as if I could somehow drown out Greg's voice. But his words kept wailing through my mind. I closed my eyes, deciding to let sleep claim me. I just couldn't cope any longer.

When I awoke, the room was gray. At first I thought I was caught up in another nightmare, but then I glanced out the window and saw that the sun had set. I'd slept through the entire day.

"How are you feeling?"

Nicholas was sitting on the chaise, watching me, just like that first time I'd woken in that room. This time he rose and came over to my bed. I watched him dip a washcloth in a small basin of water on the side table. Then, very gently, he dabbed the wet, cooling cloth across my warm forehead.

"Poor baby," he murmured melodically, his concerned gaze studying me for a long moment. "Do you feel any better?"

"A little. I think," I responded weakly.

"It's all still such a terrible struggle for you, isn't it?" As he spoke, he gently guided the washcloth down one side of my face, then the other.

"I feel . . . lost," I whispered. "So lost and alone."

He set the washcloth down and tenderly drew me into his arms, burying his face in my hair. "You're not alone. And if you're lost, I'll find you. Somehow, some way, I'll find you, my love. My sweet, sweet love."

I cried soundlessly against his shoulder for several minutes. Nicholas just held me, stroking my hair and my back, letting me cry. Finally when I was cried out, a long, low sigh broke from me, and he gently eased my head back on my pillows.

"Have some tea," he soothed, pouring me a cup from a small china teapot. He put in an extra helping of sugar. "For energy," he said.

I took several sips as he watched me closely. He looked so strong, so gentle, so caring.

"How's that?" he asked. "Is it sweet enough?"

I smiled a little crookedly. "My sweet tooth."

He smiled back, but he looked strained and exhausted. As if he'd taken on and absorbed my ordeal. I watched the smile fade from his face. "You couldn't really think I was trying to push you over that cliff."

The mask had dropped from his face as he spoke and I saw such awful anguish there that I felt his pain. We were absorbing the best and worst of each other, it seemed.

"I was...confused." Even as I spoke, I felt as if my mind was sinking into a muddle again. My words sounded muffled to my ears. And a heaviness again settled over my body, much like it had while I was reading that morning.

Nicholas was saying something, but I couldn't make it out. Something about the tea. The tea getting cold. I felt the rim of the cup pressing against my lips.

The tea. He wanted me to drink some more tea. And then out of the haze that was enveloping me, I remembered that it was after drinking the tea that morning that this same drugged feeling had come slowly over me.

Drugged. Yes, that was precisely the feeling. Not a natural sleepiness. A drug. Some kind of hallucinogen. That would explain those awful visions—

With a force that came from some long-hidden source, I struck out fiercely at Nicholas's hand. The cup went flying across the room, the tea spraying everywhere. Nicholas gave me a stunned look.

"Get out! Get out!" I shrieked. "Leave me alone. Please, please, please . . ."

After a brief hesitation, he silently rose from the bed, crossed the room and left.

As soon as the door shut, I flung off the covers. I had to act fast, before the drug overpowered me. I knew that I could only fight it for so long. My legs buckled under me the moment I got out of bed. As hard as I tried, I couldn't pull myself to my feet.

I dragged myself to the door on all fours, pulling myself up by the doorknob so that my hand stretched high enough to reach the lock. As soon as I turned it, I remembered that Lillian and Nicholas both had keys to the room. A locked door was no impediment to either of them.

Already, I could feel myself drifting in and out of lucidness. Hurry, I told myself. Do something quick. And then I saw the wooden desk chair with its tapestry-upholstered cushion and arms. It was no more than ten feet from me, but it seemed like a mile. Somehow, I had to find the strength to reach the chair, drag it back to the door, and prop it under the knob to bar entrance to my room.

Perspiration ran down my body like rain as I very slowly completed the exhausting maneuver. When, at last, it was done, I doubted I had any energy left over for dragging myself back to bed. I lay there on the soft, plush carpet, my whole body trembling. My eyes started to close, but I forced them back open.

I had to get back to bed, crawl under the covers. It was my cocoon. I somehow believed I'd be safer there. I don't know how long it took me to get to my bed, but when I finally fell onto it, my breath was coming in strangulated gasps. I saw the teapot and the sugar bowl sitting on a silver tray. With my last ounce of strength, I swept them off my bedside table, the amber liquid and snowy-white powder mixing and congealing on the rose carpet, staining it red. *Like blood being spilled.*

Lillian came to me in the night. Was she real? A nightmare vision? An apparition? To this day, I can't be sure. All I know is that her presence charged the air with an eerie, menacing force.

I saw her looming over me, staring down at me, her smile contemptuous. "You silly little fool. There's no escape. Not now. I warned you, but you wouldn't listen."

"Don't you have any pity?" I cried, but I couldn't hear a sound coming from my mouth.

"Why should I pity you? Why should I care two hoots for you? It's Nicholas I pity. How do you think I feel, seeing him so wretched and torn, day after day? Watching him be destroyed?"

"But I . . . love him."

"You don't love anyone but yourself. And he knows it. Deep in his gut, he knows it. And it's driving him mad." Her words hissed out, fury coloring her pallid complexion.

Yes, madness. There was madness in that house. Madness and terrible danger.

Lillian raged on as I lay there, helpless against her onslaught, horrified. I began to shake my head violently, squeezing my eyes shut. "Go away! Go away!" I screamed. And still I heard no sound coming from my lips. Only Lillian's voice—hard, cold, menacing, without pity.

I covered my face with my hands as burning tears broke from my eyes. Soon I was sobbing convulsively into my pillow. When at last the crying subsided, she was gone. My gaze shot to the door. The chair was still wedged in place.

I took long, ragged breaths, feeling like my whole world was unraveling. When my breathing steadied, I looked over at the clock on my bedside table. It was almost five in the morning.

I sat up in bed. My head was throbbing and I still felt terribly woozy. If only I hadn't drunk that second cup of tea. Still, I was in less of a daze than I'd been in earlier and I knew that I had to take action while I could still think at all clearly.

The phone. Yes, that was it. Sir Galahad and his yellow charger to my rescue. I would call Greg. He wouldn't care if I roused him from his sleep. All I had to do was tell him to come for me and he'd be at the house in no time flat. I almost laughed aloud at the simple solution to my nightmare.

I flicked on the bedside lamp and lifted up the receiver, starting to dial even before I placed it against my ear. I was on the fourth digit when I realized that the phone wasn't making the connection. I hung up and tried again, holding the receiver to my ear first.

No dial tone. It couldn't be. I tried again. Once, twice, three times. Nothing. I traced the line. The phone was securely plugged into the jack.

Bleakly, I stared at the dead phone. Could we have lost service in yesterday's storm? None of us in the house used the phone much, and no one had noticed. It was possible that the rain and wind had knocked down a line. A chilling terror gripped me. It was just as possible someone had deliberately tampered with the phone. Just as it was possible someone had deliberately tampered with the brakes on my car.

I heard myself cry out then, but it came as a muffled sound. I fell back in bed, my pathetic whimper having taken the stuffing out of me. I felt weak and dizzy; my body was again drenched in perspiration. Lillian was right. There was no escape. I was lost and alone. And no one would rescue me. Not Greg. Not Nicholas. And most especially, not Lillian. If only I had never come to Raven's Cove in quest of my past. If only I had let Deborah Steele rest in peace.

There was a loud banging sound. I tried to tune it out, pulling the pillow over my head.

"Damn it. She's got something propped against the door."

Emerging from my deep fog, I squinted in the direction of the voice. Nicholas's voice. Coming from the other side of my door. With a kind of stupefied fascination, I watched the door start to push open, the chair that I'd jammed under the doorknob slowly inching away.

And then I saw a strong, male hand reach around from the other side of the door and grab hold of the chair leg. After some pushing and shoving, he finally managed to pry the chair free.

The door flew open. Instinctively I cried out in alarm as Nicholas stormed into the room.

"My God," he exclaimed hotly, "I thought you'd gone unconscious. Or... or worse. Why the hell did you barricade yourself in here?"

I opened my mouth to speak, but Nicholas had already turned his head away from me. Only then, did I see that he wasn't alone. A small man with short, frizzy blond hair, dressed in a tailored business suit, had followed Nicholas into the room.

"Delusions," Nicholas told him tersely. "Just like I told you on the phone."

The small man nodded, stepping around Nicholas and approaching my bed.

I regarded the stranger suspiciously. "Who are you? What do you want?"

He smiled pleasantly. "I'm Dr. Morris. Allan Morris. Your husband called me and asked me to drop in and have a look at you. He says you've been under the weather."

"You say Nicholas called you? When? When did he call you?"

I saw the doctor look over at Nicholas before he returned his full attention to me. "He phoned me a little under an hour ago."

"He couldn't have," I countered. "The phones aren't working."

Nicholas crossed to my telephone near the bed and picked up the receiver. He held it out to me.

I could hear the dial tone even before I brought the receiver to my ear. I stared up at Nicholas. "But... But it wasn't working. Only a few hours ago..."

"There's been nothing wrong with the phones. I called Godfrey in New York last night before turning in. And Lillian used the phone early this morning to call in a grocery order."

"But, it isn't possible," I muttered. Or was it possible? Had that phone call I'd tried to make to Greg at five o'clock that morning been nothing more than a dream? Had I just imagined that the phone was dead?

Dr. Morris came up beside me and gently took hold of my wrist to check my pulse. I looked up at him.

"What kind of a doctor are you?" I asked.

I saw the momentary hesitation. "I'm a psychiatrist, Mrs. Steele. Your husband explained to me that you are suffering from amnesia as a result of a violent assault on you a few months ago. And that since you've been home, you've had a rather rough time of it."

A dry laugh escaped my lips. "You might put it that way, Doctor."

He patted my hand. "Your husband also tells me that yesterday you took a turn for the worse. He attributes it to the added trauma of an automobile accident the day before yesterday."

From the corner of my eye I could see Nicholas watching me. I grew increasingly nervous and uneasy. I tugged on the doctor's sleeve and he leaned down closer to me. "I don't think it was an...accident," I whispered hoarsely. Then, drawing him closer still to me, I added, "And something else. I'm being...drugged. The tea..."

He smiled faintly. A humoring smile, I thought. It made me angry. "I want to speak to my own psychiatrist," I demanded abruptly. "I want to speak to Dr. Royce."

Nicholas came over to the bed. "Dr. Morris is a fine psychiatrist. If you'd like me to leave the two of you alone so you can talk..."

I glared at him. "I tell you, I want to speak to Dr. Royce. I want to speak to him this minute. If you don't let me speak to him..."

"Okay, okay," Nicholas soothed. "I'll dial him up for you."

A minute later he was being connected to Dr. Royce's office. "Yes, I'm calling for Deborah Steele, a former patient of Dr. Royce's," Nicholas said pleasantly into the phone. "She'd like to speak with him if he's available. It's quite...urgent."

At the prospect of speaking to the one person I trusted above all others, I began to relax a little. But then I heard Nicholas say, "Oh, I see. A week? Yes, yes, I understand. Yes, I'll tell her."

He hung up the phone.

"What... What...happened? Where is he?" I could feel panic roll in like a tidal wave.

"He's away on a week's vacation. He just left yesterday," Nicholas replied quietly.

"No. No, it's not true. I don't believe you," I cried. "You don't want me to speak to him. Because... Because you know he'll believe me. You want me to think I'm going mad. But I'm not. I'm probably the only sane one in this house." I was shouting by then, waving my arms about, my fists clenched. To anyone looking at me, I suppose I must have looked quite mad. Even in the agitated state I was in, I could tell that Dr. Morris certainly seemed to think so.

"Please, Mrs. Steele, try to listen to me," the doctor said, taking hold of both my flailing wrists. He might have been a small man, but he was quite strong. "You're suffering from paranoia. You're having hallucinations and delusions. It's often a component of your condition. Especially given the added emotional shock of coming back home, not remembering anyone or anything from your past. I'm certain the tension has been building and then there was the car accident. I know you're very frightened. And confused."

I gave him a beseeching look. "Yes, yes, I'm so confused. I... I can't think straight. Everything is so...jumbled in my head." I looked over at Nicholas. He looked drawn and haggard, but there was nothing but warmth and tenderness in his dark eyes as his gaze locked with mine. He reached out and took gentle hold of both my hands, while Dr. Morris relinquished his firm grasp on my wrists.

"It's going to all right, darling," Nicholas murmured softly. "You're going to be fine."

I felt a bit calmer and my breathing started to even out. But then a flash of light caught my eye. It was the reflection of sunlight dancing on a fine slender steel hypodermic needle in Dr. Morris's hand. His other hand reached out for my arm.

I wrenched it away from him, struggling at the same time to wrest my hands from Nicholas's hold. "No, no!" I cried out in panic. "Don't do it. Please, please, please..."

I began to writhe wildly, determined at all costs not to let them drug me again. Once I was under, I'd be lost. At their mercy. "No, no!" I shouted.

It took both men to get me under control. Nicholas ended up straddling me on the bed, pinning both my hands to my sides. I was hoarse by then, and when I felt the sting of the injection, a pathetic whimper was all I could muster.

I remember Nicholas finally climbing off me, his fingers uncoiling from my wrists. I kept my hands at my sides. I didn't move a muscle. There was no point in trying to fight anymore. I had lost.

Dr. Morris patted my shoulder. "This will just help calm you, Mrs. Steele. Really, you'll feel so much better. Don't worry. I'll look in on you again tomorrow."

After the doctor left the room, Nicholas stretched out beside me on the bed, cradling me against him, tenderly smoothing my damp, tangled hair back from my face. "You're going to be fine, my sweet. I'm going to take care of you. You're lost now, but I'll find you. Just like I promised." He rocked me gently as he spoke in a soothing, melodic voice.

I'm not really sure if I said it aloud or not, but I heard myself say, "I love you, Nicholas." And I heard him say in return, "I love you, too."

CHAPTER FIFTEEN

Daylight pressed against my eyes. The light hurt. I threw my arm across my closed lids. I could feel the cool mountain breeze blowing in from my open window, but still my skin felt hot and clammy. All through the day, I heard them come and go from my room—Nicholas and Lillian. Each time, I pretended to be asleep.

Whenever Nicholas came in, he would always walk right to my bed, lean over and stroke my damp hair or dust a kiss on my forehead, or dab the cool washcloth on my dry lips.

Lillian, thank heaven, never touched me when she came into my room. But she stood close to my bed, staring down at me for what felt like endless moments. I could feel her eyes burning into my flesh. I could feel my own heart flutter with nascent hysteria, my whole body tensing, preparing for an assault. If she had so much as laid a finger on me, I would have struck out at her with all my might. But she didn't. In some ways her silence and distance were more of a torture for me. A part of me wanted to strike out, put an end to the tormenting expectation of doom.

Twice that afternoon, I tried to reach Greg at his house. The phone was working, but Greg wasn't in. As dusk started to descend, my panic began to build. The light had disturbed me, but the darkness brought with it terror. Finally, after a third fruitless try to reach Greg, I got Godfrey and Julia's number from New York City information. Waiting until after Lillian and then Nicholas's pilgrimage to my oom, I grabbed up the phone and dialed, praying Julia would pick up.

She did. On the second ring. I almost broke down and cried with relief. I must have been so incoherent, it took a few moments for her to even realize it was me.

"Deborah, you sound absolutely awful," Julia said with alarm. "What's wrong? Are you ill?"

"Drugged," I whispered hoarsely. "I've been drugged, Julia. I... need help. I don't know... what to do. Please, Julia..."

"Deborah, you're not making sense. Isn't Nicholas there? Does he know you're having an...attack? I can't believe that man. Don't tell me. I know. He's holed up in his den working on his book and is utterly oblivious—"

"No, no!" I cried into the phone, trying to get her to understand. "He's the... one. Oh, Julia. I'm so... mixed up. Maybe it's just Lillian—"

"Lillian. Of course," Julia snickered. "That woman gives me the willies, too. But, you mustn't mind her, Deborah. She's perfectly harmless. Just a spinster suffering unrequited love. Really, you should pity her more than anything else."

Oh, she didn't understand. And the effects of the tranquilizer were making it so hard for me to explain.

"Please listen, Julia. I'm...so afraid. I need to...get away from here."

"I couldn't agree more," Julia said emphatically.

She was going to help me. I didn't know how, since she was hours away, but I still experienced a rush of relief—until she went on talking.

"I told Nicholas he ought to bring you when he comes down this weekend for the publication party. You'll have fun, Deborah. There'll be all sorts of interesting people floating around and you can get all dolled up for the occasion. Nicholas insisted it would just be a strain for you, and

you know how hard it is to argue with him when he's made
up his mind. But you must tell him you want to come. It'
just what the doctor ordered, tell him.''

I was about to make another attempt at explaining my
perilous situation when I heard the door start to open
Quickly, I dropped the receiver in the cradle, but in my haste
to place the phone back on the bedside table, I misjudged
and the phone fell with a thud to the carpet just as Lillian
appeared.

''So, you're finally awake.'' She carried in a tray of food
Did she really think I'd let anything she'd touched pass
through my lips? She knew, as well as Nicholas, that I used
sugar in my tea. She could as easily as Nicholas have doc
tored the sweetener. I imagined she either wanted to ar
range for another convenient accident, or if that failed
again, at least convince Nicholas that I was going mad. The
irony of it. Here was this insane woman orchestrating my
committal to an insane asylum.

''I want to be alone,'' I said tightly.

''Nicholas wants you to eat something. He doesn't want
you wasting away to nothing.''

''I don't care what he wants,'' I spat out.

She glared at me with pure hatred. ''No, you don't care
about what anybody wants.''

I felt so weak. ''It's not true. Maybe I used to be that way
but I've changed. Can't you see that? Are you so deter
mined to despise me still, that you can't see that I'm not the
same Deborah you remember?''

She gave a snorting laugh. I shall never forget that laugh
nor the way her dull eyes suddenly glowed like hot coals
''Don't you think I know that? In some ways, you're worse.
More dangerous. At least Nicholas knew the score with tha
little bitch. But you've got him in a tailspin, you little im
postor. Oh, you may fool some people, but I'm one person
you can't fool.''

"What— What are you saying? You *know* I'm not Deborah?"

"That's right." Again, she gave that hideous snort.

"How... How can you be so sure I'm not Deborah?" A chilling fear bubbled up from deep inside me.

She stared at me, her gaze oddly vacuous now, her voice flat, as she answered my question. "Because I know Deborah is dead."

My mind tried to hurl her words away. It couldn't be true. Deborah wasn't dead. *I* was Deborah. *I* was Deborah.

"No." I could barely get the word out. It dropped into the air like some lifeless thing. Tears rolled down my cheeks. I stared at her, bewildered, shocked, a little sick.

"You know it's true," she countered caustically.

And I did. All the pieces that didn't quite fit, made frightening sense now.

"How? How... did she die?" My voice was a strangled whisper.

She gave me a long, dark look that made me shiver. It was a look that said Deborah's death was no accident. Nor had she died of natural causes.

I shrank away from her, the darkness invading me, turning my insides cold with horror. I knew then that Deborah had not just simply died. She had been murdered. Lillian didn't need to say it; it was written on her face. Which meant either she'd killed her or she knew who had and she was shielding the murderer. There was only one person Lillian would shield. The mercurial Nicholas Steele. The man I had let myself believe, until then, was my husband. The man I had fallen deeply, irrevocably in love with.

I awoke to a commotion on the stairs. It was sometime the next day. Not the morning though. That doctor had come again in the morning. He wasn't accompanied by Nicholas this time. I told him everything. About being drugged.

About not being Deborah. About Lillian telling me that Deborah was dead.

He gave me a sympathetic look laced with pity. And once again the hypodermic needle appeared. I cried out in despair, guessing that the doctor either thought I was a raving, paranoid schizophrenic or he was in cahoots with Nicholas and being paid to keep me drugged. Having eaten nothing for over twenty-four hours, and with the drugs still lingering in my system, I had no strength left to fight off the injection. Within minutes, I was once again sinking into a stupor.

The commotion roused me, but I was pathetically weak and unable to focus on what it was about.

But then I recognized Greg's voice. Greg was out there. He had come to rescue me. Had I called him again? I couldn't remember. My thoughts kept unraveling in threads.

I tried to focus. And then I heard Lillian's voice. She was nearer. Maybe right outside my closed door.

"She can't see anyone," Lillian was saying firmly. "Doctor's orders. She's under sedation. Come back in a couple of days."

No, no! Don't go away, Greg. Please, don't go!

I dragged myself out of bed and half crawled, half stumbled to the door. It was locked. I banged on it. And then, gathering all of the little strength I had left in me, I cried out, "Greg, Greg!"

A moment later I heard the lock turn. Greg rushed into the room, practically falling right over me as I lay spent on the floor.

He let out an alarmed gasp and then pulled me up in his arms. No sooner had he turned to the door with me than Nicholas appeared there, barring the way.

"Put her back in her bed," Nicholas commanded in a low, threatening voice.

"I'm taking her out of here, Nick. And you're not going to stop me," Greg countered ominously.

"It's over, Greg. I want nothing more to do with you. So, get out of this house now and don't show your face here again."

"I'll go, all right. But not without Deborah."

"Deborah is ill. She also happens to be my wife. You step one foot out of this house with her and I'll have you locked up for kidnapping. Lillian's already phoned into the police. If you don't want any trouble, Greg, you'll do what I say."

I heard their voices as if they were coming from some far-off place. I couldn't speak or argue. I had no voice left. The drug the doctor had shot into my arm kept tugging at my senses. I wanted to tell him—tell Greg—that I wasn't Deborah. That I wasn't Nicholas's wife. That I was...*nobody*.

I felt myself being lowered to my bed. And then I heard Greg's voice, like a cobra's hiss: "You may win this round, but it doesn't end here, Nick. I promise you that." Then he leaned down and kissed me hard on the lips, right in front of Nicholas. "I'll be back for you, Deb. Don't you worry."

"Not...Deb," I croaked, but Greg was already storming across the room, with Nicholas following him.

I don't know how much time passed before I came to again. There was only a remnant of daylight left. Nicholas was standing at the side of my bed. When my eyes opened, they met his. But not for very long. A moment later he looked away.

The next thing I remembered, he was pressing a glass of water to my lips. I was so thirsty, my lips so dry, my throat so parched. But, still, I tried feebly to push the glass away.

Nicholas's gaze returned to my face. He gave me a haunted look, then took a long sip of water from the glass.

"There," he said quietly, holding the glass out to me again. "If it will still your fears, I'll taste all of your food, too."

I started to cry.

Nicholas gently stroked my cheek. "It's all right. It's going to be all right. Dr. Morris is actually quite encouraged by all this. He feels that while what you're going through right now is hell for you, it could very well be the start of a real breakthrough. Your memory could start to come back now—"

"But you don't want it to come back, do you, Nicholas?" I accused harshly. "You don't want me to remember my past. Because if I remember, I'll know it's all been a lie. I'll know I'm not Deborah." I took in a ragged breath. "Just like you know it," I said, praying he'd deny it.

But he didn't.

He gave me a long, weary look. "Yes, I know it. I've known for some time. I suspected it almost from the first, but there was the uncanny resemblance. And the fact that you were an artist. But the differences stood out, as well. You were so much more subdued and introspective than Deborah. Not that your changed manner couldn't be explained by the trauma you'd undergone. But then other qualities between you two were so glaringly different. You were so sweet, so tender, so caring. So...loving. You had such heart." He leaned closer to me. "You may look like Deborah, but you're nothing like her." And then, in a bare whisper, he added, "Thank God."

I stared up at him, dazed.

He smiled faintly, but there was anguish in his eyes. "I love you. I don't even know what name to call you. I could never call you Deborah."

My head was spinning. "You didn't love her?"

He sighed deeply. "Oh, at first I was dazzled by her, infatuated. Deborah was so carefree, so sure of herself. And of what she wanted. She was an expert at seduction. And

vas putty in her hands. It wasn't until I brought her home
o Raven's Cove, that I slowly began to see her as she really
vas. Cold, calculating, selfish, unfaithful. But still so damn
provocative. There were times when my resistance was low,
imes when my desire got the best of me," he confessed, not
quite meeting my gaze.

But then, after a protracted silence, he took my hand and
ooked down at me again. "After she was gone, I vowed no
voman would ever do that to me again. I convinced myself
was immune. I would drown myself in my work. I would
keep to myself. I would—" He stopped and smiled at me.
"And then you appeared in my life, so lost and afraid, yet
o endearing, so enchanting. I fought it with all my strength,
his feeling that I had for you. But it only kept growing
tronger and stronger. Until there was no fighting it any
onger."

He brought my hand to his cheek. "I wanted to tell you
he truth from the start. I knew it was wrong of me to let you
;o on believing you were Deborah. To let you go on believ-
ng you were my... wife. But I was so afraid you'd leave.
And, perversely, as much as I longed for you, a part of me
vanted you to go. I was in such torment. And then there was
Greg...." His voice trailed off.

"You believed...Deborah and Greg were lovers," I
murmured. "And you thought I might be more...like her
han you wanted to believe."

He didn't answer, but I could see from his expression that
ny theory was right.

"I may not be Deborah," I said quietly, "but she's been
ere with me since I first stepped foot in Raven's Cove. She's
een a shadow between us the whole time."

"Yes," Nicholas admitted quietly.

I knew then that if I asked him right at that one moment
f he had killed Deborah, he would have told me the truth,
o matter what the repercussions.

I prayed for the courage, but just when I needed it most
my courage failed me. I couldn't bring myself to ask Nich
olas that fateful question. I couldn't take the risk of hear
ing him say the one thing I so desperately didn't want to
hear. And so, chastising myself for being a coward, I locked
the question away inside myself. But was I a coward? Or just
a woman hopelessly in love?

Nicholas cupped my chin, tilting my head up so that our
eyes met and held. "You think you're my prisoner," he said
in a pained whisper. "But you're wrong. I'm your pris
oner, my darling. I'm hopelessly in love with you. Now that
you know the truth—that you aren't my wife—there's
nothing to keep you here. And yet, there isn't anything I
wouldn't give for you to stay."

He was opening the door for me. I could leave. He would
let me go. And if I did leave? Oh, I imagined I would sur
vive, but something in me—something even more crucial
than my memory—would be lost to me. Lost to me forever.

It wasn't that I wasn't afraid. But, for all my fears and
confusion, I felt a longing then that was more searing and
pervasive than any I had ever felt before. Nicholas didn't
love Deborah. He hadn't loved her for a long time. It was
me that he loved. Me? But who was I, now that I wasn't
Deborah? At that moment it didn't matter. I was the woman
Nicholas cherished, the woman he adored. He was giving me
an identity that I clutched to my heart. Just as I clutched his
innocence to my heart. I wouldn't believe he had murdered
Deborah. That was all there was to it.

My desperate desire for him, the certain knowledge that
I didn't want to leave him, filled me with a strange exhila
ration. Slowly, my arms lifted, my hands twined around his
neck.

As I drew his face to mine and kissed his lips, I told my
self again that he couldn't have killed Deborah. It had to
have been Lillian. Lillian had hated Deborah. And she must

have seen or guessed that Nicholas's brief infatuation with his seductive but wanton wife had waned, turned to disappointment, even despair.

And, I reasoned further, why would Nicholas have told me just now that when I first arrived he suspected I might not be Deborah? If he'd killed his wife, then he would have known for certain that I wasn't Deborah. He would have known the moment he laid eyes on me that I wasn't Deborah. Unless he was being clever and cunning, throwing me off track...

Oh, but he was kissing me back, then. Such sweet, tender, loving kisses. Surely, not the kisses of a murderer.

The evening slipped from shadowy dusk into darkness. Nicholas lay beside me on the large bed. His lover's hands caressed me, gliding over my hips, sliding up along my rib cage, cupping my breasts. The whole time his hands claimed my body, his lips claimed my lips—as his soul claimed my soul. Desire pressed in on me, pulsating. I was too weak to do much of anything but lie there and drink it all in. Like honeyed nectar. And let him carry me off to the other side of pain, doubt and fear.

A jigsaw jumble of sensations enveloped me, and I felt a trembling race through my body, thrumming inside me like a spring storm. But I fought the fear. I was in my lover's arms. I willed my mind to blankness, not wanting to think about the terror and the danger lurking in the dark corners, not wanting to think beyond the moment; wanting only to feel the joy and tenderness Nicholas, and only Nicholas, could give me.

I felt his mouth against my throat, his tongue on my pulse. His fingers twined in my hair. As he pressed his naked body against mine, I could feel his muscles quiver beneath his smooth skin.

He kissed my lips with warmth and passion, then looked down at me, his dark eyes reflecting both sorrow and joy.

"I don't even know what name to call you."

"Katherine. It's as good as any," I murmured. And to myself I thought, Better than some. Better than *Deborah*. I wasn't Deborah. I wasn't Nicholas's manipulative, unfaithful wife. And I was glad. I told myself this could truly be a new start for us.

"Katherine," he whispered. "Katherine, Katherine, Katherine," as he kissed my eyes, my lips, my breasts.

And when, at last, he entered me, a sigh fluttered from my lips. Like the murmuring of my heart. A new strength flooded me. My arms encircled his neck and I pulled him down fully on me, wanting to bear all of his weight, take all of him, revel in that intimate rhythm that was ours alone.

As we made love that night, I felt myself being reborn in a new image. And I felt Nicholas being reborn, as well.

CHAPTER SIXTEEN

When I awoke the next morning, I found Nicholas looking down at me from beside the bed. He was already dressed and looked incredibly dashing and romantic in his dark suit, black shirt and tie, his long dark hair pulled dramatically back from his face with a leather thong.

"Are we expecting company?" I asked groggily.

He smiled, then bent lower and lightly kissed my lips. "I've got to go to New York for that damn book party. Do you want to come? Julia's called me and insists it would do you a world of good."

I smiled faintly, remembering my frantic, incoherent phone call two nights ago to Julia. What a roller-coaster ride of emotions I'd been through.

"Must you go?" I asked.

He sighed. "I'm afraid Godfrey would have my head on one of Julia's silver platters if I didn't."

"How long will you be gone?"

"The party's this evening. And then I've got some dreary business matters to look after, tomorrow. If I get done early enough I'll drive back tomorrow evening. Otherwise, Sunday morning."

I glanced out the window. The sky was overcast. I quickly looked back at Nicholas.

"Do you want to come along?" he asked. "If you stay, I'm afraid you'll have to fend for yourself. Lillian's going to visit an old school chum in Albany for the weekend. It's one of her only friends, and I gather the woman's under the weather and Lillian feels she ought to help her out.''

"When . . . When will she be back?'' I asked.

"Sunday afternoon. She's taking the train, and there's only one run between here and Albany on Sundays. It gets in at three-fifteen in the afternoon, and I told her I'd pick her up at the station.''

My spirits lifted, knowing Lillian wouldn't be around. I did think then that I should talk with Nicholas about his cousin and what she'd told me about Deborah being dead. And what she'd alluded to. But, I told myself, it wasn't the right time. It would be a heavy load to dump on him just as he was about to leave for the city. Besides, I didn't want to ruin the romantic mood we seemed to be sharing.

"I suppose you don't mind Lillian going off,'' Nicholas was saying. "But I do worry about you being all alone here.''

"Don't worry,'' I assured him. "I'll be fine.'' Especially knowing Lillian wouldn't be around.

"You've been through a few pretty rough days. I spoke with Dr. Morris—''

I gripped his hand. "Oh, please don't have him come again, Nicholas. Really, I'm feeling so much better.''

He smiled. "Yes, I noticed that.''

I felt myself blush. "Last night was wonderful, darling. Try to hurry home by tomorrow evening.''

He glanced out the window. "It might rain today. Or by evening, anyway.''

I followed his gaze, dismissing the clouds, refusing to have a storm intrude now. "No, I don't think it will.''

Our gazes met and held. "I wish to hell I didn't have to go,'' he muttered. "I wish I could pull off my clothes and crawl back into bed with you.''

"I'll keep the spot warm for you.''

He gathered me into his arms and held me very close. "Oh, Katherine. I never thought I would know this kind of happiness. I'm not an easy man to live with. I'm moody and withdrawn, and wretchedly jealous. You deserve better, you know. I'm not exactly a prize catch."

I stroked his dark, silken hair. "That makes two of us. I'm a woman with no past, Nicholas. . . ."

He kissed my lips. "I don't care about the past. The past is dead. It's only the future that matters. Our future together."

An involuntary shiver raced down my spine.

"What is it, Katherine?" Nicholas asked with alarm.

"No—nothing. Nothing." I kissed him back with fierce ardor. "It's just that I'll miss you."

His smile lit up his whole face. "That's the nicest thing you could have said to me."

We kissed again and then he left. As my door closed, my fingers moved to my lips. Was it just my imagination or had there been a hint of desperation and fear in that kiss—on both our parts?

Greg called me at midday. I was out in the garden and had to run back into the house to pick up the phone.

Hearing me greet him so breathlessly made Greg ask me anxiously if I was okay.

I laughed. "I'm fine. Wonderful."

"That's nothing short of a miracle. You looked like you were practically at death's door yesterday."

There was an edge in his voice that I didn't quite understand. "I was pretty much out of it for a few days," I admitted. "A local psychiatrist was treating me for stress. I'd just gotten a shot of a tranquilizer before you showed up. But, I'm much better now."

"Where's Nick?"

"He had to go into New York for a book party. And Lillian's away, too. Visiting a friend in Albany. I've got the place all to myself."

"You shouldn't be alone, Deb. I'll drive up—"

"No." I wasn't sure at first whether I was simply saying no to Greg driving up to see me, or also no to his calling me Deb. Funny, I thought, how certain Greg was that I was Deborah. He'd never even had a single doubt.

"You don't want to see me?" he asked.

There was no missing the disappointment in his voice.

"It isn't that at all," I said softly. "It's just that this is the first time I've had a chance to be completely on my own, and I think it's important for me. You do understand, don't you, Greg?"

There was a pause. "I'm worried about you, Deb. These sudden swings of emotion. One day you're down, the next day you're flying—"

"I told you. I was on medication."

"I'm still worried about you. And I still think you should leave Raven's Cove. Leave Nicholas. You saw him yesterday. I think the guy's gone over the edge."

"Please, don't talk like that about Nicholas, Greg."

There was another pause, this one longer. "You're in love with him. After everything that's happened . . . Deb, you can't really be so blind—"

"Let's not do this, Greg. I'm very fond of you. And I know once everything . . . settles down, you and Nicholas will straighten things out between you—"

"No, you're wrong. It's too late for that. He knows it and so do I. Because I see through him now—now that it's . . . too late."

I hated the sense of doom that rang out in Greg's words. He was making me cast doubt on my own feelings, reawakening my suppressed anxieties and fears. It was the last thing I wanted. "We'll talk later," I said firmly. "I'll phone you tomorrow. Maybe we can get together for lunch. There are things we have to talk about, Greg."

"Are there?"

"Tomorrow." Gently, I hung up the phone.

As the night rolled in, bringing with it the storm that Nicholas had predicted and I'd denied, I found it harder and harder to push down my fears. I kept hearing strange creaking sounds in the house. I told myself it was just the storm, but I wasn't convinced. At close to nine, I decided to go up to bed and try to fall asleep. Tomorrow, I'd wake up and the storm would be gone and hopefully, before nightfall, Nicholas would have returned.

When I stepped into my room and flicked on the wall light-switch, nothing happened. The room remained bathed in darkness—a darkness that seemed to take on texture and dimension; a living, breathing darkness.

And as I stood at the door, I picked up the whiff of perfume. I recognized the scent immediately as one of Deborah's. Ever since that first day when I'd broken that one perfume bottle, I'd never touched any of the others on the dressing table. Her dressing table. Deborah's.

Now, in the darkness, breathing in her scent, the bedroom suddenly felt uninviting, alien, pulsing with secrets best left alone. I turned away from the room, pausing in the hall, trying to decide where to go. Now the light in the hall was gone, as well. Had the storm knocked out the electricity? I tried a lamp sitting on a rosewood credenza. It didn't work, either.

And then I remembered having seen a flashlight in Nicholas's desk drawer—the drawer in which I'd discovered that paint-spattered letter opener. A feeling of dread spread through me. What about that letter opener? Had Nicholas destroyed my painting? I quickly told myself that Lillian could as easily have done the dark deed and set Nicholas up. Or rather, set me up to suspect Nicholas.

I walked into his den. The flashlight was where I'd last seen it. I flicked it on, grateful for the ray of light that sprang from it.

The letter opener was still in the drawer, as well. But it was spotless and gleaming, now. Beneath it was the manuscript Nicholas was currently working on.

I hesitated. Last time I'd picked up one of his manuscript sheets, I had been sick with shock and fear by what I'd read. But, in the end, curiosity won out and I sat down at his desk and withdrew the manuscript pages. About a dozen of them.

It was the story of a man driven by lust and jealousy to destroy the woman that he loved beyond all reason. I read only the first three pages, stopping at the point where the tortured man struck out at his lover, his fingers curling around her throat, squeezing, squeezing, until he'd squeezed the very life out of her. Then, lifting her in his arms, he carried her down to the basement. And buried her.

What madness propelled me down to that basement in Raven's Cove? Or was it my first real surge of sanity? I had to know. I had to know if Deborah was buried there. I had to know if the man I loved didn't write horror *fiction* after all, but *fact*. Was everything we had shared together merely fodder for his next horror story? Was I to be not only Nicholas's next lover, but his next victim, as well?

With only the flashlight to guide me, I cautiously made my way down the cellar stairs. Again, as in my bedroom, I picked up a whiff of Deborah's perfume. Was she haunting Raven's Cove? Was she drawing me into the sordid ending of her life? Was she leading me to discover the truth that she already knew?

I was at the next-to-the-last stair when something hard and viselike reached out of a dark corner and grabbed my ankle. I went flying, as did my flashlight. The next thing I knew, I was on the cold cellar floor, enveloped in blackness, pain radiating through my body from my crash landing.

And still there was this cold, viselike "thing" attached to my ankle. No. Not a thing. A hand. Someone was there in the darkness with me. I could hear the breathing now. And the scent of Deborah's perfume became sharper, cloying.

Panic surging through me, I kicked out furiously, managing to break free. Pushing down the pain, I tried to crawl away.

A shot rang out. I froze, then tried to dive behind some cartons. One of them toppled. There was that hand again. Not at my ankle now. At my neck. The fingers curled around my throat.

Rage energized me. I would not be a victim again. I would not let it happen. I began to fight with all my strength, clawing at the hands encircling my neck, kicking, screaming.

There was a thudding sound. The gun. I dove for it in the darkness, my assailant following my lead. I felt all around for the weapon. Only to feel its barrel being pressed against my temple.

A hideous laugh rang out in the blackness. I recognized it instantly. And then I heard Lillian hissing in my ear, "You read the start of his book, didn't you, you nasty little snooper? Oh, yes, I was watching you from outside his den. Did you really think I would leave you all alone here?"

Another laugh gushed out. A laugh filled with mad glee. "So you know the truth. It doesn't matter now. He had every right to kill her. She was a hateful, deceitful hussy. She didn't love him. She never loved him. And he didn't love her. Any more than he loves you. If he even so much as suspected you knew the truth, he'd do away with you without a second's thought. Just like he did away with her.

Strangling her. Squeezing until he'd squeezed out her last, viperous breath. And then he carried her down to the basement and buried her.''

"No, no, no!" My voice was a hoarse, tortured cry. It couldn't be true. Not Nicholas. Not Nicholas. Not Nicholas.

"But he doesn't have to do the dirty work this time," Lillian wheezed in my ear. "I'm going to save him the bother...."

She had gone completely over the edge now. She was out of control. Were they both mad? Both cousins? I flailed my arms out wildly, making contact with one of her shoulders. I heard a grunt and then the thud of the gun as it fell out of Lillian's hand again and slid across the floor. But even as I tried to breathe in a sigh of relief, my breath was cut off by Lillian's fingers, which were once again coiled around my neck.

I gasped in pain and terror as I felt my windpipe closing off, but then something incredible happened. The assault I'd suffered at the hands of that masked stranger nearly three months earlier flashed before my eyes. I remembered the attack. The man wore a ski mask. I could picture him. And then something else even more extraordinary flew into my mind.

My name. *I remembered*. My name was Elizabeth. Elizabeth Crane...

"No," I gasped, refusing to lie there cowering and helpless, as I'd done in that dark alley in Manhattan. With my memory starting to come back, so did some of my strength.

We struggled on that cold cement floor. Surprised by my sudden power, Lillian lost her grip on me. I struck out hard, my fist making contact with her chest. She grunted, but then she was back on me, a raving hellion. Her fingers were at my throat once again.

And then my hand touched a wooden board lying on the floor. I grabbed it blindly and struck out.

A low groan escaped Lillian's lips. For an instant her fingers tightened on my throat, but then they went limp and she fell heavily against me, unconscious. Terrified that I'd killed her, I quickly felt for a pulse.

I breathed a sigh of relief when I saw I had just knocked her out. And, as if by magic, the lights suddenly went back on. Just as I was getting to my feet, intending to phone for the police and an ambulance, I heard footsteps overhead, moving toward the basement door.

What if it was Nicholas? What if he suspected I now knew the truth? Would he kill me, as Lillian had said? Terrified, I grabbed for Lillian's gun.

The basement door opened. Footsteps cautiously descended the stairs.

I was trembling badly, but I held the gun as steady as I could. The question was, Could I use it against Nicholas if I had to? Could I use it against the man I loved?

But it wasn't Nicholas who came into view. It was Greg. I was so relieved, I began to cry. Greg rushed over to me, took the gun from my hand and held me against him. I broke into sobs, muttering almost incoherently, "Dead. Her body... Here... in the basement... It's true. Oh, God... It's true."

Greg was stroking my hair, my back, his voice whisper-soft. "You found her, then?"

I shook my head. "We've got to...call the police. And an ambulance...for Lillian. I...I knocked her out."

"Just catch your breath, darling. I'm going to take you away from all this madness. I'm going to love you the way you were meant to be loved. I've loved you from the start...."

I gently drew away from him. "No, Greg. You don't love me. It's Deborah you love. I'm... I'm not Deborah. My

name is Elizabeth. Elizabeth Crane. I still don't know much
more than that, but it's a beginning.''

What was funny—funny in an odd way—was Greg's reaction to my revelation. No. His *lack* of reaction.

I stared up into his handsome face. "You . . . You aren't
surprised.''

He smiled sheepishly. "I was going to tell you tomorrow.
I never did stop checking up on you. And very recently I got
this lead to. . . to Elizabeth Crane, missing from her home
in Perkin Springs, Connecticut. . . .''

As soon as Greg uttered those last words, I could picture
not only the sleepy little mountain town, but my little white
cottage. And the studio attached to it. The studio where I
painted. Tears rolled down my cheeks. It was like a light
going on in the dark void of my mind.

"Why . . . didn't you tell me on the phone this morning?'' I asked him, remembering that he still had called me
Deb. Why had he done that?

"Come on, Elizabeth. That's not the kind of thing you
tell somebody over the telephone.'' He started to draw me
back into his embrace when we both heard footsteps overhead.

"Nicholas?'' I uttered in a frightened whisper. My guess
was confirmed a moment later when he called out to me.

"Tell Nick you're down here,'' Greg hissed in my ear. I
saw him cock the gun, point it toward the stairs. I stared first
at the gun and then up at Greg's face. And what I saw there
chilled me to the bone.

"Greg, you can't mean to shoot Nicholas in cold blood!''
I said, horrified.

A strange and frightening smile lit his face. "Why not?
He deserves to die. He made Deb's life miserable. He destroyed every chance for happiness we might have had. And
he almost did the same to us. But this time I win. I mean to
have you, Deb.''

"Not Deb. Elizabeth," I corrected. But I could see then that, even though Greg knew the truth of my identity, it didn't matter. I was still Deborah to him. He was still fighting to win *her* love. He couldn't really separate the two of us. I realized then, to my horror, that he didn't want to.

"Please put down the gun, Greg. You can't seek retribution this way. Besides, I don't love you. It has nothing to do with Nicholas."

Greg's eyes were glazed. "He's got to pay. He's got to pay."

"Not this way," I pleaded. "If he did kill Deborah, he deserves a fair trial...."

He gave me a savage look that took my breath away. "You're still the same teasing little bitch. You couldn't beat him then. And you can't do it now. Leading me on. Always leading me on, toying with my affections, taking me for granted. And then laughing in my face... I told you once before you couldn't do that to me. Didn't I? You just laughed. But then you stopped laughing. I made you stop. And I'm not sorry..."

My throat constricted as the hideous truth finally sank in. Not Nicholas. Not Lillian. It was Greg. It was Greg who had murdered Deborah. Greg, who was insanely in love with his friend's wife, who must have felt such hate and fury when she laughed in his face. And so he'd struck out at her. Killed her. Then another piece of the jigsaw puzzle fell into place. That's why Greg wasn't surprised when he thought I was saying I'd actually found Deborah's body in the basement. Because he had buried her down here himself...

He glared at me, his gaze full of loathing. "I tried with you. I tried my best. I thought I could get a second chance. But you kept fighting it. That's why I rigged the brakes. I wasn't going to let him win again. You were better off dead, for all our sakes. Only you're a real fighter, baby. And for a while there, I really was your knight in shining armor. We

came so close. So close. But you couldn't let go of Nick
Even after you thought he was the one who'd doctored th
sugar." He smiled wickedly. "I did keep you guessing, didn
I, baby? Sometimes I'm so clever, I have to be careful no
to outsmart myself. Good thing I've always been lucky. Lik
finding you in the first place. That was a real piece c
luck—"

I gasped as I heard the basement door open.

"Darling? Katherine? Are you down here?"

I started to cry out a warning to Nicholas, but Greg threv
his arm around my neck, clamping his hand down hard ove
my mouth. Tears streamed down my face. In another in
stant I'd be a witness to the murder of the man I loved. Hov
could I have been so blind to Greg's true nature. How coul
I ever have doubted Nicholas? How could I bear never ge
ting the opportunity to make it up to him?

Only a miracle would save us both now. And then,
happened. The miracle I prayed for.

Lillian was coming to. Her moan caught Greg off guard
I didn't waste a moment, shoving against him with all m
might. The gun went flying from his hand, but then h
quickly reached inside his pocket and pulled out the blad
sharp letter opener that had been in Nicholas's drawe
Where *Greg* had put it, I realized now. To cast suspicion o
Nicholas when Greg had been the one, in fact, who'd mu
tilated my painting. But why? Jealousy? Did it even matt
now?

Nicholas's footsteps were racing down the stairs.

"No!" I cried out in warning. But Nicholas was alread
rushing over. I kicked back at Greg's shin with all my migh
He grunted, loosening his hold on me just enough fc
Nicholas to pull him forcibly from me. His hands clenche(
Nicholas began landing blow after blow on Greg.

"No!" I cried. "Stop, Nicholas! That's not the way . . .

I'm not sure if it was my words or Greg too beaten up to fight back that made Nicholas stop. I didn't care. I was only grateful that he did. Nicholas let go of Greg, who slumped half-unconscious on the floor. Then he rose and came to me, a faint smile of relief on his face, and mine as well, when suddenly Greg sprang back to life, knocking me down, then grabbing Nicholas from behind. With speed and maniacal power, Greg wrestled Nicholas to the floor, pinning him there.

Laughing darkly, holding the blade of the letter opener at Nicholas's throat, Greg began to gloat. "I never could be sure about that crazy cousin of yours. That's why I brought our lovely amnesiac here. To prove to her that Deborah was still alive. I had to prove it, you see. Because I thought she suspected me of killing Deborah that dark night up in her studio. After I slashed her paintings. I didn't mean to kill her. I just wanted to make her suffer, like she'd made me suffer.

"Go figure, your batty cousin thought I was you that night. Lillian thought you'd slashed the paintings, you'd struck Deborah. And then when Deborah couldn't be found the next morning, she thought it was you that murdered her. The laugh's on me."

No sooner had he uttered those last words than he began to laugh. I lay there helpless on the floor, knowing that as soon as he stopped laughing he would plunge the blade into Nicholas's throat. And then he would take care of me and Lillian.

But just as I reached the depths of despair, a crackling sound sizzled through the air. No sooner did I hear it than I saw the blood spurt from the back of Greg's head. The laugh caught in his throat, became a gurgle, than a pained moan. And then he slumped over, rolling off Nicholas, the letter opener clattering on the floor beside him.

I looked back at Lillian. She held the smoking gun in her amazingly steady hand. Nicholas rose from the ground and went over to her, gently prying the gun from her hand. She looked up at him and smiled angelically. "You're all wet from the storm, Nicholas, dear. What you need is a nice cup of hot cocoa."

I watched her walk past me and then past Greg's body, seeing neither of us. As she started up the stairs, Nicholas checked Greg, looked up at me and shook his head. Greg was dead. He had paid the ultimate price for his crime.

Nicholas put his arm around me and led me up the stairs. We could hear Lillian humming as she headed down the hall to the kitchen.

"What will they do to her?" I asked, feeling a rush of sympathy for the woman I had both hated and feared. Those feelings had vanished in the instant she had fired the gun.

"She saved both our lives," Nicholas said, in answer to my question. "Her own as well, most likely. I doubt she'll stand trial." He looked very sad but resigned. "I've tried my best to look after her, but she needs the care of experts. We'll find her a nice private hospital where she can get the help she requires, Katherine."

I smiled at him. "Not Katherine. Elizabeth. My name's Elizabeth, Nicholas. Elizabeth Crane."

The police and ambulance arrived within twenty minutes of Nicholas's phone call. The medics carted off Greg's body and a very kind and gentle policewoman escorted a dazed Lillian to the cruiser. The police promised Nicholas that they would take her to a nearby psychiatric facility rather than the police station.

We stood at the window and watched them leave in the rain. Then I looked up at Nicholas. "What made you come back tonight? Did you know about Greg?"

"I always suspected something. I think that's why I made him the antihero in my new novel."

I smiled.

"What is it?"

I touched his cheek. "Nothing. Go on. You were telling me what made you come back tonight instead of staying for your party."

He drew me close to him. "It was the rain. That's why I came back. I didn't want you to be afraid."

I smiled at him. "Katherine was afraid. But not Elizabeth. Elizabeth will never be afraid of the rain. As long as we're together."

"We will always be together, Elizabeth."

Hand in hand, we stepped out into the rainy windswept night, and stood together on the bluff. And for just a few moments, in the rain and the blackness, we kissed. A kiss that set our pasts to rest. A kiss born of the present and the future that we would share.

EPILOGUE

Nicholas and I were married two weeks later. Julia and Godfrey were our witnesses. In the two weeks before our wedding, much of my memory had returned, some of it helped by notes that were uncovered in Greg's office in Manhattan, days after his death.

As it turned out, there was reason enough for me to have resembled Deborah Steele so strongly. Deborah and I were first cousins. We hadn't seen each other in years, or even kept in touch. I admit I never had liked her. Or trusted her. Besides, she was very rich and ran in very different circles.

I, on the other hand, had lived a very quiet, solitary artist's life in Perkin Springs. I had only moved there a few months before that assault on me in Manhattan. Before then I had spent several years studying painting in Florence and having a couple of disappointing love affairs. I had never found the right man for me—until Nicholas.

Greg had discovered the relationship between me and Deborah soon after her death. I have no positive proof, but I believe now, as does Nicholas, that it was Greg who assaulted me that night in Manhattan, intending to murder me. I think he meant to plant evidence on me that I was Deborah Steele. It would have been a clever way for him to prove she hadn't died that night up in her attic in Raven's Cove, had Lillian ever come forward.

But I didn't die in that dark alley. I survived. And so Greg began his next plan. He would bring me *home*. I think he meant to do away with me as quickly as possible, setting up either Lillian or Nicholas as the culprit, but I believe he did begin to fall in love with me. Or, at least, to begin to confuse me with Deborah and the warped love he still felt for her.

But all that is in the past. Thanks to Nicholas—my love, my husband—I needn't dwell on the past anymore.

Today we're celebrating our first anniversary. And we have much to celebrate. We're expecting our first baby. Nicholas says he hopes it's a girl, but I suspect, deep down, he'd like a boy. I've told him we'll just keep at it and have both a boy and a girl. Nicholas thinks that's a fine idea. We wouldn't mind ending up with a houseful of children.

Oh, yes, and we have another birth to celebrate as well on this day. Nicholas's new book is coming out. Not the horror novel he'd begun when I'd first came to Raven's Cove. He burned that manuscript and began a new book—a wonderful romantic novel of two lost people finding each other. The ending, of course, is happy. We wouldn't have it any other way.

*　　*　　*　　*　　*

And now,
an exciting preview of

SWAMP SECRETS

by Carla Cassidy

Look for SWAMP SECRETS and two other
haunting Silhouette Shadows™ romances
available this month.

And every month from now on, watch for
two new Silhouette Shadows novels,
stories from the dark side of love,
wherever Silhouette books are sold.

CHAPTER ONE

The house sat perilously close to the edge of the swamp, as if fighting a losing battle against the gloom that radiated from the dark, thick woods.

Lindsey Witherspoon slowly drove into the driveway and parked. She pulled a sheet of paper out of her purse and rechecked the address, although there was no doubt in her mind that this was Cindy's house. Only Cindy Mae Clairbourne, with her flair for the dramatic, would choose to live in a house perched at the edge of a swamp.

Lindsey turned off the engine and sat for a moment, looking at the house where she would be staying for the next six weeks. The house itself was huge, a Southern-style mansion with a sweeping veranda that in any other setting would look dignified and stately. However, in this particular place, shadowed by huge pine trees and viewed in the eerie glow of twilight, the house seemed foreboding.

With a small laugh of self-derision, she got out of the car and stretched. Obviously she was more tired from the drive than she'd thought.

She found the key just where Cindy had written it would be, beneath a planter on the front porch. She unlocked the door and pushed it open, greeted by the hot, stale air of a house closed up for several days.

As she walked in, she fought against a sense of unease. Inside, the house was decorated beautifully, but with the heavy wooden shutters tightly closed at each window, no sunlight peeked in to lighten the gloom. She walked from room to room, unlocking and shoving open the wooden shutters, allowing in the jasmine-scented breeze and the sunshine.

She found evidence in the decor that Cindy Mae had changed little from when the two women had been room mates in college. She still apparently had a penchant for blue and peach, as most of the rooms sported the pleasing colors.

Lindsey caught her breath as she walked into one of the bedrooms, deciding this would be the one she would sleep in for the duration of her stay. Sunshine seeped in around the edges of the shutters, casting dancing shadows on the furniture. Lindsey threw open the shutter, raising her face to the sunlight that chased away the shadows and the last of her unease.

The room was gorgeous, boasting a canopy bed covered in a pastel-blue spread, and an antique dresser with a large, slightly warped mirror. But it was the French doors that led out to a small balcony that overlooked the back grounds that made Lindsey's decision to claim this room as her own.

She'd always wanted a room with a balcony.

She stepped outside and breathed deeply, smelling the heavy, perfumed scent of strange vegetation, the moist dankness of slow-moving water. It wasn't an unpleasant scent, just different than anything she'd ever smelled before.

The swimming pool was directly below, the water catching the last of the sun. Beyond the pool, landscaped grass intermingled with brilliant-colored flowers. Then the swamp, dark and mysterious, with dead cypress trees rising like giant toothpicks and Spanish moss hanging like shrouds. The swamp was already black with the coming of night, its shadows reaching out to claim all that lay nearby. It was almost as if the darkness didn't come from the fading of day, but generated from the swamp itself.

Lindsey shivered and wrapped her arms around herself, ᵈding beauty in the scene despite the chill that danced up ʳ spine. She wished she had her camera handy, but it was ⁱl packed in the trunk of her car along with her luggage. ᵉ'd love to get a shot of the swamp. *There will be time ᵒugh for that later,* she thought, once again taking a deep ᵉath.

Cindy's invitation to house-sit while she and her hus-ⁿd, Remy, were in Europe, had been a godsend. Lindsey ᵉded time to think, evaluate where she was going with her ᵉ, what she wanted for herself.

Besides, the swamp would be a perfect place in indulge ʳ passion for photography. She'd always been intrigued by ᵉ image of a swamp, although this was as close as she'd ᵉʳ been to one.

Realizing it would soon be completely dark, she turned ᵈ left the balcony. She wanted to get her luggage in be-ʳᵉ it got too late.

A few minutes later, bags safely deposited in the bed-ᵒm, she made herself a drink at the bar in the living room, ᵉn turned on the light that illuminated the pool area.

She sank into one of the chaise longues and leaned her ᵃd back with a sigh. This six weeks would be good for her. ᵉ needed time away from her life back in Washington, C., time to lick her wounds and regain her equilibrium. ᵘis Louisiana bayou was as good a place as any to have a ʳsonal crisis.

She sighed again and moved the handle to recline the ᵘnger. She closed her eyes, intrigued by the night sounds ᵃanating from the nearby swamp. There was no sound of ᵛilization, no automobile noises to shatter the night crea-ʳes' whispers.

She must have fallen asleep because she awoke suddenly, ʳ a moment disoriented as to where she was. Night had

embraced the area while she slept. No lingering glow of du
pierced the grounds beyond where the pool light illun
nated.

Yet what instantly disturbed her was the silence. The nig
sounds that had lulled her to sleep were gone, replaced by
quiet so profound it was unnatural. Even the light bree
that had caressed her face before had stopped. It was as
everything held its breath in anxious anticipation.

The hairs on Lindsey's arms rose as if in response to sor
electrical field, but she knew it was a reaction to the feeli
of being watched. She pulled herself up to a sitting po
tion, trying to pierce the veil of darkness that lay beyond t
cocoon of light where she sat.

"Hello?" Her voice sounded small, tinny in the total
lence. She squinted, sensing something...someone near
"Is somebody there?" She projected more force into h
tone and was pleased by the effect, then jumped as a tw
snapped and footsteps whispered against the grass.

Fear speared through her as she realized how vulneral
she was, how isolated. The nearest neighbor's house w
several miles down the road, and the small town of Bat
Bay was a twenty-minute drive north. She was complete
and totally alone. Nobody would hear her scream.

She reached down and grabbed the drink glass she
brought outside with her. She needed something in h
hands, something that could be used as a weapon.

She stood up, adrenaline pumping through her. "Wh
there?" Impatience battled her fear as she shielded her ey
trying to see beyond the glare of the pool lights. "Cindy,
that you?" she called illogically.

"I'm looking for Remy."

The deep voice reached out of the darkness from behi
her, surprisingly close to where she stood, making her ju
and whirl around in alarm.

He cloaked himself in the darkness, wearing the shadows
e a shield of invisibility. The only thing she could discern
out him was his height... tall... and his shoulders were
ainously broad.

"Who... I..." She was appalled to hear her voice come
t as a breathless squeak.

"I'm sorry, I didn't mean to frighten you," he said, but
s tone held no note of apology.

"I... You merely startled me," Lindsey exclaimed,
htening her grip on the drink glass, although she had a
ling the fragile glass would be quite ineffective against
s man who'd appeared out of nowhere.

"Would you mind stepping into the light? It's rather dis-
ncerting to be talking to a disembodied voice in the dark,"
e asked.

"Certainly." He stepped forward and Lindsey instantly
shed he'd remained in the shadows.

The light played on his long hair, trying unsuccessfully to
ll a highlight from the unrelenting blackness. His face was
e that compelled, all harsh angles and planes unrelieved
 any hint of softness. As he took a step closer to her she
ticed that his eyes were the color of swamp moss, a deep
sterious green. He was hauntingly handsome, carrying
nself with a rigid control that somehow suggested an im-
nent eruption.

Lindsey unconsciously took a step backward, finding his
uminated face strangely disturbing.

"Remy? Is he here?"

Options battled in Lindsey's head. If she said Remy was
me, then what excuse could she give for not going inside
d getting him? On the other hand, she wasn't sure she
ed the idea of this man knowing she would be alone in the
use for the next six weeks. She quickly settled some-
ere in between. "Cindy and Remy aren't here right now.
rhaps I can tell them you stopped by, Mr... ?"

"Blanchard. Royce Blanchard." His piercing eyes studied her, again causing a shiver of apprehension to work i[
way up her back. There was something about him tha
frightened her, an edge of madness in his gaze that unse[
tled her. Perhaps if he smiled, she thought. Surely tha
would relieve some of the harshness, minimize the predastory look in his strange eyes.

"What did you do, Mr. Blanchard? Walk through th
swamp to get there?" Lindsey forced a smile to her lip[
hoping to pull an answering one from him. She would ju
feel better if he smiled.

"I didn't come through the swamp. I camp from it," h
answered, no humor apparent. "I live there."

"In the swamp? Really?" For a moment Lindsey's fea
abated as a sudden thought struck her. "Then you mu
know the swamp very well."

"As much as one can. She guards her secrets well."

Lindsey's gaze went out to the darkness, out where th
swamp lay with all its mysteries. He made it sound like
living, breathing entity. In fact, if she listened very hard sh
had the feeling she would be able to hear it breathe, feel i
heartbeat.

She looked back at him hesitantly, wondering if she wa
crazy to even consider asking him what she was about t
But who better to guide her through the swamp than a ma
who lived deep within its center?

Besides, he knew Remy, so surely he was all right. An
man would look sort of spooky in this lighting, she ratio
alized. In the light of day he was probably very ordinar
looking, not spooky at all. This last thought made up h[
mind. "Mr. Blanchard, I'm planning on going into th
swamp while I'm visiting here to take some nature phot
graphs. I could use a guide. Would you be interested?"

He took a step closer to her, bringing with him an earth[
almost herbal scent that was strange, evocative. He stood [

r to her she could feel the heat radiating from his body.
gaze seemed to take on a new intensity and he smiled.
t the gesture didn't soften his features as Lindsey had
ped; instead it only emphasized their harshness. "It's
vious you're new to the area, otherwise you wouldn't ask
h a question."

"Why?"

His features seemed to harden and shadows found the
tours of his face as he stared at her. "The last woman
o asked me to guide her through the swamp ended up
d."

Welcome To The
Dark Side Of Love...

COMING NEXT MONTH

SPRING FANCY

Three bachelors, footloose
and fancy-free... until now!

Spring into romance with three
fabulous fancies by three of
Silhouette's hottest authors:

ANNETTE BROADRICK
LASS SMALL
KASEY MICHAELS

When spring fancy strikes, no man is immune!

Look for this exciting new short-story collection
in March at your favorite retail outlet.

Only from

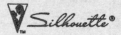

SF93

where passion lives.

**Silhouette Books
is proud to present
our best authors,
their best books…
and the best in
your reading pleasure!**

Throughout 1993, look for exciting books
by these top names in contemporary
romance:

CATHERINE COULTER—
Aftershocks in February

FERN MICHAELS—
Nightstar in March

DIANA PALMER—
Heather's Song in March

ELIZABETH LOWELL
Love Song for a Raven in April

SANDRA BROWN
(previously published under
the pseudonym Erin St. Claire)—
Led Astray in April

LINDA HOWARD—
All That Glitters in May

When it comes to passion,
we wrote the book.

BOBT1RR

SHADOWS FREE GIFT OFFER

To receive your free gift, send us three proofs-of-purchase from any Silhouette Shadows™ books from March, April or May with the Free Gift Certificate properly completed, plus a check or money order (do not send cash) for $2.25 to cover postage and handling, payable to Silhouette Shadows Promotion Offer. We will send you the specified gift.

FREE GIFT CERTIFICATE   096 KAN

Name: _____

Address: _____

City: _____ State/Prov: _____ Zip/Postal Code: _____

Mail this certificate, three proofs-of-purchase and check or money order for postage and handling to: Silhouette Shadows Promotion, P.O. Box 9071, Buffalo, NY 14269-9071 or P.O. Box 604, Fort Erie, Ontario L2A 5X3. Requests must be received by June 30, 1993. No liability is assumed for lost, late or misdirected certificates.

PLUS—Every time you submit a completed certificate with the correct number of proofs-of-purchase, you are automatically entered in our HAUNTING SWEEPSTAKES to win the GRAND PRIZE OF A THREE-DAY TOUR OF SALEM, MASSACHUSETTS, for two, including accommodation, airfare, sightseeing tours and $500 spending money. No purchase or obligation necessary to enter. See below for alternate means of entry and how to obtain complete sweepstakes rules.

HAUNTING SWEEPSTAKES
NO PURCHASE OR OBLIGATION NECESSARY TO ENTER

To enter and take advantage of the SHADOWS Free Gift Offer, complete and mail your Free Gift Certificate, along with the required proofs-of-purchase and postage and handling charge, to: Silhouette Shadows Promotion, P.O. Box 9071, Buffalo, NY 14269-9071 or P.O. Box 604, Fort Erie, Ontario L2A 5X3. ALTERNATIVELY, you may enter the sweepstakes without taking advantage of the SHADOWS gift offer, by hand-printing on a 3" x 5" card (mechanical reproductions are not acceptable) your name and address and mailing it to: Haunting Sweepstakes, P.O. Box 9069, Buffalo, NY 14269-9069 or P.O. Box 626, Fort Erie, Ontario L2A 5X3. Limit: one entry per envelope. Entries must be sent via First Class mail and be received no later than June 30, 1993. No liability is assumed for lost, late or misdirected mail.

Sweepstakes is open to residents of the U.S. (except Puerto Rico) and Canada, 21 years of age or older. For complete rules, send a self-addressed, stamped envelope (WA residents need not affix return postage) to: Haunting Sweepstakes Rules, P.O. Box 4682, Blair, NE 68009

To collect your free necklace you must include the necessary proofs-of-purchase with a properly completed offer certificate.

ONE PROOF-OF-PURCHASE

096 KAN
